To Liz and Mark,

Hoping you have as much fun
reading this as I had writing it.

Anthony S.   June 2006

FORTY FIRST TIMES
Courtship Through the Ages
Volume 1: Cavemen to 1944

By the same author:

The Messiah FCA, 2001
Julie and the Seasons of Life, 2002

FORTY FIRST TIMES

Courtship Through the Ages

Volume 1: Cavemen to 1944

Procreation without Pleasure

Anthony Scrimgeour

Book Guild Publishing
Sussex, England

First published in Great Britain in 2006 by
The Book Guild Ltd,
25 High Street,
Lewes, East Sussex
BN7 2LU

Typesetting in Times by
IML Typographers, Birkenhead, Merseyside

Printed in Great Britain by
Antony Rowe Ltd, Chippenham, Wiltshire

A catalogue record for this book is
available from The British Library

ISBN 1 84624 016 6

*'Males of necessity must insist and persist because
females to defend do desist and resist.'*
Anon

*'And if a woman have an issue, and her issue in her flesh be blood,
she shall be put apart seven days: and whosoever toucheth her shall
be unclean until the even.'*
Leviticus, 15:19–24

'Women are incomplete beings.'
Saint Thomas

*'Man for the field and woman for the hearth
Man for the sword and for the needle she
Man with the head and woman with the heart
Man to command and woman to obey
All else confusion.'*
Alfred Lord Tennyson

*'When a woman says "no" she usually means "no" although
she might just possibly be thinking "yes", "yes perhaps" or "yes
eventually". If, however, she says "yes" one should either proceed
with extreme caution or run like hell.'*
Anon

The Encounters

Volume 1: 50,000 BC – 1944

Fact or fiction?

The starting point for each chapter is a specific historical period, with its politics, wars and other major happenings; also social, religious and moral trends that influenced people's lives. The fictitious characters are then incorporated, bringing the period to life. The first two chapters are based on anthropological studies; others are inspired by events that altered the social structure of civilisations. Most scenarios, however, are more intimate and reflect the everyday life of ordinary people.

Every attempt has been made to render the historical contexts authentic. Even so, this is no socio-scientific thesis; the following text merely represents a thought-provoking and hopefully entertaining glimpse of human courtship throughout past ages.

First encounter: Atraa and Yabou
50,000 BC   Mesopotamia

She was standing by the river, not far from the security of their cave. There were seven other females and five surviving children, plus Oog with the twisted leg who no longer hunted and Agah the aged who was too feeble to accomplish anything. Urrgrh, keeper of the fire, was inside the mountain protecting the flame, rekindling it when needed, ready to light the main fire when the hunters returned with fresh meat.

Oog held a heavy branch, ready to defend should beasts come prowling, or marauders from other tribes hoping to steal their flame. Not that they would be able to protect themselves, even supposing they reached the sanctuary of their dwelling in time.

They knew the dangers, but males must hunt, because without food there was no existence. Oog had successfully protected everyone from the tiger, but when wolves attacked they only managed to reach the cave by abandoning one of the smaller children. The choice had been easy, little Mei had one hanging arm and walked crookedly since falling from the rock. Also she was female. Her mother had screamed abuse, refusing to accept the sacrifice of her child. Then she herself had been devoured, with her heavy belly she could not run fast.

She, Atraa, was bored. Although permitted to converse with grown females and share their thoughts, it was almost impossible to discuss serious things. Waving hands and making noises with their mouths worked for giving orders, but she wanted to learn whether the other females shared the same feelings as herself. Also, what they thought about males. And what males thought about them. How would she

1

understand their tribal customs, become useful, if her elders were unable to share their knowledge?

She studied the others as they waited for the males to return. As usual, in fact as always, having collected sufficient snails and acorns for the evening meal, with great difficulty because the cold season had arrived, they were minding the children, feeding the youngest with their bodies. When the children did not require attention, they sat and did nothing. Not that there was anything to do. Or was there? Banging hollow objects made exciting sounds, throwing rocks in the water was fun. But the noises announced their presence to those who might wish them harm, so they were only permitted to amuse themselves when the males were home. What did females from other tribes do? She had never encountered any, only males when they attacked seeking to steal the flame.

A high-pitched shriek emanating from one of the younger females, followed by a harsh response from a more ancient companion, indicated they were squabbling over something, probably a stupid jealousy about who picked the white wriggling things from the hair of Yabou, their leader. Or who should collect wood for the evening fire. Since Yabou decided anyway, she saw little sense in arguing.

Adults were much less fun than children, but since her body had changed she was obliged to remain with the grown females. Which was normal, because she had become like them.

Well not quite. She still had not produced a baby from inside her body. Even more important, or so it seemed, no male had inserted the thing that females did not possess. Once Aga tried, but Yabou hit him with a heavy stick. Other males stared now her body had changed, it made her feel uneasy yet excited. However, she did not especially want to be mounted, often it hurt the females. Even so, she sensed they were contented when it happened, and jealous when another was chosen. Why? Did they like suffering?

It was strange, only females produced babies, possibly because males could not produce the white liquid which fed them. Yet males made all the decisions, which was unfair since females protected and taught their babies until they became adult.

2

She felt the sensation inside her. She arose and walked towards the chosen place hidden amongst the trees. When you pushed food into your body everyone gathered together, but when things emerged from underneath you hid yourself. It did not make sense, like many other things.

She stopped walking, made certain no one could see and crouched. Just as she finished she heard a twig snap and a sssssshhhhhssshhing sound, two of the elder boys were watching her. She instinctively pushed her animal skin to cover where hair had grown then, grabbing a stone, flung the missile in the direction of the intruders, screaming as loudly as possible.

Oog arrived, realised what had happened and limped hurriedly after the culprits. Judging by the screams soon heard from afar, he was murdering them.

She returned to the stream, only to be verbally assaulted by the other females who were incensed at her carelessness. Some of their fury was directed at males in general but, as usual, it was difficult to know what thoughts her tribe members were struggling to communicate.

The haranguing ceased. She sat down amidst the others, who appeared despondent and listless. She picked a flower and slowly pulled out its petals. And then another. And then, considering this even more pointless than doing nothing, she sat and did nothing.

Oog stiffened, stood up. He had heard a noise. Everyone tensed, ready to run to the cave. Then they heard Ulua's signal, the males were returning.

Shortly afterwards they entered the clearing carrying a single pitiful carcass; the hunting had been disastrous and they would eat little that evening. She knew this was serious for if they no longer killed sufficient animals they would be obliged to sacrifice more children, abandon their friendly cave and move elsewhere.

Two females walked to where the animal had been deposited. Their task was to heat it in the flames before tearing it into small pieces so everyone could share in the eating.

Yabou, livid with rage at arriving home almost empty-handed, walked towards the crouching women; they knew what he wanted.

3

Aaga, his reserved female, shrank from him, shaking her head and pointing to her stomach. Yabou flared his nostrils, he knew what she meant, that the liquid was escaping. It was peculiar, the same liquid poured forth when they injured themselves, sometimes they died, whereas it regularly appeared from inside females for no reason whatsoever. When it happened the males were full of fear, keeping a safe distance, pointing to the night-time sun as if it was responsible, possible because the liquid reappeared each time its shape had completed a cycle.

Snarling with frustration, Yabou placed his foot on the whimpering Aaga and kicked her aside. He then scrutinised the other females. Unga advanced smiling, before turning and offering herself. Her male had been killed whilst hunting, consequently she was available to anyone who wanted her, usually when a younger female was afflicted by the night-time sun or had a distended belly. But Unga's heavy, shapeless form failed to excite her leader, who advanced towards Yrbi until Aga made warning noises. Yabou halted, unwilling to take possession, although he regularly helped himself when Aga was absent.

She watched fascinated until Yabou caught sight of her. He looked away, seeking elsewhere, then his gaze returned. He strode over and grabbed her hair, pulling her upright.

She sensed what might soon be happening, yet was too confused to manifest gratitude at having been chosen. Always assuming she would be, for Yabou seemed especially foul-tempered.

Without warning he span her round and pushed her head downwards until her face touched the grass. Intimidated, disorientated, she remained immobile, waiting. Then she felt him pushing against her, hurting until the pain became so intense nothing else mattered. Screaming, she broke free and collapsed onto the ground, squirming away from her aggressor. He, roaring in rage at such flagrant disrespect for his authority, grasped one of her ankles and yanked her backwards. Frenzied, not wanting to endure more pain, she kicked towards the cause of her suffering, her foot unintentionally finding its target.

4

She lay on the ground waiting for retribution, watching as her leader raised a heavy branch above his head before smashing it down onto her head, reducing her skull to splintered fragments of bone.

Second encounter: Uigt and Aaga
15,000 BC   Eastern Ethiopia

It was the hot season. The hunters had accumulated sufficient reserves of meat to feed everyone, unlimited supplies of fruit were growing on trees. There was no risk of starvation.

A group of younger adult males, bored with nothing to do, wished to travel beyond the mountains, discover where the ball of brightness in the sky disappeared before darkness arrived, explore where nobody had previously ventured. The time to depart had arrived. Older tribesmen attempted to dissuade them, fearing the ball of brightness would burn them as it descended, but the young males were overcome by curiosity, eager to learn what existed outside their usual hunting grounds.

So, when the ball of brightness next appeared, they had left their cave and walked steadily upwards. Previously, when wondering how to cross the mountains, Utta had pointed to a lower place between two summits. They understood, it would be wiser to walk there than climb the highest parts strewn with dangerous rocks.

Now, with the ball of brightness at its highest, far from the safety of their cave, they were approaching the gap. Advancing cautiously, scared of the unknown, they regretted their intrepidity yet were determined not to abandon their mission. Sensing no signs of danger, they entered the narrow passage. Before long, after struggling over a mass of fallen rocks, they emerged onto the other side. Far below was another valley, similar to their own although many times wider. Excited, they clambered down the steep slope, dislodging unstable rocks and occasionally sliding

7

themselves, until reaching flatter lands where trees grew.

A sudden movement startled them, they were ready to seek cover when a flying animal rose screeching from some bushes. They laughed, it was identical to flying animals in their own hunting ground! They continued walking, heading towards the bottom of the valley where they would find clear liquid and somewhere to rest during the period of darkness.

On arriving they drank eagerly then splashed themselves to become cool, for the ball of brightness had heated their bodies more than usual.

They picked fruit and found eggs. All were relieved that the animals and vegetation were identical, yet disappointed nothing different had been discovered. Having eaten, they played in the clear liquid until the ball of brightness disappeared. He, Uigt, was puzzled because it was not falling onto the mountains they had crossed but others further away. It was definitely the one which rose from the ground that morning, it had never left the sky. It was baffling, worrying, proof of magical powers. He often wondered if the same ball returned each morning or whether it was another; now he would never know.

Unused to being separated from their fellow tribesmen, their hunting trips always ended before darkness, they became apprehensive. Thankfully sounds coming from beyond the darkness were familiar, which was comforting.

Before long they were asleep.

Forms emerged from behind nearby trees without warning, clubbing them with heavy objects until they could no longer resist. He attempted to escape but two attackers forced him onto his stomach and tied his hands. It was strange; his tribesmen massacred intruders immediately, enabling them to steal weapons and trinkets at their leisure. So why had they not been killed?

What did the attackers want from them?

Forced to rise, he was pushed through the forest with a sharp hunting weapon held against his back. Seeing nothing, he frequently stumbled and once nearly fell. When encountering a low branch he was brought to an abrupt halt, the weapon entering deep inside his body. But still they did not kill him.

On arriving at the attackers' settlement they were bound to wooden posts outside the entrance and left alone. Six of his tribesmen had set off that morning, only five were prisoners. In the gloom it was impossible to ascertain who was missing. However, as light replaced darkness, he realised Utta was absent; had he escaped or been killed during the ambush?

Liquid from the wound in his back had spread down his legs onto the ground and his whole body ached. In spite of the discomfort he gazed towards the settlement, fascinated by the wooden mounds into which the attackers had disappeared. Judging by noises coming from within one of them, well he knew what they were doing. At least their tribes had something in common.

When the ball of brightness reappeared vast numbers of attackers emerged from the mounds and congregated around the fire which, to his surprise, had been rekindled by females, not males as was the custom in his tribe. On arriving, everyone prostrated themselves before the flames, emitting weird wailing sounds. Then they squatted in silence, apparently waiting for something to happen. He noticed objects scattered around the open spaces, tools and weapons considerably larger and more complex than his own; clearly the attackers had discovered things unknown to his modest tribe.

Four attackers arrived. They prodded Oug and Kui with a large stick whose point was sculptured from yellowish metal, then untied and dragged them towards the fire. To his horror, having been being bound to a large contraption, they were lowered into the flames. As they screamed in agony the congregated attackers repeated the wailing sounds and banged their hands together, then gazed upwards in silence at a ball of brightness attached to a wooden pole. It was magic, how could they remove one from the sky and keep it for themselves?

After a long wait the attackers, shouting animatedly, pulled the blackened bodies from the inferno, hacked them into small pieces and hungrily consumed them. Each head was crushed with a heavy rock, the contents being offered to the most impressively dressed males. He now understood why they had not been slaughtered during the attack.

The ball of brightness rose higher into the sky. He and his remaining companions were left alone, although a guard observed them from within the confines of the settlement. He was hot and extremely thirsty, small flying animals crawled over blood from his wound, which ached atrociously, and his arms and legs hurt from being tightly bound. Eig and Ula either moaned in abject misery or remained silent. Realising the futility of trying to escape, he resigned himself to his fate. Why had they been so foolhardy? Would the surviving hunters back home catch enough food during the forthcoming cold period, when there was no food growing on trees? Or would everyone die from starvation?

He observed the attackers as they busied themselves. Females cleared away the meal, which was normal, but others walked to where food trees were growing just outside the settlement. How lucky for them, his own tribesmen were obliged to walk great distances to gather fruit, sometimes in vain. The females not only collected food from trees, they poured clear liquid onto smaller plants growing nearby, something which mystified him until he remembered they shrivelled and died unless clear liquid descended from the sky. The attackers were feeding them! It was disconcerting to witness females performing male tasks, but it kept them busy, prevented them from arguing endlessly like females from his own tribe. It also explained why male attackers treated them almost as equals; they were performing tasks crucial to feeding everyone, especially their numerous children.

The activity of certain males was even more curious. Groups of animals, especially those enjoyable to eat, were grazing in a space surrounded by branches stuck into the ground. As the ball of brightness descended towards the mountains elderly tribesmen caught several animals and extracted the white liquid drunk by their young. Surely it was wrong to steal child-food from other creatures? But how clever to capture the beasts alive; whenever you were hungry you simply walked to their enclosure and killed one.

Two females walked towards the prisoners. One was tall, graceful with her movements, very unlike those from his own tribe. The other was shorter and unusually skinny, also older, but her face was strangely appealing. He watched them, overheard their conversation. Although the sounds coming from their mouths made no sense, their gesticulations and facial expressions were understandable; he deduced they were comparing the prisoners to their fellow tribesmen. Poor Eig and Ula obviously did not impress them, both possessed faces covered with thick hair but he, taller and slimmer, apparently intrigued them, possibly because he more closely resembled their own males.

The skinny female caught sight of the shining stone worn around his neck. He raised his head so she could examine it and the expression on her face showed gratitude. Turning, she said something to her taller companion. He repeated her sounds, not knowing what they meant. But the females understood and laughed. The skinny one observed him attentively, then slowly emitted several different noises. He realised they wanted him to repeat her sounds, except they were strangely different from his own tongue and difficult to formulate. She frowned and repeated herself. This time they understood and smiled encouragingly. He marvelled at how they described thoughts by changing the expressions on their faces, very different from the monotonous stares of his own tribesmen. The guard arrived, glaring menacingly, but the women spoke to him without fear and pointed in his direction. He was to produce a repeat performance.

Even the guard laughed.

Then he and his companions were left alone.

Before the ball of brightness disappeared the two females returned, accompanied by three others each carrying an earthenware pitcher containing clear liquid. All three prisoners were allowed to drink. He said 'thank you' in his own tongue, then looked at the skinny female. He repeated himself slowly, emphasising each individual sound. She, as he had hoped, mimicked him. He repeated himself again, and this time she copied him almost perfectly. Unable to clap his hands, he smiled at her. He said 'good' in his tongue and she copied him. Then, to the amusement of all five females, he dutifully repeated the sounds each of them uttered.

Next morning a group of male attackers came to select further victims for the flames. A scream was heard from afar as they were untying him; the skinny woman was waving her hands and pointing at the other prisoners. So, for the second time, he watched as fellow tribesmen were lowered into the flames. He noticed the attackers ate more slowly than members of his tribe; they even stopped to share food and talk amongst themselves, behaviour noticeably different from the greedy grabbing of his own tribesmen. There was something pleasing about the attackers; they may have killed his companions but their comportment was friendly, they seemed to enjoy each other's company. And, after the food was finished, they made agreeable noises together, gleefully banging on hollow wooden implements and waving their hands above their heads.

The skinny woman arrived holding the half-eaten foot of one of his companions, which she held to his mouth. He looked at her pleadingly, sadly shaking his head. Realising the reason for his refusal, she made a clucking sound and walked away, only to return with fruit. Once he bit her by mistake, only slightly, yet he instinctively closed his eyes expecting to be struck. But she only made more sounds. Opening his eyes he realised she was still offering the fruit. Having swallowing another juicy morsel he gently touched where she had been bitten, repeatedly muttering 'sorry' in his language, hoping she would understand his dismay.

She returned to the large open space with the fire in the middle. Surely it was dangerous to reside far from a cave, although the flames should keep animals away. He could see her standing facing two elderly males, gesticulating and pointing at him. They also commenced gesticulating, then signalled to some younger males who started walking towards him. They untied his bonds and led him into the settlement. He stumbled, his legs were not working properly,

12

but they prevented him from falling. He was brought to a halt in front of the elderly males, one of whom espied his shining stone. Although less intricate than ornaments adorning the attackers, its colour and shape were distinctly different. He unhooked it, handing his most precious possession to the imposing grey-haired attacker. He then looked towards the skinny female, pointing at his necklace. The male looked perplexed, frowned, smiled with understanding and handed the stone to the excited female who, in front of everyone, approached and touched his mouth with hers.

He wondered what her gesture meant. In his tribe females were forbidden to touch males without permission, and then only to tend wounds and scratch where they were itching. Back home such comportment would result in severe reprobation.

He decided to grasp the skinny female, assert his authority, but she was engaged in an intense discussion with the elderly males. One of these walked away, returning with the remains of an arm, all that remained of his former companions. The stump was held to his mouth, he was being invited to eat. He was about to refuse when it registered that the offer was symbolic; by accepting to consume the flesh of his companion he would be signalling allegiance to his new tribe.

Males in his tribe generally had a preferred female, although they could mount anyone they chose except those reserved for Bouga their leader and she from whom they had emerged. This created jealousies because certain females were mounted frequently whilst others, especially the older ones, were never selected. Attacker males, on the contrary, seemed to remain with one female, sharing a mound with both her and her children. Even more intriguing, the males attended to the children, which was stupid. Or was it? He knew that females only produced children if they were mounted, thus males made babies. Not females. So, if a female was always mounted by the same male, he alone could be the cause of her children. Thus it was not completely stupid for him to help raise them.

Regardless of their different customs, it was he who should be choosing his female. Of course he would not normally have selected

13

someone so scrawny, certainly not as old, but the choice was her or death. He wondered if her male had been killed or whether she had never been selected due to her shrunken body. Infuriatingly, he was unable to pose questions using their strange sounds. In any case, she pleased him considerably more than the ill-tempered members of his own tribe, including Auba, his preferred female. Yes, sharing a mound with the skinny attacker would surely be enjoyable, far better than being lowered into the fiery flames. So he bit on his companion's arm. It was delicious and he was starving, so he helped himself to another portion.

Having swallowed the last tasty morsel, he touched the skinny female on the mouth and held her hand. Several females emitted whooping noises and stamped their feet in unison. A white-haired male placed his hands on their heads, presumably accepting their union. An elderly female beckoned him, indicating he was to enter one of the mounds. She washed his wounds and helped dress him in clean garments then, when everything was to her satisfaction, he was escorted outside. Someone pointed to the skinny female and uttered the sound 'Aaga'. He repeated the name and she, without further hesitation, excitedly led him away from the others.

Instead of walking to nearby trees she entered one of the mounds. That was another strange habit, the attackers only seemed to mount each other when concealed inside the mounds, not outside with others watching. Not for the first time the attackers' behaviour baffled him.

She stopped near where animal skins were placed on the floor, the moment had come. To his astonishment she removed her garment without hesitation, though with evident embarrassment, exposing an almost hairless body significantly less shrivelled than expected. With a quick movement he removed his recently donned tunic and span her around, ready to force her head downwards and mount her. But she resisted angrily, then calmed down, holding him in her arms and touching his mouth repeatedly with hers, before pulling him down to the ground. Disorientated by her inexplicable behaviour he allowed her to guide his hands onto her breasts. She yelled as he grasped

14

them violently, as was his custom, for it was essential that males demonstrate their domination. She grabbed his hands but, instead of removing them, showed how to softly stroke her body which resulted in her breathing in great gasps as if fevered. Then her hand gently encased that which confirmed he was male. Both surprised and embarrassed he was attempting to wriggle free when she gazed straight in his eyes and smiled, so he relented and allowed her to continue, especially as he was experiencing agreeable sensations.

Looking across at him, grinning happily, she indicated he was to climb onto her. Puzzled, he hesitated, uncertain how to proceed. So again she guided him. And, whilst he was inside her, their mouths touched and stayed touching, and he experienced a multitude of delights previously unknown to him.

Third encounter: Sokaris and Idria
2,145 BC   Herakleopolis, Egypt

He stood at the window gazing beyond the palm trees and mud-dwellings that surrounded the palace, his eyes focusing on distant sand-dunes shimmering in the afternoon heat. The spring drought would soon be replaced by the annual inundation of the Nile whose expanding waters deposited alluvium on their fields, manniferous earth without which crops could not grow during the period they called 'emergence', when the desert heat was least intense. After two years of failed floods a bounteous harvest was essential as the nation's food reserves were practically exhausted.

They had prayed for deliverance, the country's temples resounding with incantations as worshippers arrived with ceremonial offerings. Surely the gods would listen, for never had such a magnificent civilisation graced the world. A thousand years ago the Egyptians had emerged from primitive village settlements to build an empire so vast it defied human imagination. Yet its continuing greatness depended upon respecting the wishes of the gods, safeguarding the absolute power of the pharaohs and forging a wealthy disciplined society capable of maintaining an invincible army.

As eldest son of King Sesostris II, Pharaoh of all Egypt, both god and king, it was his inviolable duty to propagate the dynasty, provide an heir to the throne. To achieve this his father had negotiated a marriage contract with an Antef prince residing in the southern region of Thebes, more appropriately governing it much to the chagrin of his father in Herakleopolis, glorious capital of Fayoum and supposedly of the entire Egyptian Empire. Choosing his bride, future queen of the realm, had been omni-important, a major step to obviate hostilities fermenting between jealously ambitious cliques inhabiting their despairingly fractious nation.

Heirs to the royal throne traditionally married within their own family to ensure purity of royal lineage, notwithstanding prevalence to deformed or still-born children. To solve a dynastic crisis his great-grandfather, on the premature death of his father and ruling pharaoh, had unhesitatingly married the latter's widow, his very own mother, and had sired four still-born daughters before the gods granted that a male infant might survive.

His own mother, however, was straying beyond the age of fecundity whereas the body of his elder sister Hatshepsut indecently excited him. Consequently his father's imposition of an unknown outsider had caused consternation and displeasure, however justified the decision. With growing threats of invasion from the Hyksos in the east and the unpredictable Bedouins from Libya in the west, compounded by unrest amongst their multifarious population of servitors, especially the intractable Jews, it was critical to consolidate a ruling oligarchy powerful enough to enforce cohesion throughout the realm. The bride herself, as his father explained, was of little consequence assuming she produced an heir. It was her father's political influence that counted. During their extended and sometimes acrimonious negotiations the prince had emphasised the excellent health and guaranteed chasteness of his daughter; to eliminate possibility of defilement she been both excised and sewn. If her first-born son carried his name he would support whole-heartedly the permanent bonding of their families and, by implication, abandon ambitions he might have concerning succession to the imperial throne.

The deities had been consulted, especially Osiris, god of earth and vegetation, to ensure bountiful harvests, and Ré the sun-god and creator of men; also Hathor, goddess of love, to ensure the marriage would be blessed with happiness. After endless meditation and pouring over scrolls of papyrus inscribed with astrological charts, the high priest ecstatically announced the benediction of the union and

18

confirmed the propitious date. Then a messenger arrived from Thebes, the timing coincided with the bride's six days of wearing the 'blood bandage' during which everything she touched would be tainted with impurity, including the pharaoh himself, and she would be unable to respect her nuptial obligations. A secondary date submitted by the priests was less auspicious, yet there was no suitable alternative.

Sensing his reticence at marrying a stranger, his father insisted his son constitute a harem subsequent to the nuptials; after all, monogamy only applied to females excepting prostitutes, a wise and necessary precaution to superintend paternal parentage. Relieved, he recalled earlier words of wisdom spoken by his father, advice offered when he was still advancing towards manhood, when his governess discovered dampness where his virility reposed during the night and joyfully informed his father, who proclaimed the royal concubines at his disposition for satisfying eventual desires. His father, having advised against conversing with them, which was pointless for they harboured few thoughts within their heads, also explained it was imperative to arrange her demise if a royal concubine displayed signs of impregnation. Contraception was reliable, sheaves made from animal bladders for males or the insertion of acacia tips or olive oil into females, but it reduced the pleasure. Disposing of infants after birth was a possibility but sacrificing male children was resented by the gods. Some masters accepted bastard children into their entourages; for a future pharaoh such practice was best avoided. Consequently the preferred solution was discreet elimination of the future mother. Iridis, a palace guard, arranged such matters, his compensation being the right to partake of victims before slitting their throats. He also procured replacements, which were in plentiful supply.

Of course, as his father asserted and he himself subsequently discovered, concubines were uninspiring bed-partners; having had their sex organs disjoined to prevent pleasure they failed to communicate sensuality to their partners. Unexcised Asiatic and Jewish professionals working in the city were vastly more

19

enterprising, knowing exactly how to stimulate their partners towards ultimate release, rendering the act of possessing a woman a much-appreciated distraction from palace intrigue and official ceremonies.

He wondered how an Egyptian wife would differ from concubines and professionals. During their first encounter she would be a maiden, so it was unlikely his masculinity would be tested. Or could such an indignity happen? For example, did those from his own people possess innate knowledge of performing as wives and, especially worrisome, understand what was expected from a husband? Furthermore, his future wife would presumably be endowed with a personality. How to address her? Unfamiliar in such matters, his royal prerogative of infallibility was at risk. His father had been of little assistance, stating that females were females whatever their race or religion; it was for him to impose his masculinity. And now it was too late to seek advice elsewhere; within hours he would be married. Hopefully the gods, having blessed his union, would assure its success, protect him when he confronted his wife.

Turning his gaze from the shimmering sand-dunes, he summoned his servants. The time had come to prepare for the ceremony.

The trumpets blared forth, achieving an aura of magnificence befitting the enormity of the occasion. He stood waiting in front of the altar, facing the high priest, sensing his bride had entered the temple, was advancing towards him. He turned as she arrived, surprised at the meagre height of the veiled form. He knew she was no child, the marriage contract attested fifteen years old, unusually advanced in years for a bride. Her father insisted he had been awaiting a suitor worthy of her exceptional qualities; if nobody had been forthcoming she would have been offered as handmaiden to the high-priestess.

His attention returned to the altar. The wedding ceremony had commenced, he must concentrate on the interminable exchanges to be intoned before the shrouded shape alongside him was pronounced his wife and princess of the realm.

20

He was all but fainting from fatigue when the final supplications were chanted to Osiris and Ré, Isis and Horus, also Bès to ensure safe delivery of their male children. Trumpets triumphantly announced that the gods had united the two mortals standing before them. The high priest indicated the groom should lift his bride's veil. Her face, apart from tearstains, combined inexpressiveness with forlorn fatalism. Princess Idria was a nonentity. At least physically. Meanwhile her unknown and potentially perturbing personality represented an underlying threat to his royal prerogative; that night he would be sharing his bedchamber not with a slave but a future queen.

As the banquet increasingly disturbed the stillness of the night, as sobriety became rarer than cool breezes in midsummer, as cherubic servant girls unknowingly tempted him with delights unrelated to the roast pigeon and honeyed cakes being served, as the undulating swirling of the dancers stimulated manly inclinations which would not be satiated that night by their innermost charms, he grew increasingly convinced his bride's personality was as much a misnomer as her physique. Admittedly he should instigate the dialogue, help his princess overcome her inhibitions and reveal her intellectual attributes. But he possessed no suitable thoughts to transform into words; never before had he conversed socially with a female other than family members. He did inquire as to her tastes in prose and verse; she affirmed an affinity for both yet declined to disclose preferences. He queried her predilection to playing the flute or lyre; her perfunctory response indicated familiarity with musical instruments, in fact with music in general, but she shunned sharing her thoughts. So he renounced, finding solace amongst his political advisers.

However, as he kept reminding himself, he had a pressing duty to accomplish; a stained cloth must be displayed attesting compliance with two fundamental clauses of the recently negotiated marriage settlement.

Unable to postpone the moment, he led his princess away from the festivities. The bridal bedchamber was empty, the bed ominously waiting. There was a moment's respite as she summoned her servitors and was escorted away to be prepared. Changing into his night-garment he remarked that his masculinity was grievously indisposed to respect contractual obligations, however laboriously they had been negotiated. Uneasiness became disconcertion when, climbing into bed, he espied the ceremonial linen awaiting its requisite evidence.

She returned in a night-gown. This revealed her diminutive frame marginally more than her formal wedding robe, only to confirm there was little to reveal. She stood standing before him, awaiting instructions. Should he undress her? Should she undress him? Should they undress themselves, or each other? Should he watch, or politely look away? Since his bride was staring at the floor, displaying neither initiative nor enthusiasm, it was unlikely she would solve the conundrum.

Asserting himself, he requested respectfully yet firmly that she enter his bed. She obeyed, installing herself as distantly as possible. Should he speak, for example at least enquire whether she was prepared? Or should he imperiously impose his authority? He glanced at the immobile form, then moved towards her. She shivered, no she had trembled. He approached nearer, inadvertently brushing her hand. She emitted a hissing sound, otherwise her body remained rigidly motionless.

Then she spoke.

'My Prince, please be patient, explain my duties.'

Stupefied at being addressed, he retreated in confusion.

'Please do not be aggrieved, I only wish to accommodate my husband to the best of my abilities.'

'You are aware of your obligations?'

'Such matters have not been disclosed. Only you, my master, may indicate how I comport myself in your presence.'

He was confounded, never had a female formulated a request for guidance; either she was proficient or she was rejected. Yet he could not dispose of a wife for lack of aptitude, only infertility. Her request displayed pragmatic wisdom.

Except he had no idea how to respond.

'I am unable to formulate precise instructions, though I am in appreciation of your concern for my well-being.'

'It is only normal, you are my master and it is my duty.'

He hesitated, uncertain how to proceed.

'I beg that you be gentle. It has been explained that a wife enduring pain cannot attend nobly to the wishes of her husband.'

He remained silent, attempting to hide his disarray. Whereas his modest encounter with the priest's knife had heightened potential for enjoyment, her absent organs prohibited pleasure and encouraged discomfort. However, since women with their tendency to indiscipline could not be entrusted to respect the indispensability of fidelity, surgical intervention was both unavoidable and justified. Even so, although committed to asserting his masculinity, he no longer wished to single-mindedly pursue self-satisfaction, as would be expected, but instead to heed her supplications, at least to the extent this was possible.

He decided to move towards her, prove he was indeed her master and husband. Then he halted, for such a gesture might possibly distress her. So he indicated she should approach him before recalling the mistimed dissipation of his virility.

They lay together, hardly moving, sensing each other's presence. Her hand gently touched his shoulder and then moved towards his chest. He felt trembling, became aware how such a gesture must have required inordinate courage. So he turned towards her and awkwardly yet softy kissed her cheek. She smiled and he felt hitherto unknown emotions of contentment.

His virility still absent, he enquired what other information she had received concerning her matrimonial duties. Several times he smiled at the naivety of her tuition, yet he remained silent; was it consideration for her well-being or his own disconcertion that rendered him unwilling to reveal the true nature of the infliction awaiting her?

He enquired about Thebes.

He was enchanted by the gentle yet sweetly cynical commentary of living in her distant and different society. It was strange that someone so bursting with observations and impressions had remained stoically silent during the matrimonial celebrations. So he asked her why.

'I followed my mother's counselling that a person learns nothing from speaking, only from listening and especially to males, for their words are wiser than those of females. So, since I must assimilate everything about your society, I listened and purported to learn during the evening.'

'And what, may I ask, did you learn?'

She smiled shyly at her husband, almost slyly, a mischievous gleam in her eyes, and proceeded to answer his question.

Dawn was softening the intensity of darkness in the bridal chamber. He had slept intermittently, memories of trysts with pirouetting dancers and voluptuous ladies of pleasure profaning the innocence of sleep. As nocturnal slumbering transformed to wakefulness he perceived that his remembrances had stimulated more than his mind. She was awake, his masculine pride required comforting. He moved towards her and exerted his rights as husband and master as gently as possible. And, when she experienced the inevitable pain, he almost weakened and begged forgiveness.

Fourth encounter: Hylas and Myrtale
412 BC   Athens, Greece

The softly sensitive skin of Bettayia conveyed emotions mortal words could never express. Her lover stirred, moved closer, momentarily merging the intimacy of nakedness into a single expression of love. Then she withdrew, breaking the invisible cohesion.

She opened her eyes. The afternoon sun shone through the window with voyeuristic intensity revealing two ageing bodies sweating from efforts as intensely physical as emotional. Bettayia was sitting motionless, the fierceness of her ardour tinged with sadness. Without a word, their next union was already confirmed, she rose from the bed, dressed and exited the love-chamber, returning to her husband Androculis, wise and renowned chronicler, preserver of the myths and well-respected citizen of the most remarkable civilisation ever to grace the world.

Whereas she, wife of Thesus, famed orator and magistrate of Athens, stayed within the confines of her husband's residence, its women's quarters or gynaeceum, *her social prison. She recalled her first marriage to Dyonisis. Initially he imposed his presence three times each month until she became fruitful, as was decreed, immediately discarding her until she was again ready for impregnation. The mortification of being assailed physically, then enduring three seasons of nausea and acute discomfort until the ultimate abasement of childbirth was every woman's destiny. But why? It was as if the gods frowned upon procreation. Aphrodite, Eros and even Hera, tempestuous goddess of marriage and wife of Zeus, had ignored her pleas for dispensation. How could they condone such injustice, decreeing male sperm contained future life but obliging women to suffer the purgatory of incubation?*

After a second son was born she was abandoned, confined to supervising the household and raising her husband's children. Then Dyonisis was thrown from his horse. In compliance with custom she wed the most senior unmarried member of her father's family, not out of concern for a grieving widow but to ensure return of her marriage dowry. Thesus, a widower whose male heirs had perished in the Peloponnesian wars, welcomed Dyonisis' sons as his own, herself and her daughters as extraneous parasites. He visited her bed a couple of times – was it out of duty or curiosity? – then overlooked her existence. Shortly thereafter he married off both her daughters, Artemis even before her fifteenth birthday, leaving her alone with the servitors.

She was forty years old. Although citizens often lived to a greater age she suspected the remainder of her life would be of brief duration. There was a cumulating weariness within her body; was it illness or fatigue from a tormented mind? In any case, having produced sons her life's work was accomplished, her continued existence an irrelevance.

She coveted the ignorance of women like Bettayia who had received no formal education beyond domestic management, whereas her own father, after the tragic death of his son, taught her to read and write in spite of society's condemnation of such practice. He introduced her to medicine, explaining that illness was caused by microbes and not the wrath of the gods; he expounded the fundamentals of democracy and the workings of the polis, and he shared his love of Homer and Sophocles. However, once married, she was confronted with the dreadful reality of being female. Whereas Bettayia and other wives accepted the poverty of their social standing with equanimity she, peremptorily denied access to knowledge, suffered incessantly.

Sighing softly, she arose from the bed. Soap, water and a comb removed external evidence of recent indulgences which, although practised widely, remained beyond normality. Or did they? The cleavage that split society into misunderstanding halves was between men and women; was it not logical that supreme love be confined to each sphere of influence, that intimacy between opposing sexes be limited to the necessity of impregnation?

Wiping clean her leather dildo, she wondered how a simple object cobbled from animal skin could generate such intense release. Except that the life, the urgency, the passion it communicated emanated not from its unforgiving rigidity but from the hands, the very soul of Bettayia. Not surprisingly the original upon which it was modelled, disfiguring the groins of an unfeeling husband, had generated neither joy nor excitement, only pain and resentment.

She placed the instrument in a drawer where it would await Bettayia's return. Never had she, never would she, provide her own satisfaction because self-induced pleasure constituted an abandonment of shared love for the ignominy of sexual solitude.

When dressing she respected the dictates of Thesus and encased her bosom in the garment that lifted a woman's breasts, for an ageing wife reflected adversely upon a husband's advancing maturity.

The sea-breeze brought chilling dampness to the mainland; it was early spring and the embrace of winter had not relinquished its hold. Sitting in the shelter of the terrace she watched the clouds scurrying overhead. Why? Because there was nothing else to do. Sometimes she gazed at a cloudless sky seeking the miniature holes through which stars shone at night. Whenever possible she listened to the wind in the trees, sometimes as it caressed them, occasionally when it whipped them with frenetic fury. How could something invisible display such strength? Unless, as claimed, wind was the breath of the gods and storms a manifestation of their anger.

She knew so little about so much. Men were inordinately proud of their odes, their poems, their myths and tragedies, yet how could she appreciate the splendour of Hesiod, Plutarch and Homer, learn from them, if denied the possibility of discussing their signification with others? Admittedly, on formal occasions when wives were invited, she attended presentations at the theatre. She was fascinated by the drama yet sensed the dialogues implied knowledge unknown to her. Sadly this was considered normal, for a woman's mind must remain pure through ignorance just as her body remained chaste through denial. Did not Pericles proclaim 'the best woman is she of whom men speak the least' and Xenophon advise that husbands and wives remain strangers to avoid frictions? Wives were inferior, one could not shun the facts, but why did husbands glorify the divergences instead of condescendingly overlooking them?

Concubines were also considered bodies without brains, servile suppliers of sensuality, whose responsibilities complemented those of a wife whilst insulting every one of them. Only the hetairai, women of pleasure and ladies of leisure, entrepreneurs of erotica, provided both social as well as physical intercourse to males. Refused formal education like other women, they learned from corresponding with distinguished guests during frequent evening festivities, adroitly outmanoeuvring their benefactors in the game of mutual self-gratification.

Wife, concubine or heteiras? Which was preferable? Incapable of answering her own question, she sought her linen threads; weaving would occupy her until nocturnal slumber provided release from daytime lethargy. She heard footsteps – her son Hylas was approaching. From the expression on his face he was not attending his mother; knowing of her presence he would have undoubtedly ventured elsewhere. Yet he greeted her politely and responded to enquiries about recent deeds and future plans.

So his training with Androculus was terminated. Upon attaining puberty sons of social dignitaries were attributed to older males with whom they followed an apprenticeship in the intricacies of physics, politics, literature and philosophy. She knew from hearsay that the curriculum did not limit itself to enriching the intellect – it included initiating the body because, so males assumed, only another male could instruct youths in the multifarious physical manifestations of love. Such distorted hypocrisy infuriated her. Why, following what warped logic, could male sodomites proudly stroll hand in hand *when women were censured for equivalent activities? Because husbands had legal ownership of a wife's sexuality which, accordingly, was theirs alone to dispense.*

Evening imposed its shroud of darkness on the outside world and she sought warmth and brightness inside the building.

He was convoked for jury service. Admittedly no democracy thrived without an irreproachable judiciary but polis leaders like himself were burdened with innumerable other responsibilities. Those upstart mercantile traders were to blame, their increasing influence was scarcely complemented by appreciation for the finer points of running a democratic oligarchy. He, Thesus, born into a noble family of landowners with impeccable lineage, should be granted unlimited freedom to administer Athens for the benefit of all.

The Peloponnesian War was a disaster, victory unattainable. The population, taxed to the limit, could not absorb another imposition. Even his finances were suffering. He would have willingly divorced his wife to economise needless expense but the marriage dowry departed with her, another archaic polis law that required amendment. To stop further depletion of the nation's wealth they should negotiate peace, however unfavourable the terms. Notwithstanding, after so much heroism, so many gallant soldiers making the ultimate sacrifice, including his two sons, it was unthinkable to contemplate anything other than final victory. Self-delusion, once an unwise luxury, had become an indispensable companion.

That evening he would cast aside such irritations; his adopted son Hylas was to be initiated into the Phratry. He had arranged a wonderful surprise, fitting proof of a father's pride and affection.

Having dined with her insipidly uninspiring sister she was walking within the confines of her quarters when the wind ceased hustling amongst the cypresses. She distinguished voices; her husband and son were talking in the main garden prior to another evening's merriment.

The former, proud his adopted son had completed his

29

apprenticeship with Androculus, was offering something special; the moment had come to experience a woman. Sons from modest families visited the city's brothels but Hylas deserved better. Far better. Myrtale, a hetairas *attending that evening, one of his favourites, would initiate him that night. Being with child, she no longer risked fecundation, consequently she would make available her true femininity instead of the habitual orifice. When Hylas asked how, therefore, could she be pregnant, the reply was that certain* hetairai *assumed such risk if the recompense was sufficient. Assuming she survived childbirth the wanton wretch could benefit from her ill-gained wealth at leisure.*

Hylas thanked his father, it was a wonderful indication of paternal love, and promised he would learn abundantly from the encounter.

The banquet was reaching its climax, when musical and intellectual exchanges replaced culinary considerations.

There was need to foster gaiety for the discussion had dwelled lengthily on the Peloponaesian War which had waged inconclusively for twenty years, decimating their population to such an extent that Athens could no longer sustain the over-abundance of widows and orphans. The humiliation of Delium and Mantineia, last year's debacle in Sicily during which many noble sons perished, the despotic military efficiency of Sparta which was impossible to contain; would the war ever terminate? When would the city's leaders realise their obstinate pride was destroying that which they so desperately wished to protect? However, as Myrtale, heteiras of impeccable reputation, it was her duty to promote merriment, not berate polis intelligentsia for refusing to accept sober realities. Payment of her generous fee depended upon it.

Admittedly she was contracted primarily for making available her body. However, as she continually reminded herself, unlike the thousands who sold their sexuality to dissipated males in sordid brothels, she alone had been chosen by a famous magistrate, not out of kindness but for social graces capable of rendering evenings as enjoyable as the nights that inevitably followed. Her current

30

assignment was especially satisfying; it would not be Thesus taking his pleasure but his adopted son Hylas. *Receiving the virginity of a high-born male was an honour, sexual initiation being a never-to-be-forgotten passage in a person's life.*

Her thoughts were interrupted as a debate raged amongst the guests.

'But Androculus, theories inapplicable in practice are dangerous distractions.'

'So solutions must be found to permit diligent application, prevent the foundations of our democracy from crumbling into anarchy.'

'Then explain how families of herktemoroi, declared slaves for non-payment of debt, can avoid starvation unless their sons are inducted into the army and daughters into our brothels.'

'Thereby paying for the sins of another.'

'Please, dear brethren! Remember we are gathered to welcome Hylas into our Phratry. Forget the conflicting world outside, instead enrich our minds with music and poetry!'

And Cleisthenes commenced reciting stanzas from the latest play of Aristophanes before proceeding to the much beloved Death of Simonides written by Sophocles before the world became afflicted by eternal strife. Then hired auletrids danced to the accompaniment of flutes playing airs so delicately intricate only the most refined citizens of Athens could possibly acclaim them.

She shuddered at the heartlessness of some of those present, especially Thesus. *Her hard-earned income repaid her father's debts, thereby protecting his family, including herself, from the degradation of servitude. It was for that reason she had accepted the risk of pregnancy.* Looking towards the arrogant and insolent white-haired male, father of the intruder inside her womb, she felt relieved she would not be servicing his desiderata that night.

She discreetly observed those dining, hearing but only partly understanding their words. Her master was agitated and extremely inebriated, sharing his bed that night would be brief and brutal, there would be no gentle moments before the snoring commenced.

She understood that Myrtale, the arrogantly opinionated hetairas, would be receiving the adopted son. Which of the concubines, therefore, would he choose? Amphorate was indisposed, Hera had been claimed the previous night, so it could well be her turn. Which was worse, being mauled by somebody one detested or lying unheeded in an empty boudoir? The latter, because nothing was more humiliating than the unsubtle smirking of a competing concubine.

Lying in bed unable to sleep, recalling sublime moments shared with Bettayia, she distinguished noises from outside. Somebody, no, two people, were traversing the terrace, her son and an unknown woman, no doubt the heteiras. A faint squeaking revealed their entering the building, subsequent sounds bore witness to their presence in the bedroom evacuated when her daughter married.

Listening, she distinguished the sounds of lovers exploring each other's bodies. She was surprised by the duration of the exchanges – both parties, especially the woman, seemed to be enjoying themselves, there was an inexplicable absence of haste to accomplish the final act. She imagined her adored progeny in the arms of a woman. What was he thinking? Did he respect his partner or consider her flesh to be exploited without compassion?

She sensed increasing urgency in their movements until the accompanying sounds confirmed her son had achieved manhood in the simplest and yet most complex of ways.

Fifth encounter: Mounia and Romulus
49 BC   Rome, Italy

The market was crowded, overflowing with citizens of the greatest metropolis in the world, a city seething with military power, literary expression and social cognisance. Also political intrigue, injustice and misery. Buyers surrounded the displays seeking gastronomic delicacies and household essentials, incessantly haggling in an attempt to reduce inordinate prices down to something affordable. Stalls offering unfamiliar produce from afar generated the most excitement as wealthier citizens sought luxuries including amber from barbaric regions north of the Danube, incense from Arabia and silk from China.

One stand was relatively quiet in spite of the exceptional quality of its merchandise. Few Roman households could afford slaves, especially fresh arrivals from overseas. Whereas families with more modest fortunes acquired rejects from consular and senatorial households, prospective purchasers inspecting the wares on display were determined to acquire the best whilst preventing their social emulators from outmanoeuvring them in the process.

A family was goaded onto the platform; their facial features indicating origins in north-eastern Africa, possibly Ethiopia. The male was tall and muscular yet he showed surprising passivity for someone forcibly uprooted from his rightful heritage; although lacking requisite aggressiveness for the arenas he should be ideal for labouring in the fields. The female, squat with muscular shoulders and broad hips, was accustomed to transporting heavy burdens. Again a good quality product. The daughter was an equally fine

33

specimen, and her lithesome body would shortly be ripe for her master's bedchamber.

The dealer lashed his whip in their direction, ordering them to strip. She hesitated but her father, already naked, begged her to obey. The dealer made a sudden move, threatening attrition for her lack of discipline. Sobbing, she untied her sash. As the garment fell to the ground she placed one arm across her chest, the other against her lower abdomen. The whip lashed towards her. She instinctively removed her hands, standing fully exposed, failing to hide her humiliation as completely as she failed to hide the promise of forthcoming womanhood.

Why had she been taken from her village? Life had been so enjoyable, especially the meals she shared with her family and games played with the other girls, also watching dancing whenever there was a marriage or death to celebrate, which more than compensated for the wearisome days cultivating crops upon which depended the survival of her tribe.

Admittedly she had recently been initiated into the world of women. The dressing up, the singing and dancing, the excitement amongst her fellow villagers; she knew they were celebrating something important. Then, one by one, the fortunate girls were invited into the wooden building where the village elders held meetings. Her turn arrived. She was placed on a wooden table, her arms and legs securely held by four women, including her mother. The oldest female of the village advanced with a sharpened knife and, before she could react, could resist, could protect herself, its blade sliced deep into her tender flesh. She screamed as much from shock as from the pain. A cloth was placed where the blood was flowing and she was carried to a bed where she lay for two miserable days wondering why she had been mistreated. Then, as the discomfort disappeared and life returned to normal, she forgot the distressing experience.

Not long afterwards there was gossip that Elplem, younger son of the village leader, had taken an interest. He was tall and handsome, the best hunter of the village. Although proud and excited she doubted she was ready to become a bride; her body had not expanded outwards so how could she provide milk for her children? Then, when the horrible strangers entered the village pointing weapons at anyone who attempted to escape, Elplem had hurled a stone. Immediately surrounded, he had been speared to death while she watched.

Terrified, the other villagers had offered no resistance. Much to their astonishment they were neither killed nor tortured, nor were the women interfered with, although several of the strangers eyed them avidly. Then somebody discovered Levlieh had no vision which, so she learned afterwards, rendered her unsaleable. The strangers had taken their pleasure one at a time before slitting her throat.

The lashing of the whip brought her back to the present, to the men studying her nakedness, to wondering what further affronts awaited her. They were scrutinised from all angles before the dealer prised open their mouths so everyone could inspect inside. Then, without warning, she was lifted by the legs. Everyone gathered around, eyeing where they should not, nodding in satisfaction.

What was happening, who were the people inspecting her? They were obviously superior to her villagers, arrogant and authoritarian, treating those in chains like domestic animals. But why, instead of stealing their belongings (not that they possessed many) had they themselves been taken from the village? What was required of them?

They had learned from a guard who spoke their language that prisoners were sometimes fed to hungry lions or forced to kill each other while spectators cheered. It was unbelievable, despicable, disgusting. But why had nothing terrible happened to them? Nothing made sense. Her parents prayed to their gods, pleading that they intervene to rescue them from the evil inhabitants of the enormous village in which they were being held captive. But nobody came, possibly because her parents had forgotten the correct words of the prayers.

The next morning she stood with her parents as a crowd of men shouted and gesticulated. Afterwards, as he transported them in a cart, the person who had chosen them, called an overseer, explained why they had been brought to the big village called Rome. They had been acquired by a senator, whatever that was, who now owned them. So long as they instantaneously obeyed every order, every instruction, every command, they could consider themselves lucky to have been integrated into the household of such a noble citizen.

Arriving at the senator's imposing villa, the chains binding her parents were removed. Her father was escorted away to outlying buildings which housed those labouring in the vineyards, males and females not being permitted to communicate. Distraught with worry for her father, she accompanied her mother to the kitchen where they would help prepare food and tidy away after each meal.

Realising that nourishment was guaranteed, if only scrapings from plates served to their masters, that she would be living in quarters more opulent than her village hovel and that she would be working with other abducted people, she considered herself relatively lucky. At least she assumed she was, for until commencing her duties she was suspicious of her masters; for example why had they studied between her legs at the market? And why, if slaves were so fortunate, why were they dragged from their homes instead of being invited to work for the masters?

She and her mother rapidly assumed their new duties. Shortly before their arrival two slaves had been badly injured when a shelf in the storeroom collapsed. Unable to work, they were sold to a merchant living in a nearby town called Tarquinii. The person supervising them, a particularly despicable Galician, had so severely punished one of the remaining slaves after a catastrophic banquet, that she was confined to her quarters. Hence the urgent need for replacements.

Apart from endless toiling the most vexing aspect of their existence was the prohibition to indulge in any manifestation of their former lives, such as dressing in traditional attire or singing native songs. Homesick, full of hatred for those who had abducted her, she vowed never to forget her origins. However, in spite of her rebellious state of mind, she refrained from displaying incivility to those ordering her around; fear of punishment was too great.

Several months after her arrival she was informed of her good fortune; with another girl she was to train for working inside the villa. Supervised by an elderly servant called the paedagogus, *they helped tidy their masters' residential quarters. They cleaned the marbled and mosaic floors, carried linen to the wash-house, transported vast quantities of water to the rooms where their masters washed and relieved themselves.*

Their greatest thrill was being allowed to watch as servants and trusted slaves served at table in the peristylium, *an open-air courtyard with a fountain and luxuriant vegetation. Observing the vast quantity of victuals she imagined they were preparing for a banquet, whereas a mere scattering of the master's entourage presented themselves at the appointed hour. Admittedly they were superior but surely their bodies, however corpulent, did not require such vast amounts of nourishment? The diners clamoured for more even before their plates were emptied, shouting abuse if their wishes were not instantly respected by the scurrying attendants. By the end of the meal, revolted by the sordid spectacle, she decided preparing meals was less onerous and avoided contact with her foul-tempered masters who, notwithstanding, proclaimed themselves superior to everyone else.*

She learned much from the paedagogus, *whose delight at gossiping overcame reticence for conversing with slaves. The master and mistress slept in separate chambers, as was normal. The former habitually welcomed visitors during the night; one of her duties would be to clear away evidence the following morning. His wife received nobody because, in accordance with Roman law, her husband could kill her for such indiscretions. She had few occupations during the daytime other that preparing her toilet and indulging in extravagances – for example acquiring perfumes, cosmetics and silken garments, jewellery, statuettes and articles of toiletry; the more exotic and expensive the more she purchased. Two servitors attended solely to the mistress' toiletry, once in the morning and again when she returned from the baths and prepared herself for the evening.*

She listened attentively to the paedagogus, *deeply mystified by the incomprehensible comportment of her masters. Her confusion was only further increased when, sometime later, he announced the mistress was no longer in residence and her two servitors had been dismissed.*

She was always pleased to return to her quarters, share experiences with her mother, someone who understood. Then the only link to her former life was sold to another household because she had forgotten to add lemons and spices to vegetables cooked in utensils made from lead, which frequently dispensed an unpleasant taste. The senator had been acutely embarrassed when the incriminating food was served to distinguished guests and had insisted that the guilty person be severely punished.

Sharing her room with an unfriendly stranger, she cried herself to sleep each evening, wondering if she would be happier if dead.

Her training completed without further misadventure, she was incorporated into the team serving at table.

The first meal was a nightmare. It was a tumultuous banquet organised to celebrate a son, sixteen years old, participating in the ceremony of toga virilis *at the Forum. He had been permitted to shave for the first time, had received an adult haircut and was duly proclaimed a Roman citizen. And now family and friends had gathered together to celebrate all night.*

They realised it was her initiation, her first experience, yet they yelled with impatience if she failed to cater instantaneously to their ravenous caprices. The more she accelerated the less the complaints, but the greater the risk of spilling food or upsetting cutlery. Thankfully her nimble limbs enabled her to survive without incident. Her only mishap was when, having espied an empty plate, she advanced to offer replenishment. The guest spewed forth a torrent of abuse, adjudicating she was fully capable of deciding when to order; how dare a lowly specimen of humanity interrupt the important conversation she was having. And the woman pointedly asked for a delicacy being served by someone else.

As weeks became months, as the cool damp of winter replaced summer, she became familiar with the master's family, also some of the regular guests. She memorised their tastes, predicting when and what they would order. During evening festivities discipline frequently disintegrated into disorder as wine befuddled minds and manners and lechery displaced social decorum. The servers were forgotten so long as plates and glasses were overflowing. Carefully surveying the overseer and their increasingly inebriated masters, servants and slaves managed to consume generous quantities of food intended for guests. Everyone, however, fastidiously refrained from drinking wine; the penalty for drunkenness was well known: public flogging followed by eviction from the villa after receiving an invitation to attend another banquet where the guests were lions and they were the victuals.

She felt sorry for the musicians who played lilting odes and ballads on lyres, flutes and harps. Nobody listened as they sang of ethereal love, more often unrequited than consummated. As the evening advanced their simple yet sensitive airs became indistinguishable amongst the raucous sounds of revelry.

She preferred the more intimate meals organised in the villa's trielinium. *Usually there were nine attendees who lay on comfortable couches as they consumed a surfeit of gastronomic delicacies. But they remained sober, discussing a wide range of subjects. Reference was made to the colonisation of recently conquered counties; there was trouble in Gaul, although recent uprisings had been crushed. More alarmingly, internal political strife was threatening the stability of the Republic. After the death of Crassus it was rumoured that both remaining members of the* Triumvirate, *Pompey and Caesar, would seek absolute power. Civil war was inevitable. Consequently it was vital to swear allegiance to the eventual winner. Whoever that might be. Otherwise the discussions explored a diversity of topics most of which lauded the grandeur and splendour of Rome. But not its decadence.*

Listening, barely understanding, she felt humble, helpless, nondescript. Perhaps it was inevitable that lowly people like herself became slaves, serving important masters as they struggled to administer a far-flung empire.

When spring arrived she was promoted to attending individual family members and guests, serving them exclusively, even helping with their toilet between courses. For the first time she was recognised as a person, inferior and dominated, but someone who provided useful assistance.

One evening, after the dining room had been cleared of the vestiges of a relatively quiet family gathering, she was returning to her quarters when a servant accosted her, announcing her convocation to attend one of the masters, an elder brother of the senator. She recognised his name, she regularly served him in the trielinium. A much respected consul, he was ill-mannered and disgustingly obese, someone who consumed vast quantities of food, dribbled down his toga and occasionally vomited onto the floor near where she was waiting to be summoned. Recently, whilst serving him, she had felt his hand touching her legs underneath her short tunic.

She was escorted upstairs and along a spacious corridor, then practically pushed through an open door into a bedchamber. The servant disappeared, leaving her alone with the elderly male.

'You are Mounia?'

She nodded. Although she understood their language, she was still unable to converse fluently.

'Apparently you have never known a man?'

She looked at him uncomprehendingly.

'Well, have you known a man? Answer me immediately.'

She shook her head.

'Excellent. Since you serve well at table and are no longer a child, you may experience me as your first male. I hope you are truly grateful for the honour bestowed upon you?'

She stood facing the grotesquely rotund master, too shocked to respond.

He waddled menacingly towards her, furious at again receiving no answer. She stepped backwards, surely he was too old to engage in such activities? Although, she now realised, she was no longer too young.

'Please, you me wish to marry?'

'Marry an ignorant peasant like you? Of course not, you stupid simpleton. In any case, I am already ... I have no intention whatsoever of marrying you, just allowing you to benefit from my knowledge in such matters.'

She stared uncertainly in his direction, not fully convinced by his logic yet aware that refusal would result in terrible retribution.

'I have little time to devote to your apprenticeship, remove your clothes and enter my bed.'

She clutched her tunic. Back home girls remained untouched until marrying otherwise the gods punished them. The custom was obviously different in the society of her masters. And not entirely illogical. In her village boys were taught to craft weapons and hunt animals, girls were trained to prepare food and mend torn clothes. It was intelligent that experienced people share their knowledge with others, so why not teach women how to please a future husband? Her masters were far more intelligent than members of her tribe, she should feel grateful that someone so important was willing to initiate her. Regrettably the teacher was ugly and smelt unpleasant. But of course! If he was repugnant, there could be no possibility of having romantic thoughts about him.

'Undress!!! Your disobedience is most distressing in view of my generous offer.'

'Please, is it necessary to remove my garment?'

'Of course, you stupid idiot. Remember, I own your clothes, so if you do not comply I will confiscate your entire wardrobe. Do you wish to serve naked at table tomorrow?'

She unhooked her tunic, offering implicitly to the master that which she once believed would be reserved for one special person.

'On the bed.'

She complied, intrigued at discovering what happened after marriage but wishing her teacher would be more considerate towards her.

'Lie on your back and close your eyes. You are not authorised to see me naked.'

She obeyed.

41

'You will widen your legs as a sign you wish to be taken. I, most touched by your gesture, will be honoured to comply with your wishes.'

Her thighs remained clamped together.

'I am waiting for you to offer yourself to me.'

She had lived at the villa long enough to realise he would not wait interminably. Even so, she hesitated, sensing disappointment; surely he should be loving and kind towards her? Of course not! He was a teacher, signs of friendship were inappropriate, he was there strictly to educate her. So she complied.

'Please you understand I try to be good pupil but perhaps not succeed. You must be gentle, I hurt wish not.'

'I decide such matters. The more you suffer, the more you are showing your appreciation for my generosity. You understand?'

She did not, but people who applauded when humans fought to the death or were savaged by lions obviously thought differently from an uneducated girl like herself.

She heard him advancing towards the bed. He placed a hand where the old woman had cut with the knife.

'Ah, I see you have been sliced! A ridiculous custom, even apes do not descend to such levels of stupidity. Well, do not blame me for the absence of pleasure you are about to receive.'

Forgetting his instructions, she partly opened her eyes to catch sight of the fleshy mound of Roman consul towering above her. Please, she prayed, please may I give satisfaction and learn much from his attentions.

She spread her legs even wider to ensure he understood her willingness and appreciation.

Sixth encounter: Hamish and Fiona
650   Callander, Scotland

The westerly gale whipped the waters of Loch Venacher into a fury; wavelets no longer lapped its shores, they pounded it with hostile ferocity. He, Collin, crouched alongside his brother Alexander, blending into the heather and gorse. The rain lashed continuously against their clothes, without effect, because the material was already sodden; they had been waiting an eternity.

Normally they would have climbed the majestic slopes of Ben Ledi, seeking hare and grouse. The wind, however, was veering northerly. Higher up, hidden amongst the swirling clouds, sleet and snow were falling in profusion, rendering access well nigh impossible and extremely perilous. So they had chosen the lower yet equally dangerous slopes of Beinn Dearg.

Here the threat came not from the forces of nature but Hamish, son of Ewan, fierce and feared master of Callander, whose fiefdom claimed surrounding glens including the peat-infested terrain upon which they were hunting. They had discussed the situation, but desperation blinds even the most cautious of men, the desperation of having to feed undernourished women and children before they succumbed to the frozen rigours of winter. Their sheep had been savaged by wolves, their pitiful crops of rye and barley had rotted from weeks of continuous rain, and the few salmon they had caught were long consumed. Either they hunted or they starved to death.

However great the need for food, they were regretting their decision to hunt near Loch Venacher. Not because of the weather – fierce storms were frequent – but because the wind camouflaged all sounds. Admittedly it facilitated their stalking by deafening animals to human presence, but it rendered them equally oblivious to noises made by humans, other humans, the game-wardens of Hamish of Callander, men to fear, men to avoid at all costs.

It appeared beside the clump of gorse to their right. With one graceful movement, perfected by years of practice, he flung the netting and pulled the entrapped animal towards him. Before he could wring its neck, shapes arose from behind an adjacent ridge and hurled themselves downwards in their direction. Abandoning netting and ensnared rabbit, they ran.

As expected, youth and agility enabled them to leave the yelling pursuers far behind. Then Alexander tripped on a root and plummeted headlong into a hidden hollow, practically disappearing beneath the ebony waters overflowing from it. He tried to rise, but screamed in agony as a splintered ankle buckled under his weight.

'Leave me, save yourself!'

'No, never!'

'Do not be a fool, run!'

He looked at his elder brother, the person he most adored, his friend, guide, mentor and teacher, and realised there was no alternative. So he ran. And only stopped when he reached the collection of hovels they called home.

He entered not his dwelling but that of Alisdair, the village carpenter, changed into dry clothes awaiting his return, hid the waterlogged evidence of his exposure to the elements under wood-shavings and commenced to calmly fashion a spoke from the wheel of an oxcart. Only the trembling of his hands and deep breathing bore witness to activities other than sedentary woodwork. Nobody spoke a word, they understood what had happened, what was happening, what would shortly occur when the game-wardens arrived.

As indeed they did.

'Where is he?'

'Whom might you be seeking?'

'The infernal poacher, he who was accompanying Alexander, son of Malcolm, the thief we have just captured hunting rabbit on our lands.'

44

'Nobody from our village is absent, you must be mistaken.'

'What about Alexander, the thieving bastard.'

'I was given to understand by himself that he wished to collect wood.'

'In the pouring rain?!'

'When none is left, wood dampened by the weather is preferable to none.'

'Liar!'

Angus, son of Bruce, chief warden of Callander, gazed around the smoke-filled hovel, recognising many of those present for they were neighbours, neighbours who mistrusted, disrespected, occasionally despised and frequently insulted each other, but lived in relative concordance until poaching on Callander lands resulted in violent retribution.

'You!'

Receiving no reply, he strode across the room and grabbed her by the arm.

'You are hurting me.'

'You are Fiona, sister to Alexander.'

It was a statement, not a question, for he knew her identity.

'You will return to Callander with me. Only when the miserable wretch accompanying Alexander submits to our justice, will you be released.'

'And if this imaginary person does not materialise?'

'Knowing Hamish of Callander, she will be decreed guilty and dangle by the neck in the company of her contemptible brother.'

The rain had ceased. Instead, violent sleet squalls savaged the barren uplands, occasionally descending to batter habitations cowering beneath the protective flanks of the Trossachs and Menteith Hills. The wooden construction that served as home for Malcolm and Moyna, plus their three children Alexander, Collin and Fiona, shuddered as hail lashed its outer walls, threatening to flatten the roughly hewn and unstable structure.

Inside, the villagers were discussing yet another tragedy afflicting their community, where suffering composed the daily routine and survival was a luxury.

'They know both of you were attending.'

'No! Only that we were two in number, my identity is secure.'

'Alexander will tell.'

'No! My brother may be poor but he is proud and honourable.'

'Nobody resists their torturing.'

'Pity upon him, and us all!'

'I will present myself before they arrive to seize me. I will plead my purpose was to stop Alexander from poaching, convince them of my noble intentions, ask pardon for trespassing. And then return home with Fiona.'

'Fie upon your naivety. They want blood, not justice.'

'But they would spare Fiona.'

'So she might return home to starve amongst us. If no other solution prevails, Fiona dies so you may continue to provide for us.'

'Never!'

'You will first reflect the wisdom of my words. Then you will obey.'

He heard the commotion, sensing from sounds permeating his private apartment that something of import must have occurred. The strong, virulent voice of Hamish could be heard above the fracas. Damnation to him. For he, Tristram, eldest son of the recently defunct Ewan, was titular ruler of Callander, not his arrogant, self-opinionated and swaggering younger sibling. Except that, since their father's interment, one could indeed suppose that Hamish ruled their fiefdom. Because that is precisely what he did, only involving his elder brother in ceremonies necessary to validate dubious confiscation of land or condemn people not as logic and morality would instruct but in accordance with the illicit interests of Hamish himself.

He continued pacing before the fire, frozen limbs distracting his concentration. Hearsay spoke of a transparent shield placed across windows which permitted light but not winds to enter a building. The

Angles imported it from Flanders. He should make enquiries with merchants in Stirling because the draughts infiltrating his rooms chilled the flames in his hearth even before their heat reached him.

Hamish entered without the politeness of knocking.

'Caught one of them!'

'Could you please be more explicit?'

'Alexander, son of Malcolm, poaching rabbit on our lands near Loch Vernacher.'

'Is that not land our grandfather confiscated?'

'Yes.'

'For what reason?'

'Because of the good hunting!'

Realising discussion would be pointless, he returned to more imminent matters.

'What are the exact charges?'

'Caught poaching our family's game. In accordance with the law, they both hang.'

'To which law might you be referring?'

'The one we formalised with father before his death.'

'I was not party to such deliberations.'

'That is your problem. Anyway, the law is decided and must be enforced.'

'You say *both* must hang?'

'Yes.'

'But you have apprehended only one.'

'Yes?'

'So whom might be the other?'

'Possibly the younger brother, Collin. We will soon know!'

'And how, might I enquire, will you shortly be learning of his identity?'

'We have a hostage, Fiona, unmarried sister of Alexander. It is simple; we lift her clothing and explain that if he protects the identity of his accomplice his sweet little sibling will be soiled as befitting the circumstances.'

'You would not ...'

'Do not fret! Watching me prepare to unravel her maidenhood will loosen his tongue!'

'If he refuses?'

'Then the sister hangs with him, preferably first so he may witness the consequence of his silence.'

'And if he confesses, gives you the information?'

'We arrest the person identified as guilty, hang both of them.'

'And the sister?'

'We still take our pleasure, perfectly justified considering the trouble her family has caused. Then we accidentally slit her throat.'

'But that is murder!!'

'No, the elimination of an irritation.'

'I will not have it!!'

'Do not allow childish morality to interfere with the imposition of justice. Would you invite every crook and felon to invest our lands by publicly pardoning those caught stealing our game?'

'Of course not. But ...'

'There is no "but" to worry yourself about. Just leave matters to me.'

And his brother exited the chamber, no doubt planning to celebrate his capture of human game in a manner both boisterous and inebriated.

'I wish to see the prisoners.'

'But, Sire, your brother gave instructions ...'

'I am not interested in his instructions. Fetch them both.'

'Please, Sire, Alexander, son of Malcolm, is in chains and your brother possesses the key.'

'Then fetch the woman.'

He waited her arrival, deep in thought, incensed at his brother's baseless cruelty. He agreed justice must be imposed but that meant deference to morality, in other words equating punishment with the seriousness of the crime. Furthermore, however impoverished and downtrodden, there were limits to what peasants would endure before rising up to ouster self-proclaimed despots. With the Scots

48

leaving Ireland to occupy much of the western highlands and Northumbrians forever pushing their boundaries northwards, he and Hamish could eventually depend upon those very same peasants for protection.

Add to this there was trouble brewing amongst the seafaring Danes and Vikings. The time had come to strengthen relationships with neighbours, reinforce their kingdom's ability to defend itself. His fellow countrymen should bury their differences, not their kinsfolk. Yet their king in Inverness seemed indifferent to the survival of his nation.

His brother, likewise, thought little of such matters. To him nearby Dunblane and Stirling were dens of debauchery whereas each represented a bastion of influence that should be exploited.

Travellers spoke increasingly of a new god. No, his son, who had descended to earth somewhere in a distant land. He was Jewish, whatever that meant, and his mother had given birth without having known a man. Surprisingly the god was not Thor, he was somebody else whose name he had forgotten. Worship of his son was becoming widespread, even in Rome. Of course the Romans were long since departed from Britain, having been replaced by Saxons, Angles and Jutes who now occupied the southern lands. Apparently even they were becoming believers and were constructing numerous places of worship called cathedrals.

Although the happenings were muddled, the words of this mysterious son of a god abounded with common sense. One should be friendly with neighbours, pardon those who annoyed you and not intrude upon other men's wives. Then you rested every seventh day, although it was unclear whether you could still hunt game and take pleasure with women. He had forgotten the other recommendations; being unable to inscribe words in permanent form was frustrating.

A Saint Augustine (apparently saints were messengers from heaven) had settled in Canterbury; another named Columba had constructed a large stone building for his followers on the western island of Iona. Perhaps he should visit, learn more about their beliefs, determine whether their ways should be introduced in Callander.

Except that Hamish would refuse.

He wondered about the villagers whence came the poachers. They were neither Picts, like himself, nor Scots, so they must have arrived from the south before settling near Loch Venacher, living a pitiful existence on land unclaimed until his father took a fancy to hunting rabbit and grouse.

A knock on the door interrupted his reflections. The gaoler entered, pushing forward the requested prisoner. Her hands tied tightly, she would have fallen if he had not stepped forward.

'You may leave us.'

'But …'

'Out!!'

And they were left alone.

He studied the shivering creature as she stared downwards, purposefully avoiding his gaze, her ragged clothes still dripping damp from her journey through the driving rain.

'What is your name?'

She looked up, surprise registering on her face. Evidently she had been expecting someone else.

He walked to the nearby table and sought a knife.

She lurched backwards in terror.

'If you inform me of your name and promise not to escape, I will release your hands.'

She stood there, uncomprehending.

He replaced the knife on the table.

'Fiona, daughter of Malcolm and Moyna.'

The knife remained on the table.

'I promise not to escape.'

He sliced the rope, uncovering wrists bleeding from the vicious and unnecessary strength with which she had been bound. He led her to the fire, supporting her as the flames warmed her body and caused the dampness impregnating her clothes to evaporate.

Leaving her briefly, he fetched a jug of fermented mead. She hesitated, then, fear of fainting overcoming pride, she consumed his offering.

'I summoned you not to propose nourishment but to understand what happened this afternoon.'

She remained silent. Then spoke.

'I'll no inform.'

'I understand. Please instead tell of your past.'

As clothes dried on her body, as mead permeated her veins, she recounted the little she knew about her family.

'So you mother is descended from Erwin of Carlisle?'

'Yes. We lived in peace and happiness until the Saxons invaded, annihilating our army at Catterick. We escaped north to the Pentlands, only to be ousted by the Northumbrians as they marched towards Edinburgh. That is when we arrived near Callander, installing ourselves on lands owned by nobody until your father ransacked our village, massacred our men, abducted their women and confiscated our lands. Since then we have been living, more often dying, near where my brother was … was collecting wood.'

'But you had no title to those lands.'

'Nor did your father.'

He pondered her words, aware of the validity of her reprobation, amazed a girl peasant should be so versed in such matters. Although, upon reflection, she was of extremely noble descent, Carlisle being a considerably more prominent burgh than Callander.

'What happened to the women?'

'We know not. Violated, murdered. Possibly some survived. We believe your father sired children with several of them but this cannot be proven.'

He winced at her words for he had harboured similar suspicions.

'What do you want of me, who are you?'

'Me? I am Tristram, son of Ewan.'

'Younger brother to Hamish?'

'No, his elder brother.'

'But…'

'Yes, my brother decides matters related to administering the burgh, including the imposing of justice upon poachers.'

'Who decided it was your land?'

51

'My father.'

'He is the thief, not my brother.'

He looked at her, admiring her fortitude, realising she displayed little of the vacuous peasant looks he so reviled. In fact, she was far from unattractive.

'It is not for us to question history.' Except that respecting history was crucial to imposing justice.

A short silence ensured, permitting both to warm themselves beside the fire. Their eyes met, he smiled. But there was nothing in return, although possibly her scowl became less intense.

'What is your age?'

'Seventeen.'

'But you are not already married?'

'No! My father says there will be no more unions, no additional children, until we can feed ourselves.'

He looked away disconcerted. People should not endure such poverty whilst his fellow burghers habitually feasted and drank themselves senseless.

'Now I have answered your questions, might I go free?'

'If the second poacher surrenders, then I would expect my brother to release you.'

'And then he will hang both my brothers?'

'You admit it was your brother?'

She closed her eyes in dismay, realising she had supplied the information he required and had so deceitfully obtained from her.

'Now that you know, you unscrupulous rogue, I hope you are contented. But freeing me will serve little purpose, I could never again face my parents.'

Before he could respond she staggered and then overbalanced, falling towards the fire. He helped her into a nearby chair, refilled her cup with mead and waited until she regained her composure.

'What happened to the rabbit?'

'I know not. No doubt your game-wardens will consume it when celebrating my brother's capture.'

'But if we consume the rabbit no proof remains that your brothers were indeed poaching. Trespassing, assuredly, but poaching requires trapped animals as proof. Perhaps, if your whole village promises never to stray on our lands, I can persuade my brother to show leniency.'

'You are the head of the clan. It is your decision.'

'Yes, but not really. As I have indicated, my brother decides on my behalf.'

They were interrupted by a servant requesting whether his master would be dining. He commanded that food be brought for two.

'I apologise for assuming you would dine with me; I should first have requested your opinion.'

'As your prisoner, I have no choice.'

'True. Although I would not wish to impose myself upon you. Do you accept?'

'No. How can I sit partaking of victuals whilst my brother is starving in your dungeon?'

'He shall be fed.'

And, true to his word, he issued the necessary orders, much to the amazement of his dinner guest and the consternation of the gaoler.

It was late, the meal had been consumed in an atmosphere of tension, although fleeting moments of understanding were discernible towards the end of the evening. Each had learned from the other, both were amazed how little they appreciated their respective existences. She had never heard of Columba, nor of his teachings, proving Britons maintained their traditional beliefs. Yet there was tolerance in her thoughts.

Finally, when she swayed from fatigue, he summoned the gaoler.

'I return the prisoner. Please ensure that she is as comfortable as possible in her cell, with sufficient covers to keep her warm. It is not necessary to bind her hands. Am I understood?'

Not only did the gaoler understand, it was clear he resented interference into the application of his duties. However, not daring to refute his master, he sullenly led away the prisoner.

'What the damnation have you been doing?'

Hamish had stormed into his brother's apartment on learning of the latter's intrusion into affairs that did not concern him.

'I have been collecting information from one of the prisoners in order that justice may be properly applied.'

'My prisoners.'

'No, our prisoners. The girl is innocent and I order you to release her. Furthermore, you have no proof against the other prisoner.'

'We have the rabbit he caught which, for your information, tasted excellent washed down with our best ale. In any case, proof is irrelevant.'

'Proof is fundamental if justice is to be imposed. You will therefore drop charges of poaching, instead assessing a minor penalty for trespassing.'

'How dare you! Such matters are my prerogative.'

'No longer. As chief of our clan I refuse to tolerate your perfunctory application of justice. If you listened to messages preached by the new Jewish son of a god you would accept my reasoning, appreciate its valid foundation.'

'By the love of Thor! You cannot take seriously the pathetic, ramblings of some foreign bastard fisherman! Peace and security are earned through fear, by eliminating troublemakers before they cumulate power, not sitting down to exchange feather-minded pleasantries.'

'One should seek to respect one's enemies, overcome divergences through understanding and not mindless slaughtering.'

'You talk like an aged grandmother. You and that puerile peasant peacemaker from Arabia! Do you realise he speaks of forbidding what men do to their womenfolk!! He is a misguided troublemaker. And so is anyone eagerly contemplating his idiocies. In any case, he is dead.'

'After the girl is released I intend to voyage to Iona to better comprehend the new teachings; you should accompany me.'

'This is intolerable! You leave me no choice. Malcolm! Iain! I, in accordance with powers invested by our father, disinherit my brother

54

of the title of Master of the Burgh. Henceforth, I replace him. You will chain him in the stockade until such time he formally accepts my authority or is banished.'

'You cannot do this!'

'Yes I can. Our father always doubted your ability to rule in his stead. He, therefore, accorded me the right to destitute you if your conduct threatened the well-being of our fiefdom. Your asinine interventions this evening are ample proof of your unworthiness.'

Alone, barricaded in the storeroom, he contemplated whether to accept submission or seek a different life elsewhere. He thought of his conversations with itinerant monks from Iona, remembered their gentle and warming messages of hope, wondered whether he should join them in their mission to spread humanity throughout their land. He also thought of Fiona, daughter of Malcolm, acknowledging he had been charmed by her gentle and noble personality even though she had manifested no such appreciation for him.

The following morning he was ordered to attend his brother in his quarters, his brother's quarters. In other words, his rightful quarters. On arriving he was surprised to notice both prisoners in attendance, the male Alexander, shackled, bruised and bleeding, forced to stand in spite of his shattered ankle, and the female, the sweet Fiona, with wrists so tightly bound her hands were whitened from lack of blood.

'My dear brother. You have been summoned to witness justice in action.'

He remained silent, aware that an argument of words was doomed to failure.

His brother addressed Alexander.

'Yesterday you were caught poaching on my lands in the presence of another person. I request that you provide the identity of this person.'

'I was alone, collecting firewood.'

'Liar!'

'I was alone, your men must be mistaken.'

'With the intervention of your sister, I intend to incite your memory to recall information so conveniently forgotten.'

He turned towards the girl. 'Untie her wrists. Excellent. Now, place her over the table. No! Not face downwards, I prefer she witness her humiliation. That is better. Now fasten her hands and feet to the table.'

The girl moaned as the rope scorched her flesh.

'Tighter!'

The girl screamed.

'Fine!'

His brother picked up a heavy baton, walked towards the bound prisoner, slid the wooden instrument under her skirt and lifted the material until her knees were visible.

'Yes, as I expected, a fine rounded body, astonishing for a supposedly starving peasant. Now, Alexander, son of Malcolm, if you do not immediately deliver the name of your accomplice I will, with this rod and while you watch, personally deprive your sister of something she surely protects with immeasurable pride and determination.'

'No!'

'I request that my brother keep his silence, he is here to witness, nothing more.'

He noticed the prisoner look towards his sister, whose eyes were closed with shame at the visual aggression of her pudency.

'It was my brother Collin. However, he was in no way helping me, he was arguing I should hunt elsewhere.'

'Liar!!!'

'It is true'

'But thank you for the information!'

'I assure you that I have spoken the truth.'

'That is doubtful.'

'What about my sister?'

'She remains to keep me company.'

'But you promised ...'

'If I recollect, I promised to deprive her of something precious if

56

the information was not forthcoming. I cannot recall accepting to refrain from such distraction if the requested name was provided.'

'You bastard.'

'That statement is incorrect, as my mother would undoubtedly attest were she attending.'

He turned menacingly towards the table, still holding the heavy baton.

'As my dearest brother keeps insisting, justice must be fair. Since the prisoner was not personally present on our lands, instead of punishing her with this somewhat unforgiving instrument, I will execute the sentence in a far friendlier manner.'

Everyone was forcibly ushered from the apartment, the game-wardens departing excitedly to apprehend Collin. As he and Alexander were being escorted to the dungeon he envisioned what would be taking place in the confines of his apartment, where Hamish, younger son of Ewan and self-proclaimed Master of Callander, having closed the door, would be advancing towards the table.

Seventh encounter: Olwen and Elfreda
875   Exstead, Wessex

'Clonk!'

'Once more and you will be victorious!'

'Clack!'

'Ha! Almost missed!'

'Clonk'

'Clack'

'Clokk ...'

Spectators cheered as Alfred's conker disintegrated into smithereens.

'That is five more beans added to your seven, making ...'

'Eleven!!'

'A dozen!'

Alfred glumly handed the beans to Percival whose conker had split asunder his pride of possession. The winner proudly lifted his trophy, still uncertain how many beans he had cumulated.

'Next Sunday you must challenge Osmund; with his many beans you are village champion!'

'Yes, but he is a fierce fighter, it would be better to ...'

'Hey! you gaggle of good-for-nothings! There is wood to be collected before nightfall, water to be fetched from the well. And, Olwen, your father asks that Aelfries' mare be gathered from the upland pasture, she will be re-shod on the morrow. Upon me! Grown boys playing games better suited for unweaned infants.'

'But it is the day of rest!'

'Wood and water would be in plentiful supply if you had not idled during the days of labour.'

And Reginald departed to where the village elders were congregating to discuss matters such as how many pails of water Percival might take from Harald's spring, the bushels of wheat considered just settlement and whether this should increase in times of drought. Or, following the death of Aelstald, how to better organise their wheat and barley fields, the current dispersion being a higly-pigly confusion of inconvenience for those pulling ploughshares.

As his friends scuttled away he, Olwen, son of Emlyn the blacksmith, set off as instructed. 'Grown boys' indeed! He was eighteen, tall enough not be considered short, and handsome according to his mother. Admittedly others had not commented so favourably, although Hilda possibly brooded with favourable notions. Irritatingly, the opinions of maidens such as her were of great import for he would shortly be marrying one of them.

But whom?

From what others recounted, the choice was of feeble import if she be strong for toiling in the fields and performing domestic chores, also for raising children. Which made sound sense. Yet there was a perplexing difference between husbands, careless of their wives, and unmarried males extremely taken by maidens, usually one in particular.

Etheldreda was the favourite. She possessed long flaxen hair and smiled shyly yet in an encouraging way. Also, although one should not be contemplating such considerations, her bosom was most prominent. When she approached everyone gazed admiringly then, as she moved away, they heeded her well-rounded lower portions. Did she know they were watching? Was such behaviour a sin to be confessed? Nobody sought the opinion of Father Joseph in case he reproached the shamefulness of their ways.

The snorting of horses announced his arrival at the upland pasture. It was late, he must hurry. Mercifully it was not sufficiently cold to encounter Jack Frost, fearful kinsman of the Devil, but elves, fairies and trolls would soon emerge from wherever they hid during daylight. And he was afraid of them, very afraid of them.

He struggled to catch the mare, she was fidgety as if possessed by an evil spirit, then he clambered astride and trotted down the muddied track towards the village.

His thoughts returned to the village maidens, those eligible for marriage. There was little point in pursuing Etheldreda, she would never prefer him over Alfred or Eadwig, nor even Percival. Although her bosom was less voluminous, Grace was equally unattainable, there being a haughty unfriendliness about her. Hilda was short and overly plump, with bright curly hair. She giggled frequently and swirled her dress so you could vision her ankles, something they surmised done purposefully to catch their regard. She was disposed to chatter with him, which was pleasing, except she conversed with all the boys, sometimes hailing them before they addressed her, which was incorrect. Everyone enjoyed her company yet nobody romanced about her. Could it be her excessive roundness or did only unapproachable maidens excite men?

Elfreda was sturdy, not plump, with strangely black hair which some claimed had been darkened by a witches' spell. Consequently she was shunned by males, who feared demons lurked inside her. Yet she acted normally, was hard-working and came from a well-liked family.

And finally there was Rowena and Seonald. Their families once lived in Wales but they were purchased by the Bishop and now cultivated his fields. Which meant, so said his father, that nobody could marry them except sons of other slaves.

He had forgotten Saelfreda. However the girl was sickly, she had maw-worms which exited from where she relieved herself, meaning nobody would pursue her.

Of course he might never marry, for he was a Briton. Whereas most of his kinsmen had fled westwards to escape the invaders from across the sea, his family remained because a woman was about to give birth. The Saxons had appreciated their skills hammering iron and weaving delicate tissues, so they were spared. When Ailfric the

61

blacksmith died and nobody was willing to replace him, the village elders offered the position to Elfgar, his great-grandfather. Although apart, they lived in harmony with the Saxons, most of whom, like him, had never known a home other than their village. His male friends considered him like themselves but now, for the first time, he was confronting the local maidens.

Darkness was descending in earnest, so he was greatly relieved to discern the flickering lights of fires kindled to warm the houses of his fellow villagers and cook their evening meal.

He scurried across the windswept common-land to the longhouse where meetings were convened; that evening a cleric representing the Bishop of Exeter was visiting with the latest Pastoral Letter. Unusually and alarmingly he was accompanied by the king's reeve. Puffing, he entered the expansive wooden structure where the meeting was about to commence.

'I apologise for my tardiness, but Dunstan's barn is ancient; with the strong wind he feared for its stability and I was lashing the timbers.'

There were murmurings of understanding.

The cleric, brandishing the Pastoral Letter, arose and addressed the villagers. After the habitual preamble he broached matters of importance:

'The Bishop wishes that repairs to the church roof be performed without delay. A special levy of ten hours labour and three pence for purchasing materials is made on all male adult inhabitants.

'Women and maidens over thirteen years old will cover their heads before entering their place of worship.

'A new font will be delivered next spring, proof of the Bishop's boundless generosity towards his subjects.'

So far so good. In other words, matters could have been worse.

But the cleric was not finished.

'The Bishop particularly reminds his followers of the following previously communicated edicts:

'It is not permitted to grind wheat or harvest fruit on the Sabbath.

62

'Merely thinking about matters of the flesh is sinful and must be confessed.

'Intimacy with one's wife is limited to procreation; it is forbidden when a wife is with child or nourishes her infant.'

The cleric smiled benignly at his audience before continuing.

'The Bishop announces the following additions to previously introduced rules of conduct:

'Father Joseph is informed forthwith of all planned betrothals; details of marriages are recorded in a church register on the day of the ceremony. Any union deemed to be based on carnal attraction will be refuted.

'Physical desire is a manifestation of the Devil, a link to the Original Sin that occurred in the Garden of Eden. If pleasure is felt by either husband or wife, however unintentionally, their intimacy ceases forthwith to forestall the Devil from claiming their souls. To minimise such risk candles are extinguished upon entering the sleeping chamber and coarse clothing is retained throughout the night, the husband only briefly lifting the material to accomplish what must be done. This should be achieved expeditiously because delaying augments the risk of pleasure in the female, the ultimate sin that ensures descent to the hell-fires of Hades.

'A married woman caught alone with an adult male other than her husband, father or brother, is to be publicly denounced. If physical contact is proven she shall suffer nine lashes and be divorced by her husband, who keeps children from their union.'

Despondence filled the hall as the list of non-sinful pleasures was again diminished. The Lord Almighty must have remarkable eyes to observe the behaviour, sinful or otherwise, of every human residing on earth. Assuming he could, 'loving thy neighbour', as preached by Jesus, was something to be henceforth undertaken with the utmost of caution ...

The cleric continued:

'Only one position of coitus is not sinful.'

Reginald had a point of concern. 'Should not our livestock be persuaded to modify their practice?'

The cleric commented that as only humans were answerable to God, animals could procreate in such manner they considered appropriate.

'To conclude, I have excellent news! I have procured for Father Joseph a copy of the works of the Venerable Bede, at last you will possess a calendar noting the days of each saint, also the different months and occurrences of feast days!'

'Oohs' and 'aahs' at this astounding announcement momentarily overshadowed despair concerning future relationships with the opposite sex, always assuming these would continue to exist.

The cleric seated himself and the king's emissary arose.

'I commence with news from around our great kingdom of Wessex. In spite of brilliant tactical manoeuvring by our armies, the Vikings advance westwards and northwards. East Anglia, Mercia and Cumbria are well established within the Danelaw. The very existence of our nation is at stake, we must defend ourselves. We are therefore gathering together a great army...'

A shuffling of feet emanated from the audience, for beloved sons regularly departed to fight the invaders, never to return. The Bishop's eulogies about ascending to heaven appeased momentarily until they realised nobody remained on earth to till the fields and harvest their crops.

'...to permanently crush the aggressor. Sons of slave-labourers and bondsmen will be selected, as is fair, but I requisition two able freemen over eighteen years of age from your village. You have valiantly supported our king in the past; I know we can continue to rely on your patriotism.'

He could, because they had no choice.

The speaker progressed to more mundane affairs:

There would be additional levies on next summer's harvest to provide funding for defending the realm against the Vikings. Alms for the poor were increased forthwith by one eighth. Greater effort must be made to maintain pathways and bridges in an excellent state of repair. And finally: 'Long live King Alfred!'

There was an audible sigh of relief as the emissary sat down, followed by a grim gloomy silence.

Christmas Day. The morning sermon contained fewer admonishments about sins of the flesh, more messages about a wondrous existence in heaven if they resisted devilish temptation whilst residing on earth. After the midday meal they gathered around an outsized bonfire and consumed roasted chestnuts. Then everybody congregated in the longhouse for dancing and merrymaking.

Each family arrived together in accordance with custom. Before long younger children wandered off into a corner, where they played. Unmarried adults assembled facing each other, young boys one side and the maidens opposite them. Sly and not-so-sly glances were exchanged, with many a young male scheming how to find himself in the company of the maiden of his choice and, if he succeeded, what he might possibly speak about.

Reginald recited verses from Beowulf, its tales of courage and honour bringing tears to the eyes of those listening. Then the musicians gathered on a raised portion of the floor, plucking and strumming in anarchic confusion before launching into the first tune.

He was learning the fiddle, the instrument played by his father. Some of the melodies he knew, others refused to stay in his mind. He would join the musicians after his marriage when no longer occupied by chasing maidens. More precisely, when no longer permitted to chase them.

Meanwhile, dallying with them would be his principal occupation. He looked around the room.

Percival and Osmund were in attendance but sadly silent, for they had been selected to fight against the Vikings. With two brothers already fallen in battle, he had been spared. However handsome his friends might be, no maiden would occupy herself with someone soon to be killed or maimed. Which meant two less competitors.

Rowena and Llewelyn were eyeing each other; as slaves they had no alternative because marriage with bondsmen or freemen was forbidden. Alfred and Etheldreda were glued into each other's gaze; never would he discover how her copious bosom might look although, he recollected, nor would Alfred, the Bishop having outlawed such visual transgressions of female privacy. Would Alfred be permitted to touch it? Nothing had been mentioned … Since the activity would presumably be pleasurable, the response was sadly evident.

That left the plump and over-friendly Hilda, Elfreda with the witch's hair and the haughtily unsmiling Grace sitting opposite Eadwig, Oswald and himself. Three versus three.

Forget Grace, she was unattainable, and ignore Hilda who was not to his liking. Which left Elfreda. They once met at the communal oven and talked stupidities, his fault, he had been unable to formulate sensible ideas. But she had not appeared bothered. Since then, he occasionally reminisced about her, not sinfully, well perhaps sometimes, always experiencing sensations of contentment.

He glanced in her direction.

She looked towards him then abruptly elsewhere when realising he was gazing towards her.

The soft folk melodies were replaced by a more swirling dance tune, the moment had arrived. He arose and, in the ensuing muddle of confusion, found himself jigging with Hilda.

He arrived home wearied from labouring in the sun. Firstly Osbert's fruit trees had required pruning, if left untended they grew branches instead of apples or pears. Then he tended his family's grapevines which grew in organised disarray and required regular attention. He wondered, God being so Almighty, why He could not disentangle his own grapes, but he dared not enquire of Father Joseph.

Hilda was standing near the porch. It could not be coincidence, she was waiting for him.

Since the Christmas festivities she behaved as if their betrothal was decided. Recalling the multitudinous sins she committed whilst jigging closer than advisable, sparsely little remained to be consummated if they married. Then, when she urgently visited outside, Elfreda had risen to accept his invitation almost before his intentions were communicated.

From that moment he had thought and dreamed of Elfreda.

Inadvertently and entirely on purpose he encountered her as often as possible. Once, accidentally and as planned for weeks in advance, his hand brushed hers. She withdrew instantly, smiling oh so sweetly whilst he pretended to apologise. And then, equally unintentionally and on purpose, she brushed his arm with her elbow. That evening he had relived their encounter whilst trying to sleep; no, whilst remaining awake until exhausting every single one of his remembrances.

Soon afterwards their shoulders unintentionally touched accidentally, causing her to drop her pail of water on his foot. Every time he inspected the scar he remembered her gently wiping away the blood with her kerchief, eyeing him sorrowfully as she apologised. He would never forget her joy when he returned the kerchief rinsed so very carefully by his understanding mother.

And now, several months later, the village council would debate their betrothal.

'Greetings, my dearest Olwen!'

He grimaced at Hilda then, finding his passage blocked by her overlapping rotundness, came to an unwilling and obliged halt.

'Let us commence!.'

A hush descended upon the gathering.

'Firstly, the argument embittering Ainval and Morton. Last autumn the aforementioned repaired the latter's fencing, receiving as payment two geese and a sixteenth of a bushel of honey. Morton claims the fencing now sags discernibly. I have inspected the supposedly inclining object and confirm a deviation from upright. Ainval claims inconsiderate people leaning on his fencing has caused the problem.'

It was voted that Ainval repay Morton one goose and straighten the fence, for leaning on such constructions was normal when villagers chatted with neighbours.

The pathway leading to nearby Stratton had subsided near Waterdown meadow and the king's ealderman had declared their village responsible for ensuring proper repair. Since nobody ever volunteered for such tasks the council would designate those responsible.

'And now to less arduous matters. Firstly Giles requests on behalf of his younger son, Eadwig, the hand of Grace daughter of Ainval. Do I hear objections?'

There were none.

'Secondly, Emlyn requests on behalf of his son, Olwen, the hand of Elfreda daughter of Dunstan. Do I hear objections?'

'Yes!! Olwen is a Briton, not Saxon as ourselves. I hesitate to permit a marriage between two different peoples; who knows what mischance could occur. Their children may enter this world as elves or manifestations of Lucifer!'

'Not unaware of brewing attractions I have carefully considered the matter. Father Joseph preaches that all humans are equal in the eyes of God, so bonding between children of differing origins cannot be against Our Lord's wishes. Furthermore Father Joseph confirms an absence of abnormalities afflicting those referred to as "intermingled" children. Also, in accordance with proclamations of our beloved Bishop, efforts must be pursued to eliminate incestuous couplings, difficult to avoid in small communities. A union between a Briton and Saxon can only be beneficial.'

Dunstan interjected. 'We Saxons alongside other tribes, not neglecting the Romans, invaded the Britons' peaceful land and unjustly killed and displaced many of them. For generations they have understandably detested us, viewing our arrogant ways with sadness. Yet we share the same countryside, both swear allegiance to King Alfred. We cannot continue to repudiate each other. Olwen is an upstanding lad and hard worker; I am therefore proud to condone his betrothal to my Elfreda, who deeply respects the young lad.'

'And therein lies the problem.' Father Joseph regularly attended village meetings, for should not the Church involve itself in every facet of people's lives? 'Such maidenly infatuation will ignite temptations of the flesh if their union proceeds. Remember that desire is the work of the Devil and must be cast asunder before permeating our souls. Consequently Elfreda, possessed with concupiscence, should be repudiated by her intended and banished from our community.'

'A moment of your time!!' Elfgar, father of Hilda, rose to address the meeting. 'Olwen is promised to my daughter. For many moons he has been courting her, talking alone with her, informing her of his intentions. In no way might he renounce his obligations and wed another.'

'Olwen, is this true?'

'In no way, may it please you. It is only natural I have conversed with Hilda, our paths cross frequently and I offer her the same courtesy as other villagers. But never have I made personal approaches, displayed intentions other than simple friendship.'

'In any case,' interrupted Ailfric, 'my younger son Elrick fancies the maiden Hilda and would be pleased if the council accepts his demand in matrimony upon attaining eighteen years of age.'

He sank back in relief, thanking Elrick for his weirdly strange yet much appreciated taste in young maidens. He smiled as the council, after acrimonious debate, approved both unions, his father's request only being accepted after Father Joseph agreed, most gracelessly, that Elfreda's feelings towards him, although unusually strong, were in no way unseemly. Claiming his beloved's hand would be a formality, although bargaining over the 'bride price' could be less straightforward. Then there would be the 'morning gift' offered to his wife after receiving proof of her maidenly virtue. He must enquire how one substantiated such a matter ...

Those, however, were inconsequentialities. Thereafter he might dare brush his betrothed's shoulder without pretence of carelessness.

The guests hooted and hollered, clapped hands and stamped their feet as he escorted away his bride. They mounted the stairs to their bed-chamber, she crossed the threshold first, then he entered and bolted the door. He held her hands and courageously kissed her on both cheeks.

'Unaware how to behave, I defer to practical sense. I will glance away whilst you undress and enter the bed. You will then close your eyes until I have entered alongside you.'

'Should you not extinguish the candle? Father Joseph intones unceasingly upon such matters.'

'You would be unable to locate the bed in the dark. Then I, incapable of seeing anything, would be unable to find you!'

He turned and stood staring at the armoire, listening to the rustling of clothes, conjecturing yet unable to imagine what sight would fill his eyes if he were to look.

It was his turn.

Climbing into the bed, he sensed her moving away until she was in danger of falling onto the floor. Then, to his delight, she moved hesitantly but purposefully towards where her husband was waiting.

'Did the "wise woman" explain what should happen?'

'Yes. Yet I remain confused.'

Silence.

'My dearest husband, do you?'

'Do I what?'

'Know what should happen?'

'Not entirely. My father recommended I observe bulls and cows, although you should be facing me instead of pointing your ... well. Fidaddle! Whatever, you should be facing towards me.'

'Why?'

Silence.

'So I can gaze into your eyes.'

'That is improbable since we are supposed to extinguish the candle.'

Silence.

'Do you, are you, I mean ...'

'Yes?'

'Well, do you resemble a bull?'

'If you mean do I have a tail and walk on four legs, then I cannot confirm your question.'

'You are teasing me!'

'Yes!!'

'Well?'

'It is not impossible that my body compares in some ways to the beast to which you have referred. However, such information is of little interest unless … Well, do you compare to a cow?'

'I am not in the habit of saying "moooow" nor slobbering as I chew the cud, if that is your point.'

'That is *not* my point!'

'Cows and myself share certain similarities.'

'How do I find it?'

'How dare you!!'

'But …'

'I regret my words. For, if I believe correctly, that is what husbands should seek.'

He moved towards her and collided with an elbow. Much to his confusion his hand then encountered her bosom, causing her to wriggle in discomfort.

'Why did you displace your hand?'

'You were writhing in pain.'

'I was not; your touch was most agreeable.'

'But you must not experience pleasure!'

'But we are married.'

He was unconvinced. Was it possible that this black-haired daughter of a Saxon might be incubating manifestations of devilry? Yet perhaps, for their first night together, just once and never again, enjoyment would not be dreadfully sinful, especially as he now resembled a bull in one very critical manner.

His hand delved underneath the roughshod material of her garment, seeking but not finding because she was shaped very differently from a cow. From her sighing and squirming, if pleasure was indeed a sin, she would have much confessing to perform next Sunday.

He was about to renounce when a hand, one unmistakably not his, guided his wrist towards its destination. How in the name of thunder would he place his thingamajig inside such a despairingly narrow entrance located in the most impossibly inaccessible of places?

But he did.

Eighth encounter: Guilhem and Anaïs
1194   Beaucaire, Languedoc

Spray from the puddle splattered the fetlocks of his horse, an irritation of little consequence. Maddeningly, the muddied mixture had also sullied his leather boots. His indignation was not directed towards cleaning his riding apparel, Paolo his valet performed such tasks, but at the thought of approaching her, conversing with her as dampness disfigured his otherwise impeccable countenance. After all, being the son of Comte de Rainol de Beaucaire was something to be proud of. Especially if you were him.

Which he was.

Not only was he that dignified nobleman, he was one of Languedoc's foremost troubadours, whose *albas* and *anti-cansos* were glorified by those cognisant with the poetic perfection of his melodies. Other singers, from itinerant *jongleurs* to noblest *seigneurs,* memorised his stanzas, especially in Languedoc, emblem of Europe, which rightfully surpassed other regions in cultural and social acclaim. They could shiver in their dank northern chateaux, consoling themselves with the accoutrements of power, but those inhabiting more meridian regions savoured the true joys of gracious living: a clement climate, boundless fruit and vegetables, prose, verse, music and the magical singing of the troubadours. Plus ladies of faultless virtue sweetly enchanted and sorely tempted but never corrupted by the lovelorn songs dedicated to them.

But only because the singers themselves acknowledged the futility of their quest. Yes futility, for only unattainable love could be extolled when omnipresent clerics exercised unassailable power with

73

unwavering single-mindedness, imposing dire chastisement on mortals straying from the narrow path of righteousness as defined by themselves, because God was almighty and His will must be obeyed.

Only one civilisation equalled, nay surpassed, Languedoc in cultural splendour: the Moorish Empire stretching from the Sahara through Andalusia towards the Pyrenees. Their poetry, finesse of melodies and elegance of philosophising outshone all else. Yet Catholic clergy castigated their heathen persuasions, decried their annihilation of Crusaders and condemned their system of numerals for including the zero, evil representation of non-existence, without substantiating such animosity with justifiable thought.

His thoughts returned to his personal crusade. Although a mud-soaked horse bore witness to an arduous journey gallantly undertaken in order to pay his respects, he himself must be beyond reproach. Otherwise how could she, whose beauty dulled perfection, ever accept his adoration with due consideration? Na Clara la Vicomtesse de Tarascon, wife of a nobleman whose social graces outweighed his impressive political authority. How she enthralled with her gracious presence, laughing voice and grace of movement. Even his most subtle stanzas could never capture the sublimation of her being. Let chevaliers debase themselves with physical gratification. He, lovelorn troubadour, would become Na Clara's spiritual *contendedor,* find fulfilment within the highest degree of spiritual love.

Except that somebody else now competed for his heart and mind, although on a more terrestrial level; Mademoiselle Azalaïs, daughter of Na Clara and progeny of her husband the Vicomte de Tarascan, from whom he intended requesting her hand in marriage.

Praying the dampness despoiling his boots would disappear, he continued his journey towards his destination and his destiny.

His path meandered across the basin of the River Rhone. Tarascon might not cumulate the economic power of Arles or Toulouse but it cultivated comparable literary refinement. With its strategic position on the banks of the Rhone and his family's vast agricultural estates situated between Tarascon and Nimes, the marriage to Azalaïs had been ordained not in heaven but in the political manoeuvrings of their respective fathers. Bearing in mind that the powerful Duc de Cavaillon had recently wed a cousin of the Vicomte de Tarascon, the consolidation of their families into one political union would place the entire Rhone valley under their dominance, from the foothills of the Massif Central to the River Durance.

And yet... And yet. His heart, his soul, his pride, his respect of romantic love, all insisted his wife be wooed and won from the heart, not the negotiating table. Because Azalaïs, unwitting pawn in a game of politics, was hardly enamoured by her pretender, having displayed disapproval when he brushed inadvertently against her evening gown. Then, when singing a *salutz d'amor*, had she not sat stiffly from disdain?

Upon making her acquaintance he had been disappointed by her unremarkable physique. Yet she was graced with refined facial features and her form, faintly distinguishable beneath her layers of silk, was not without interest. No powders and creams covered her face, for they were artefacts designed by the Devil to ignite wantonness, 'poultices of lust' according to Saint Jerome. In any case, lotions only veiled the finesse of natural beauty.

Yes, after due reflection, Azalaïs not only suited his father's materialistic preoccupations but displayed physical attributes not incompatible with corporeal satisfaction.

Notwithstanding her emotional coldness, she had conversation. Instead of gazing demurely amidst silent blushes, like most aristocratic maidens, she responded keenly to his overtures, especially when he spoke of singing. So he convinced himself that her comportment was borne of frustration, a reaction to social strictures which forbade the revealing of veritable emotions. When he escorted her down the aisle into the bedchamber, the merging of minds and bodies would transport them to paradise on earth.

The dowry had been agreed, prolonged haggling sorely testing his simplistic approach to financial manoeuvrings. He was incensed when his father declared him a desirable suitor, someone able to seek elsewhere if the endowment was inadequate. Was a wife nothing more than a charnel chattel? Forbidden to marry the woman he passionately loved, he would at least insist upon respect and affection. Hence the importance of assessing the sensitivities hidden behind the protective beauty of Azalaïs.

The pecuniary procedures settled he could concentrate on the social aspects of their betrothal. These, apart from the formality of requesting her hand, were the specific purpose of his visit to Tarascon, a visit delayed until the certificate of maidenhood had been ceremoniously delivered. Another confirmation had been delivered, with no ceremony whatsoever. Money had exchanged hands, information was forthcoming from one of her maids, that undressed her mistress still acclaimed the same graceful shape as when corseted. Furthermore, she displayed no physical deformities likely to impede the accomplishment of her marital duties, including the harbouring of unborn infants within her body.

They arrived at the banks of the Rhone. The ferry was anchored on the opposite shore. He sat under the branches of an olive tree, drank wine to quench his thirst, and continued his contemplations.

Of course he had known other women, young widows sacrificing their souls in exchange for a ladle of gruel. Also, the occasional not-so-young widow. As his father joked, female flesh was the sole commodity whose price reduced as its weight increased. Yet older women compensated lack of lithesome limbs with tenderness, refuting his verses interchanging romance and beauty. He had equally bedded daughters of tenants unable to settle their rents, wenches too young to marry yet able to accommodate a male, nubile flesh permitting perfunctory discharge without the complication of emotion, females who validated Saint Thomas' claim that 'women were incomplete beings'.

He had refrained from such encounters since his maturing mind became infatuated with Na Clara. Otherwise, how could he gaze towards the object of his adoration as he sang her praises? However, as marriage to Azalaïs advanced from indistinct prospect to forthcoming eventuality, his thoughts returned to the physical facets of procreation. Unlike peasants his spouse would inhabit separate

76

quarters and custom decreed a husband attend his wife. During those visits she would presumably expect attentions more subtle than invigorating tumbles. *Sacré Dieu*!! Their union would achieve the idealistic perfection of his songs, enabling affection to blossom into true love. It must. Because passion was the germ of creativity, those without it were creatures of mediocrity. Never, never, never would he live without passion.

His reflections were interrupted, the ferry had berthed. Shortly thereafter he dismounted before the imposing entrance, handed the reins to the waiting lackey, and entered the building wherein awaited Na Clara and Azalaïs.

Neither was present to welcome him, the honour being accorded to her brother to obviate social impropriety. For if a woman greeted a gentleman his social status was reduced to an irrelevance. In any case, women were incapable of handling such duties.

He observed his host carefully; his father's prognosis appeared justified. The pallor of his skin, the reddish hue of his watery eyes, stooped shoulders, all bore witness to deficient health. His father had confessed to haggling less than warranted over the dowry because of the brother's increasing infirmity. The sole and unmarried brother's increasing infirmity. The title and family fortune should shortly transfer to the eldest daughter, Azalaïs or, should she marry, to her husband.

Formal niceties about his journey, the state of the roads after recent storms, all progressed with due procedural circumstance. The real conveying of information would occur later.

Having exhausted the formalities of social dictum, his host smiled sheepishly and indicated that perhaps, having installed himself, he would be disposed to join members of the household for refreshment.

The gathering was surprisingly modest, a mere dozen adults including his intended fiancée. He first paid his compliments to her parents, his heart pounding as he faced the Vicomtesse, mistress of his heartstrings. He then turned to their daughter, bowed courteously, briefly touched her gloved hand with his lips and indicated how honoured and delighted he was to be in her presence. She insisted the honour was hers, smiling in a manner strangely lacking in warmth and captivation. Then, as social mores dictated, he intermingled with the assembled company and treated his intended wife as an irrelevancy.

After a sumptuous feast an itinerant *jongleur* distracted them with acrobatics and renditions of several *cansos* plus a recent *salutz d'amor* by Arnant de Mareulhand. The Vicomte then proposed that his distinguished guest honour them with of some of his own oeuvres. His false modesty, pleading inability to follow the eloquence of the professional *jongleur,* fooled nobody.

His valet arrived with their viola and flute. After a selection of unaccompanied verses he interpreted a *fin'amor* about a young man's adoration for a lady of elevated rank, during which his eyes gazed inconsolably at the Vicomtesse.

> *When I see the leaves falling from the tree*
> *Whoever may grieve or sorrow*
> *I find it much to my taste.*
> *Do not think that I want to see either flower or leaf*
> *For she scorns me*
> *She who is the one I most desire.*

Then, no clerics being present, he sang a somewhat more daring song, one describing a suitor's eagerness for a peasant, such outpouring of masculine attentiveness being permitted if the female was of lowly origin and the singer's ardour illusory. As he sang, he glanced at Azalaïs who returned his look with ambiguity, expressing censure rather than appreciation.

The entertainment concluded, he was authorised to escort his chosen lady around the garden. Alone at last, yet never hidden from the prying looks of her governess, they walked away from the patio.

At least they could not be overheard; he could finally inquire of her true sympathies.

'My dearest Mademoiselle, it is with the greatest joy that I find myself in your gracious company.'

'But it is I, your betrothed, who experience feelings of great contentment at the honour you accord my humble self.'

As she responded to his homilies he was conjuring how to broach a subject significantly more delicate than discussing their mutual appreciation at being mutually appreciated by each other.

'Although I have waited this moment with impatience, my thoughts have turned on numerous occasions to our previous encounter and to this moment of renewing our relationship. I must also remark on the splendour of your garden. You must convey my compliments to your parents.'

She agreed to convey his compliments to her parents.

'But such splendour pales in comparison to your beauty, how can a modest flower be anything but outshone by the glow emanating from your eyes, the radiance of your smile and the melody of your voice.'

He stopped and sniffed gently at a rose, inviting her to do the same.

Which of course she did.

During which time he scrutinised her form which displayed a delicate and discreet sensuality. Wherein lay a perplexity. Clerics intoned procreation was a duty to perform without recourse to pleasure. Yet his future wife, would she not receive physical gratification from offering herself? And, if so, would it be contrary to God's will? Hugues de Saint-Victor proclaimed 'conception was not possible without sinning' whereas others decreed the vagina to be the 'Devil's doorway', implying only those living in celibacy could rightfully claim a place in paradise.

She stood up, the rose duly sniffed.

Furious at his cowardice and running out of superlatives, he goaded himself to communicate the concerns he must share with her.

'You speak of our being betrothed. However, although our respective fathers have spoken, I have not formally requested your hand.'

She looked at him, startled and concerned.

'Please, nobody becomes my wife merely to settle contractual engagements. I will only submit my request if you wholeheartedly desire to marry me. If this be so, take my hand a second, no one can see. If you comply then I, the proudest man in the world, will immediately seek audience with your father.'

After a long hesitation, he felt her hand in his.

Momentarily.

Fleetingly.

Without feeling, without warmth, without enthusiasm.

Nothing, just a hand.

They continued their promenade in silence. A slight breeze ruffled the leaves.

'Please, if you are inopportuned by the cold we can retire to the protection of the patio.'

She refuted any tendency to feeling chilled, hardly surprising in consideration of the afternoon heat. But he had displayed concern as a gentleman must invariably do. Courtesy, even more than words of endearment, was the outward manifestation of an innermost love.

Silence.

'Women and flowers, the most exquisite of miracles, beauty beyond mere inspiration. How futile are my poems when attempting to describe the sweetness, the fragility and the mystery of two of God's most perfect creations. I hope the paucity of my stanzas does not distress you.'

'Sire, pray do not exaggerate our modest charms, women are but humans who manifest neither the strength nor courage of men.'

She ceased talking; they had arrived at the patio.

Night had descended to embrace the countryside with its mantle of invisibility, seeking out each mountain and valley, town and dwelling, courtyard and chamber, only failing to impose its presence where candles insolently resisted its intrusion.

The banquet to celebrate his betrothal incorporated singing by a *jongleur* with spectators responding enthusiastically to each verse. Then a group of musicians played *estampes*, folk melodies that permitted people to dance merrily although with due deference to

80

propriety of mind and spirit, the town's ecclesiastical hierarchy being present.

Later, as the revellers rested after their exertions, he requested permission to speak alone with his betrothed, her governess in discreet attendance.

They talked about their forthcoming union, guests to invite and how the ceremony should reflect their respect for each other.

'Please Sire, I beg of you, might I sing my songs at the reception?'

'You compose?'

'I do.'

He studied his fiancée, surprised at her admission.

'Do not show displeasure. I adore the *ballades* and *rondeaux* I learned as a child. It is therefore normal I compose, sometimes writing personal words to existing airs, although I have arranged melodies of my own. The Comtesse de Die has gathered fame with her *cansos*, surely I may strive to emulate her achievements.'

The rising popularity of troubadours had initially engendered harsh reprobation from the clerics, justifiable as songs of undying love served to propel ladies towards their admirers' bedchamber and into the arms of adultery. However, the extreme delicacy of more recent texts, sung by virtuosos as virtuous as their compositions, permitted those adulated to show appreciation without aggrieving the clerics. Yet here was his fiancée not only composing but expressing therein a woman's sentiments. Society might concede but the clerics would be scandalised.

She was about to say something, then stopped.

'Please, you may speak, I would be most interested to share your thoughts.'

She blushed.

'I especially appreciate *fin'amors*, where love persists without physical impertinence. Has not Ibn Hazm, the Moorish poet, claimed that a union of souls be a thousand times more beautiful than one of bodies? Sire, I beg that our marriage reflect love as recounted in your songs and never be desecrated with iniquities of the flesh.'

'But our children?'

81

'Mary bore Jesus without recourse to bodily defilement; let us prove ourselves worthy of similar honour. Remember *"nuptias non concubitus sed consensus facit"*: marriage confers the right but not the obligation to indulge in intimacy.'

It was too late to argue the naivety of her wisdom. After the nuptials he would introduce her to the requisites of procreation even if, through misguided ignorance, she proved indisposed to pursue such activities.

She smiled sweetly as she sat opposite him in their boudoir, sewing intricate patterns into the finely woven material.

'You are tired, my dearest wife. Allow sleep to relax your mind, prepare yourself for the tomorrow.'

Azalaïs rose, tidied away her sewing and made for her private bedchamber in the eastern wing of her father-in-law's castle, where they were currently attending the Comte's birthday merrymaking.

After her departure he sat alone. Their marriage a year previously had been a festival of elegance and social celebration. Their singing enchanted even the dourest clerics; never had guests witnessed such harmonious bliss. Yet her compositions remained unsung. He had been prepared to concede but their fathers, incensed, outlawed such distorted comportment, declaring women only warranted respect within literature, not in society.

After the wedding guests had departed, in the seclusion of her chamber as he prepared to perform the ultimate rite, she became aware of his intentions.

'No! You promised never to impose intimacy. We will share our days in mutual contentment but our nights must be separate in order to prevent temptation from besmirching our harmony of existence.'

'But ...'

How to broach the subject of providing evidence of her departed maidenhood? He glanced towards the whiteness of the towel, she understood and shuddered. So, behaving as a gentleman must, he sacrificed his own blood to save her humiliation. No, his humiliation.

During the ensuing months he had raised the matter on several occasions, each time receiving a more violent negation. She reminded him of church edicts imposing abstention on Thursdays in memory of Christ's arrest, Fridays in memory of his death, Saturdays in honour of the Resurrection and Mondays in commemoration of the departed, with similar interdictions during fasts and festivals.

Unwilling to violate her, he resorted to persuasion.

'Did not Saint Paul declare that women should defer to men since they had been created for his benefit?'

'That does not prevent a husband from respecting his wife.'

'But, Madame, uniting our bodies is the greatest expression of love.'

'It is an act of bestiality.'

'But it is your duty as a married woman.'

'I am sorely vexed you contemplate the despoliation of my physical self. Do you consider me as a mare waiting to be impregnated? The act is so repugnant in both its concept and execution I am amazed even peasants find satisfaction.

'But if you father and mother had not ...'

'How dare you insult my parents!!!'

'I assure you nothing was further from my mind.'

'Let us pray together then sing one of the *cansos* of Bernart de Ventadour in the hope that joining our voices in unison will calm your agitations.'

Having sung the requested song, they had retired to their different bedchambers, as far separated in mind as in body.

And now, in Beaucaire, as his father's birthday celebrations drew to a close he felt fatigued, exasperated at riposting allusions as to why no impending joyful occurrence was announced, terrified his entourage might entertain accurate speculation as to the reason.

Furthermore Azalaïs' persistent refusal to accede to his demands had delayed his intention to transfer affections from her mother to his wife. Consequently and disturbingly, throughout the evening's merrymaking his heart had pounded each time Na Clara approached whilst his wife's presence left him unmoved to such an extent that claiming marital rights barely interested him as a male, only as a husband. Enraged at his wife's obstinacy, aware his father habitually arranged personal divertissement to follow banquets, he weakened to temptation and summoned the valet, requesting similar distraction. The manservant regretted the impossibility of procuring someone worthy at such short notice. Unable to sleep, he pursued his latest *fin d'amour*, imaginably the most melancholy of his compositions, only to be interrupted by the valet; his father, having invited the Comtesse de Tarascon to his chambers, had declined his selected wench.

Unable to contain his despair, he vowed to wreak his revenge on the unfeeling fickleness of women. Sweet revenge, fitting revenge, justified revenge and a double revenge. His wife, the painstakingly prim Azalaïs, would perform her marital duties with or without wishing to do so. But only after having been cuckolded by her husband.

Addressing the manservant, he ordained that the unwanted female be fetched.

Thus, as the château slept, as the night advanced silently towards another dawn, a peasant girl was brought, someone whose family failed to pay their rent following her father's untimely demise. She was introduced as Anaïs. In the darkness it was difficult to visualise her pretensions but the plump firmness of her flesh and all-embracing odour of her womanhood triggered desires long suppressed. He placed her on the bed, removed her simple garment and took possession of a body well used to rough manipulation.

As he discharged his manhood his thoughts were removed, so very far removed, from those pertaining to the beauty of unrequited love as sung in his *cansos* and *fin d'amors*.

Ninth encounter: Humbert and Estella
1385   St Vaury, France

They trudged through the rain-swept countryside, thousands of them, fighting to protect their king and country from the invader, the tyrant King Edward of England, who had invested vast tracts of land around Calais, occupied most of Aquitaine and was now marching from Bordeaux to subjugate the rest of France. Explaining why he, Marcel Saimpol, modest yet valiant peasant, had been obliged to abandon his wife Estella and suffer induction into the army.

The general, riding in isolated splendour on his white stallion, had inspired them with promise of victory; at Poitiers they would crush the enemy for once and forever. Victory was assured for God was on their side.

And now the moment of glory had arrived.

Weighed down by armour, his feet sinking into the squelching mud, progress was slowing. He peered ahead; thankfully the enemy lines were almost reached.

His companions-in-arms accelerated towards the waiting adversary, shouting oaths with increasing ferocity as they mounted the ridge. However, when enemy arrows started flying, their bellicosity faded into frightened screams as they crumpled onto the ground, tens of them, hundreds of them. Still the arrows sought them out, yet he could not relinquish his pace, those behind would trample him. Henri, to his left, gurgled blood as an arrow pierced his neck, Jacques running ahead flung out his arms as an arrowhead exited his back. By the grace of God he himself had been spared, the enemy was straight ahead, the combat could commence.

85

The archers dissolved from view to be replaced by cavalry who hurled themselves down the slope. He saw the Englishman's weapon as it lunged towards him, only to disappear from view. Then its blade reappeared, dripping splinters of bone. He tried to breathe but nothing happened. He was falling. Thankfully the English soldier had departed elsewhere. Or was it he who was no longer there?

She lay on the bundles of straw and threadbare covering that served as her bed, had once served as their bed. For Marcel had departed with the other soldiers, never to return. Then tiny Marie succumbed to the smallpox, leaving her alone during daytime, desperately abandoned when night descended.

She had been so happy during their two years of marriage. Admittedly their life represented little more than labouring for the nobleman who owned their grazing pastures, yet those brief moments in each others arms were so wonderful. He had been so tender, so protective, so caring. Oh how she longed for his embrace, his shyly offered endearments, his gentle teasing if her breathing were to hasten.

She occasionally touched where her husband once visited, ceasing when stimulating familiar sensations for such actions were reproved by the Church. But she knew her hand would return, for the need was intense, greater than her fear of descending to Hades. Rumour spoke of herbal remedies to cure such womanly distraction, but she dared not enquire for fear of arousing suspicion.

How did her elder sister Marthe cope with widowhood? She had remarried as soon as was dignified, but five years ago suitors were plentiful. Then her second husband succumbed to pneumonia, since which time she attended midweek confessional, strangely disconcerting behaviour since no outward manner of sinning was apparent.

'But my dear Abbé, celibacy may have been decreed by Pope Siricius for reasons only obliquely linked to sound theology. Notwithstanding, nuns must respect their vows, for as brides of

Christ any man breaching their chastity is cuckolding the son of God.'

He nodded in agreement in spite of its implications, for nuns were women and denying them the possibility to provide pleasure to males was a distressing loss for society.

'Although, dear brother, Paul of Tarsus and Clement of Alexandria, the most unsavoury of characters, instigated the church's phobia for matters of the flesh, not Jesus of Nazareth. Their theological mis-interpretations continue to deform debate in Rome and Avignon.'

He was discussing ecclesiastical matters in the private lodgings of Père Emmanuel, Evêque of Guéret, a modest market town bordering the bleak and sparsely inhabited mountains of the Massif Central. His twelve kilometre journey from St Vaury had been memorable for the continuous rain and numbing gusts of wind, his welcome upon arriving equally unforgettable due to a blazing fire, exquisite cuisine and the instructive intellect of his interlocutor. Earlier ill-humour had dissipated into contented self-satisfaction, especially as his host was sparing no effort to humour his distinguished guest.

Which was to be expected, for was he not Père Augustus, custodian of the illustrious Abbaye de St Vaury, a position gained through underhand assaults on the careers of more worthy colleagues? He viewed his less-than-charitable actions as justifiable revenge for being initiated into religious orders against his wishes. Whilst his eldest brother prepared to assume the dukedom, the second pursued a military career and the third combined financial usury with entertaining himself at court, he, known as Humbert de Beauvilliers until cowled and tonsured, had been hustled into religious orders by an overbearing father. The Almighty, demonstrating lamentable lack of judgement, may have willed his integration into the Church but He would have difficulty imposing a life of denial on his recalcitrant recruit.

Hence his acceptance of the position of Abbé at the isolated St Vaury, where cultural limitation was moderated by gracious living, power and influence. No, God retained the power, leaving him the influence which he could exercise far from the stalking grounds of papal emissaries. Oh! the pleasure of denying and humbling, occasionally even depriving sinners of their very existence. All in the name of God, who could intervene to disavow his servitor's actions whenever he wished, but never did.

His reflections returned to the after-luncheon discussions. Père Emmanuel was addressing him.

'My dear Abbé, sadly you missed our most recent inquisition tribunal. Yesterday three witches were burned, as ugly and demented as representatives of the Devil should be. Oh how they screamed! The voices may have been their own but their blasphemy emanated directly from Lucifer The outer garment of one shredded as flames engulfed her body, momentarily the crowd witnessed breasts pendulating in the lewdest of manners as she twitched and twirled from God's punishment.'

'Once again our church has not failed in its glorious duty.'

'Tomorrow two widows will be pilloried for stealing food. They will assuredly repent as they scream their suffering to the waiting crowd!'

He learned with regret that no public chastisements were planned that afternoon. To console himself he would visit the public baths, pay his respects and a small fee to Genevieve for a soothing massage.

Père Emmanuel had further matters on his mind.

'The case of Frère Mathieu causes much controversy. He speaks possible heresy by contradicting the placing of chastity belts and the prohibiting of married women visiting unattended males. He argues that preventing women from sinning counters biblical logic; instead they should be accorded access to temptation, receiving praise if resisting and paying the penalty if weakening.'

'I see the foundation of his argument and reject the notion of blaspheming, for Frère Mathieu merely seeks greater understanding.'

Sensing disavowal of his opinion, he engineered a change of discussion.

'How go the confessions? What misdeeds do your parishioners invent that they might further their moral destitution?'

'Much of the same, only more! Widows of soldiers lost in battle unable to procure a second husband no longer contend with desires transmitted from Eve and ignited during their original nuptials. Admissions of wicked thoughts and consorting with males continue to animate the confessional and self-generated pleasure is as common as clouds on a rainy day. Our women are perturbed and must be constrained with undeviating purpose of mind even if the cause lies with a deficiency of husbands rather than rebellious spirit.'

'But the house of relaxation your diocese manages so charitably, surely it provides appropriate relief?'

'Yes, but indeed no. For we cater for over-eager males, not their female counterparts.'

He had overlooked such an evident limitation to a brothel's range of pursuits. 'At least you provide generous relief for society's masculine misfits.'

'But of course. Proverbs might claim "anyone keeping company with harlots squanders his substance". However, was it not Thomas Aquinas who considered harlots the sewers of society without which pollution, he meant illicit sexual practice, instead of being safely evacuated would rise to sully that society's every facet.'

'If only Eve had not weakened to temptation ...'

Sitting outside her dwelling on the bench carved for two, exhausted after a day's toiling, she inadvertently turned to where Marcel should be sitting. Soldiers returning home announced that thousands had made the ultimate sacrifice at Poitiers; although 'thousand' was foreign to her notions she imagined the enormity of the slaughter. She must face reality, adapt to widowhood instead of waiting for a miracle that would never happen.

That night her hand returned to the forbidden place. She must find a husband, but how? Not a single candidate remained in their village of Magnenton, nor in nearby Mondon, for eligible males were either wed or buried.

She used to confess receiving occasional pleasure from her husband, insisting how in exchange she bore the pain with fortitude. The priest had not seemed unduly perturbed. Yet she refrained from speaking of her more recent transgressions for the punishment would surely be of greatest severity, perhaps public burning in the company of witches. Yet God must know of her culpability, his retribution would be far greater if she failed to confess ...

She would seek advice from Marthe.

Marcel, oh how sweet and pure he had been. At least the Lord had rewarded him with early access to paradise, something for which she was thankful.

'Father, forgive me, for I have sinned.'

Back in St Vaury, the numbing repetition of the confessional was under way. Half-listening, so exploits worthy of confession would reach his ears, he reflected upon the daily administration of his abbey.

Frère Erasmus was the main upset; recently he had been disturbed sodomising a novice priest. If only his friend had been receiving he could plead violence against his person but it was he energetically thrusting perversity upon the youngster. The hearing was the following morning. How could he temper the indignation of his colleagues, prevent rumours from reaching Limoges or even Avignon? He much appreciated the company of Frère Erasmus, both for theoretical discussion and battles of the chessboard during which bishops interchanged roles with more powerful queens and popes replaced kings. How could he protect his companion from the wrath of ecclesiastical retribution which clamoured to forestall reoccurrence by removing a portion of the culprit's anatomy? His prayers for guidance remained unanswered, the Lord Almighty no doubt considering the incident a minor misdemeanour unworthy of attention.

He read the relevant papal decree:

Mutual masturbation	*1 year penance*
Oral release	*7 years penance, life if repetitive*
Sodomy	*7 years penance*

The Church's philosophy was that societies failing to eradicate sexual deviation faced disintegration. Strangely, having decreed death as fitting punishment for adulteresses, the penalty upon males for comparable crimes was mere penance. A papal logic difficult to grasp, yet comforting in its existence.

How to best solve the affair of Frère Erasmus? Seven years was a lifetime for someone his age. Perhaps the novice could be convinced to declare that, suffering acute itching, he had presented his underneath for thorough inspection. Or, having sinned, he had implored the accused to mete punishment in the most degrading of ways. Yes!! The incident would be resolved to everyone's satisfaction.

He pondered another problem, one causing concern to his counterpart in nearby Bénévent l'Abbaye. One of his monks had confiscated Church parchment to inscribe poems, works of dubious merit:

Sweetest innocence and untouched purity,
Condemn one to boredom and wasted obscurity,
But let maidenhood be tenderly torn,
And a woman of beauty is wondrously born.

Was it theft of Church property, blasphemy or moral iniquity? And how to make the punishment fit the crime?

In the gloom of the confessional the word 'sister' caught his attention, for incest was a sorrowful crime. No, the younger sister of the confessor was caressing portions of her body only husbands should attain. Should she be exorcised or simply confess? He explained that her soul was being tormented by the Devil. However regrettable the occurrence, the sister had not herself sinned. As a sign of understanding she was invited to attend the midweek confessional.

The next sinner pleaded forgiveness for having spoken unworthily of her husband, the following admitted to coveting her neighbour's strawberries. Enough was enough. He glanced towards the nave; the line of sinners was despairingly long. Aggrieved, he replaced himself with the aforementioned Frère Erasmus, someone well disposed to pardon sins relating to the flesh.

91

Washing clothes at the fountain with her younger sister Estella, she suddenly felt faint. Could the plague be returning to punish her? And everyone else, for the pestilence of her youth had eliminated sinners, of that there was no doubt, but also those of noble spirit including blameless monks from the abbey.

She stopped wringing her linen, stood up and collapsed, confirming her suspicions. Her second husband had died more than three years ago but neighbours attending the midweek confessional had become with child in similar circumstances. The priest intoned that fidelity to the memory of their defunct spouses had been heeded in heaven; sperm deposited long ago had been miraculously returned to life, permitting impregnation. It was a wonderful gift, their husbands watching from above must be greatly overjoyed.

And now she had been blessed. It was indeed a magnificent gift, but not without practical inconveniences. Since her husband's death she, like other widows, had added tending animals to the multitude of domestic tasks. How could she milk cows and shear sheep with a bulging belly? Furthermore, she must abandon the midweek confessional that so uplifted her wearied soul.

The world ceased spinning. She gathered together her laundry and prepared to return home. Dearest Emile, how happy I am for both of us.

Early evening vespers were finished, they would shortly gather for the frugal meal so painstakingly cooked by Frère Jerome, *canard trouffé de foie gras* and *tarte aux mirabelles à la crème de chèvre* being the culinary fortification chosen to help them resist the nocturnal vigil awaiting them. He had been informed of a distant monastery whose dining-room was accessed by the narrowest of chinks in a wall; monks presenting a belly too extravagant to pass returned hungry to their cells, a certainty for those of St Vaulry.

Alone in his office he considered directives arriving from Avignon enunciating songs of praise to be performed on feast-days. Church music was becoming ever-increasingly intricate. Even though transcribing annotations onto parchment provided invaluable guidance, the musical artistry of the scores insistently outclassed his choristers' musical abilities. Furthermore, living in cloying damp surroundings, working in the cavernous kitchen and shouting instructions whilst building outhouses fashioned vocal cords too roughly hewn to respect the harmonic delicacy imagined by the music's creators. Departures from the purity of

Sanctus, Sanctus, Sanctus Dominus
Deus Sabaoth.
Pleni sunt coeli et terra gloria tua

were such that singers feared visits from liturgical composers more greatly than Vatican inquisitors.

They were still struggling with plainsong and monophonic psalms when parallel and free organum were introduced. And now scholars from Saint Martial in Limoges encouraged melismatic organum whilst Notre Dame in Paris proclaimed the unequalled greatness of its motets. It was polyphony in theory, cacophony in practice.

Yet he must not abandon the education of his brethren, and not just in matters of melody. Persistent reports were reaching St Vaury of itinerant emissaries from Rome arriving unexpectedly to verify the compliance of papal edicts. Non-conformists were paying heavily for ethical laxness. He must be cautious, consult with colleagues; the era of theological liberty was perhaps drawing to a close.

Thankfully tomorrow was Wednesday, the midweek confessional was approaching. Smiling, he descended towards the dining-hall.

'My sweet Marthe, that God should bless you with such a miraculous gift! Of course I will care for your animals, share every moment of your happiness.'

'Dearest Estella, your Marcel disappeared two years ago, your problems are equal to mine, yet you are ready to support your sister

in time of need. To show my appreciation I propose you replace me at tomorrow's confessional!'

'But I have not been summoned!'

'But yes, the priest rec ... Nay, I am confused by my fatigue.' How could she reveal indiscretions spoken during her most recent confession? Yet her sister had indeed been invited.

'They are expecting me, yet I cannot attend. They would be pleased if you replace me.'

'I have not sinned, how can I therefore confess?'

'You talked of touching yourself where it is forbidden.'

'Perhaps it is true. But how are these confessionals, why do people talk in hushed voices when considering them?'

'Enter into my kitchen, away from prying ears. There I will explain.'

He strode circumspectly from his office towards where the midweek confessional took place, a seance reserved for widows tormented by inner yearnings.

Assuaging their problem in the most natural way, effective and pleasurable, could cause scandal, so he had adopted a ruse practised widely throughout the land. Having demonstrated remorse, the pitiable wretches were instructed to pray for forgiveness. If their pleas were answered, the Almighty would visit as a man and confirm his benevolence by providing the release they so yearned.

Now the Almighty was obviously too over-occupied to intervene personally. However, since no mortal could replace Him without prior acquiescence, a sign was necessary. Which was simple. Having asked the penitent to expose herself, confirming her readiness, He signified approval by causing a suitable swelling amidst his manservant's loins.

As sinners were leaving, duly satiated, they received stern warning that revelation would engage the wrath of God. If miraculously they became with child, they should praise Him for his extraordinary generosity.

By alleviating the deprivations of widowhood the practice

prevented god-fearing women from falling prey to dementia and witchery, and ultimate burning at the stake. Such interventions were indeed for a worthy cause.

He arrived where the first woman was waiting.

Having confessed her sinful actions she waited for retribution, only to experience relief when her interlocutor expressed understanding and granted the possibility of redemption from the Almighty himself.

Trembling with apprehension, she was led behind the altar and guided into a private chapel. On arrival she was blindfolded and placed facing the Virgin and Child, her uncovered lower regions pointing heavenwards as a sign of supplication. Being deprived of sight was worrying, but she was safely surrounded by men of God. Also, everything was occurring exactly as Marthe had described. She prayed for forgiveness, prayed for her husband to return, prayed that the yearnings would subside, prayed and prayed and prayed. And whilst praying she begged, as had been granted to her sister, that if God personally intervened to exorcise the demon defiling her, she would experience the immeasurable pleasure she craved.

Then she heard sounds. Praise to the Lord Almighty, for His love and generosity were boundless.

Tenth encounter: Elizabeth and Charles
1571   Shaftsbury, England

She sighed as she finished page three hundred and fifty seven and advanced to page three hundred and fifty eight. England effused with palace intrigue and political scandal, Parliament blithely voted self-serving laws to curry its own favour, and Catholics, briefly returned to favour by Queen Mary, were being ousted into obscurity and exile. Protestants, Lutherans, Calvinists, Puritans and Presbyterians, a sinister hotchpotch of anti-papist reformers, plotted to outmanoeuvre Queen Elizabeth's Anglicans in spite of risking premature dispatch to their maker, those descending to hell being offered a fiery foretaste of the purgatory awaiting them upon arrival. Meanwhile Europe's nations, unused to coexisting peacefully, rapaciously expropriated the unknown world whilst plotting future treacheries against each other.

Whereas she, on instructions from her father, Member of Parliament and wealthy land-owner, or vice-versa, apparently one spawned the other, was obediently wading through Cicero and Homer, with Walter of Henley's Husbandry *included for light relief – literary irrelevancies compared to the seething excitement of the real world.*

She discussed such incompatibilities with her mother.

'Dearest Mother, of course I will comply with Father's ordinances, yet cannot you procure literature more relevant than classical antiquity, for example Lais *by Marie de France or Hue de Rotelande's* Ipomedon, *for I wish to understand the concerns of our nation, become involved.'*

'*Dearest Elizabeth! Must I insist once again that such matters do not concern you, conversation between ladies being limited to domestic matters and discussing other ladies, those unwisely absent.*'

'*Who know as little as us, thereby ensuring we never advance in our search for knowledge!*'

'*Which is normal, for matters beyond family and household are not our domain.*'

'*It is far from normal! No, I correct my words. It is indeed normal, but neither logical nor acceptable.*'

Her mother sighed as she had on innumerable other occasions when conversing with her unique, precociously stubborn and delightfully adorable daughter.

'*I return to my question of literature, do you ...*'

'*Of contemporary authors not declared salacious or blasphemous by your father, and they be few, I have heard reference to poems by Marlowe and Sidney.*'

'*Who write irrelevancies in a dialect daringly poetical yet falsely real.*'

'*You speak more like their sonnets than their sonnets speak of themselves.*'

'*And so might you!*'

Mother and daughter momentarily forgot the acrimony of their debate and burst into peals of merry laughter.

'*Ovid, Homer, Chaucer, Malory ...*'

'*I have read them several times.*'

'*You can improve your French.*'

'*England is practically at war with France.*'

'*Spanish is a delightful tongue.*'

'*Yes, but the country is Catholic.*'

'*True, I overlooked the disparity between their phrases of eloquence and the heresy of their papist beliefs. Although, since one may separate a head but once from its supporting shoulders, they cannot punish their heretics with greater severity than us.*'

'*Where have you learned such fascinations?*'

'*My brother, the bishop, when holding an empty glass of port*' *previously refilled, does occasionally pronounce on worldly matters.'*

'I wish very much to familiarise myself with the running of our estate, for one day I will inherit it.'

'Your husband will receive the inheritance until it is transferred to his son when you are widowed.'

'Only if I marry.'

'Of course you will marry!'

'Why?'

'Because ...'

'Yes, Mother?'

'To enable your husband to produce an heir.'

'And why, my sweetest Mother, does he produce the heir and not me?'

'Elizabeth, your disrespect of common purpose dismays me.'

'But I merely question stated facts.'

'Do not enforce open discussion of such indelicacies, which shall be accepted as well-founded without reflecting upon demeaning details.'

'If they be "well-founded", then please explain why I share your blue eyes, lightly-tinted wispy hair and immodestly sized feet?'

'Elizabeth!! That is enough blasphemy!! Such theorems are decided by wise men and remain unquestioned.'

'Except by myself. I will enquire of my father concerning his opinion.'

'He will only rebuff you.'

'Yes, but in an excitably enjoyable way. Perhaps the ensuing dialogue will be imposed by him but the wrangling should be equivalently amusing for both. At the same moment I will speak about learning of our estate.'

The clement weather permitted a change of routine; she could read Cicero in the formal garden instead of their 'embroidery salon', the room reserved for ladylike pursuits of leisure. Surrounded by the four walls of the manor, she was protected from roaming vagabonds, highwaymen and escaped felons; also the wind, except that the herbaceously festooned garden resembled more a prison than a place of repose.

Page four hundred and thirty seven.

Her father's voice was heard indicating displeasure about an inconsequentiality although, from the tone of his forceful voice, one could imagine a stupendous calamity resulting from the offending person's deeply-entrenched imbecility. Then footsteps were distinguished advancing towards her.

'My dearest Elizabeth, you wish to converse with me?'

'Only on the condition my father would wish to converse with his daughter.'

'But of course! Always assuming she is of a relaxed and understanding nature.'

Was he jesting or cynically serious?

'But I never am! When was I last docile to your arguments!'

'You should have been a son.'

'Never upon your life!! A daughter I will remain, with her innumerable qualities and occasional defaults, whilst being taught the responsibilities of a gentleman. For I wish to assist overseeing the estate, learn about my heritage.'

'Dearest daughter, I and my overseers handle such concerns, there is no need to worry yourself…'

'Perhaps no obligation, but I wish to involve myself, render my life meaningful.'

'Impossible! Women do not involve themselves in such activities.'

'Mary reigned for nearly six years, Elizabeth has replaced her. If women might be queen, then I can manage an estate.'

'Mary, in spite of being Catholic, was a disaster, ruining our country, whereas Elizabeth will never last.'

'Why? Are you plotting against her?'

'Elizabeth!!!! If you must joke, please whisper your misplaced fantasies; already here is proof of your inability to handle worldly affairs. As for our queen, who may indeed be a woman, she is surrounded by the wisest of councillors, male to the last man.

Perhaps she will survive a while, especially with William Cecil to counsel her. For your information, he superintends the civil service.'

Unfamiliar with the wherewithal of the civil service, she dared not enquire as to the reasoning behind her father's opinion.

'Have you perused Utopia *as advised?'*

'When I have completed Cicero I will dutifully commence Thomas More's novel.'

'It is not a novel!'

'Both works prosaically relate imagined happenings, whereas the reality of today inspires me.'

'Referring to the realities of today, I have invited James Tilworthy and his family for dinner next Sunday. It is time you became better acquainted with his son, bearing in mind your long-standing betrothal. Even if his family lacks a certain dignity of lineage, its position within the corridors of economic influence more than compensates, especially now that Cedric has completed his apprenticeship in London and has intimate knowledge of commercialising wool in foreign lands. As such, he is perfectly suited to assume management of the estate. You understand my implications?'

She did. Considered incapable of handling anything, her maidenhood was being contracted to a future estate manager.

'Dearest Elizabeth, I hope I can count on you to make me proud!'

And her father departed to involve himself in affairs other than compromising the ambitions of day-dreaming daughters.

Having triumphed over the literary long-windedness of Cicero, page four hundred and sixty-two being inscribed with words of congratulatory accolade, THE END, *she craved fresh air and a chance to contemplate the ominous signification of Cedric Tilworthy attending dinner on Sunday.*

Dainty clouds danced and pranced like spring lambs in the brilliantly blue sky as their carriage negotiated the country lane. Chatterby, her once-upon-a-time nanny and present-day chaperone-cum-confidante, sat in muted silence, no doubt furiously frustrated that private thoughts could not be overheard by even the most cunningly curious of gossipmongers.

She, Lady Elizabeth Melville, was twenty-four years old. Since becoming betrothed to Cedric Tilsworthy on her twelfth birthday she had preferred to overlook the incident. Never had Cedric or anyone else touched her, and never had she wished that such an incident might occur, for men were vain and uncomprehending. Admittedly she had committed the indelicacy of imagining how it would be to lie with a husband but with little success. Chatterby, under intense questioning, explained that married persons were prone to comporting themselves like rabbits in springtime. Husbands, after having imposed their attentions, generally slept soundly, often snoring, which was difficult to accommodate. Even so, wives became used to their presence, even missing them when absent, at least those with good fortune, for enduring an inconsiderate husband was worse than spinsterhood.

Conversing with gentlemen had created sensations neither sinister nor pleasurable, with one exception: Charles Hardcastle, the recently appointed family parson. He was soft in his manners, unassuming in his attentions. As they became acquainted, he lodged in the manor house and encounters were frequent, his presence rekindled daydreams about possible night-time happenings. Incomplete day-dreams. For, in spite of Chatterby's revelations, the manners of marriage remained mysterious.

Although over-age had she lived in the previous century, she was young for today's brides, at least those pertaining to the gentry who married when nearing twenty-five. From what Chatterby indicated, two reasons explained the change in habitudes. Firstly, sons of nobility were obliged to forge a career before marrying, instead of depending upon family heritage. Secondly, the misogynist teachings of Catholicism had been replaced by the somewhat more egalitarian applications of Protestantism, wherein males respected a woman's inferiority instead of displaying indifference to her existence. Marriage was becoming a partnership between souls of differing sensitivities. At fifteen, the age her mother married, no personality *was formed, whereas ten years later a maiden was an entire person who must needfully be wooed into acceptance.*

Charles had surely interpreted her inclinations, for she was naively lacking in discretion. So she accosted him, remaining as circumspect as possible, which was far from completely so, and he expounded how theological practice was at variance with the practicalities of agriculture and trading.

'But the clergy must comprehend all facets of society.'

He explained the church was responsible for spiritual guidance, not commercial and financial manoeuvrings.

'In an age where women can be queen, a wife could manage an estate whilst her husband theorises.'

His manner confirmed she had overstepped her mark, had encroached upon a subject reserved for masculine enterprise. Yet he had not denied affection between them, on the contrary.

As a greyish cloud churlishly hid the sun before floating eastwards towards ultimate evaporation, and as the sheep baa-aa-aa-ed in the fields, she realised the choice was between Mrs Cedric Tilworthy, Mrs Charles Hardcastle or Lady Elizabeth Melville eternal spinster of Shaftsbury. She must urgently talk with her father, before it was too late, before ...

Human voices, agitated and aggrieved, interrupted her thoughts. To the horror of Chatterby and to the consternation of their two male escorts, a group of labourers surrounded them, obliging the carriage to halt. One looked up accusingly into her eyes.

'My wife and baby are dying and you spend your days trotting aimlessly round the countryside.'

'Careful, Amber, she be his Lordship's daughter.'

'Daughter of the thieving bastard who levelled our forests and enclosed our common lands to graze his sheep, stealing our means of living.'

'Amber! Control your tongue, for they be ladies and you a simple sheep reeve.'

She looked down at her accuser; he appeared more desperate than dangerous.

'Please, I beg calmness. You speak of your wife and daughter, what is their illness?'

'Hunger!! And everything else that follows.'

'Where are they, do you live nearby?'

'My Lady!' All were stunned at her question but only Chatterby had dared interject.

'I would wish to ascertain with my own eyes the veracity of your comments.'

'But, my cottage be unfit for ...'

'Let me decide.'

It was not, being unsuited for anything remotely human. Only the hens and goats seemed at ease amongst the filth, also the rodent scurrying into the gloom of a cobwebbed corner. She advanced to the bodies huddling on the bed of festering straw and dagswain coverlet; did the smell emanate from them or fungal vegetation?

The mother coughed horribly, yet no blood emerged from between her lips. There was hope. She picked up the infant, its clothes damp from urine and stained with faeces. A miniature mouth sought her breast, hunger overcoming maternal recognition.

'When did you last eat?'

'Yesterday. But I am not hungry, for dandelion soup be most nourishing.'

She turned to her senior footman.

'Jenkins you will deliver milk, eggs, bread and sweet potatoes, dry straw for the bed and wood to repair leaks in the roof; also faggots and kindling wood. We ourselves will choose blankets and clothes, which you will bring concurrently.'

'But your Ladyship!!'

'Yes?'

'N-n-n-nothing.'

'And you, Amber, you will remove the filth from your home, ready to receive what we will deliver.'

'But that is for my wife to accomplish!'

'Is she capable?'

Amber gazed at the shivering creature to whom he was married.

104

'I will do it, just as you request.'

Outside the cottage she breathed deeply, appreciating the freshness of air untainted by human, animal and vegetable decomposition. Other villagers accosted her.

'What about my Annie?'

'My roof also leaks!'

'Please, listen, you must understand, because I am personally in no position to respect your wishes. However, I promise to speak to those with responsibility.'

She saw them hesitate, then renounce as they realised she was speaking practicalities. For she was a woman.

'I will return tomorrow to ensure that my instructions have been implemented.'

Driving home she quizzed Jenkins on how such misery could exist. He explained that Holland was blockading English wool exports, seriously compromising farmers and merchant traders, the former defending their finances by disengaging labourers and increasing the rents of those remaining. Meanwhile food prices rose rapidly but not wages, leading to hunger and serious rioting around the countryside.

By the time she reached the portal of her family's residence she had committed herself to confronting her father upon the subject.

'I apologise most humbly for our tardy arrival; a horse went lame and a replacement had to be saddled.'

She looked around the reception hall; twelve people were present, ignoring servants. Herself, her parents, their neighbour the Right Honourable Arthur Althersham with his wife Emma and daughters Celia and Rosemary, her mother's elder brother His Reverence the Bishop of Warwick, visiting the diocese, and the Tilworthy family including daughter Sissie and son Cedric.

With dignified due diligence they completed the social niceties of hosts greeting guests, then moved into the drawing-room.

James Tilworthy addressed her father.

'So, Jonathan, what is this I hear about the farm-labourers'

105

rebellion being calmed, riots cancelled because of the intervention of a lady of charity.'

'I beg your pardon?'

'Delivering food and clothes to save a baby's life, wood to repair a leaking roof and offering hints of further kindness!'

'The rebellion has ended?'

'Not entirely, but it has seriously quietened.'

'What the damnation is this nonsense?'

'Father, perhaps I ca ...'

'Be quiet, child!'

'No, my dearest Lady Elizabeth, pray continue your discourse, for I believe you are not foreign to such occurrences.'

'What the devil? Elizabeth, explain yourself forthwith!!'

She complied in spite of the incivility of the command, pleased to announce her involvement yet scared of her father's response. Which was not delayed.

'How dare you interfere in matters of running my estate! Your stupidity has in all probably sabotaged longstanding dealings to subdue the labourers.'

'Would you have refused aid if you had been approached?'

'Of cour ..., naturally I would have shown concern.'

'But not helped?'

'That is my affair.'

'Since you express outrage, you cannot confirm charitable action on your behalf.'

The expression on her parent's face could have been accompanied by smoke and fire bellowing from his nostrils. Before his displeasure exploded into fury, she addressed the bishop.

'Dear Uncle, what would Jesus have done if He had been in my position?'

A heavy silence filled the room.

'He would have shown the same mercy as you.'

'Proving I was correct in my actions?'

'Not entirely, for our Saviour has powers of discretion beyond those accorded to unmarried daughters of English nobility.'

'Why?'

Her father answered on behalf of the bishop. 'Because you are unfamiliar with handling the estate and have no inkling how to comport yourself.'

'Which is why I plead to be taught.'

'Enough!! There are ladies present, let us behave in a dignified manner. Sissie! I believe you play the clavichord with increasing dexterity?'

'Yes, I am taught at the Guild school. However, my favourite instrument is the virginal upon which I play such favourites as "Greensleeves" and John Bull's "In Nomines" settings. I pray daily that the master of the school's wait, our orchestra with seven musicians, will allow me to play lead! I would wish to join the church choir, but such honour is reserved for boys and gentlemen.'

Much to the relief of those in attendance, the senior manservant announced that dinner was being served.

After luncheon the gentlemen debated business and politics in the library. Elizabeth joined the ladies in the embroidery room, sipping herbal tea as she listened half-heartedly to their exchanges of gossip and attempts at scandal-mongering.

When the men emerged Cedric Tilworthy suggested she accompany him for a stroll.

'So you will return to the village and ascertain how your charitable actions are benefiting the labourers?'

'That is my intent.'

'Even if your father refuses permission?'

'I am free to visit our family's estate.'

'Please do not be affronted, but your comment does not constitute a clear response to my enquiry.'

'In such case, I would send Chatterby.'

'Ha! You have a determined mind.'

'You have been warned!'

'How do you mean?'

'The reason you are accompanying me is not to obtain exercise but *a consequence of dealings between our mutual fathers who desire to ratify our betrothal in marriage.'*

'An occurrence which would please you?'

'Possibly not. Although favouring the condition of marriage, I am strongly adverse to the imposition of a husband for reasons financial, political or downright cynical.'

'Do you believe I would accept a wife imposed by my father?'

'Would you refuse your father's wish?'

'That would depend whether she be fair and of good character.'

'Thereby eliminating my unruly, unconventional self?'

'By no means!! I consider you utterly delightful, your forthright personality charms me enormously and, if I might mimic your "unruly, unconventional self", I find you highly pleasing to the eye.'

'But ... What must I do to dissuade your ardour?'

'I cannot imagine, for it grows with every minute spent in your presence.'

'We would argue.'

'About what?'

'Running the estate.'

'For what reason?'

'You would prevent my involvement?'

'No.'

'My father advised that such falsifications would unfreeze my heart?'

'Yes, but ...'

'Continue.'

'I swear that my declaration supporting your involvement truly corresponds to my thoughts on the matter.'

She was increasingly perplexed; they were supposed to be disputing opposing opinions, not averring harmonious agreement. How to rebuff him before he assumed acceptance of their marriage? She decided to set a trap.

'How do you foresee a wife?'

His face expressed astonishment, for she had exceeded the boundaries of social etiquette. Yet his intensity of purpose only seemed to strengthen at her indiscretion.

108

'Lady Elizabeth, finished are the times of infant brides devoid of personal significance. I see my wife as an accomplice, someone for whom I will have much affection, with whom I will share the pleasures of raising a family whilst dividing the responsibilities of running a household and family business. Disagreements will be resolved with an equality of spirit, not predetermined masculine dominance.'

She stopped walking and gazed in astonishment, for his words sounded excitingly heretical yet wondrously sensible. Then she realised it was she, not him, who had fallen into her trap. She must douse his ardour before it was too late.

'Lady Elizabeth, will you accept my hand in marriage?'

Either she became Mrs Cedric Tilworthy or she revealed the truth.

'I cannot, for my affections lie elsewhere.'

'Father, you wished to see me?'

'Yes!

She seated herself facing his lordship, ready for the worst.

'You are aware of the saying "Two errors a rightness do not constitute"?'

'Thus refusing the hand of Cedric does not compensate for helping those poor labourers?'

'Yes. NO!!'

'Dearest father, you are not habitually indecisive.'

'My dearest daughter, after much reflection I am prepared to instigate your apprenticeship of running the estate. To commence you may learn to write and study matters of financial administration. However, you will follow my dictates as long as I am alive, for twin masters are worse than none.'

'May I return to the mother and child?'

'You may. You see, I can be generous!'

'Begone!! You now realise that contented labourers work better, bring in more revenues.'

'How, I mean ...'

'Cedric explained it to me.'

Her father sighed in exasperation, then smiled.

'*Elizabeth, you are both my favourite daughter and the son I so regrettably lost in the London plagues. However, that does not pardon your unaccountable rejection of Cedric's offer in marriage. May I enquire as to your reasoning?*'

'*My heart yearns for another.*'

Her father required several moments to regain his composure.

'*And who might be this interloper?*'

'*Charles Hardcastle.*'

Her father considered the implications.

'*And how does he consider the situation?*'

'*I believe he harbours similar inclinations, but hesitates due to the modesty of his situation.*'

'*A sign of undoubted intelligence.*'

'*Thereby indicating his suitability?*'

'*NO!*'

'*For what reason?*'

'*He is denuded of financial resources.*'

'*I will inherit more than adequately.*'

'*That is irrelevant. To be blunt it is his theological leanings that bother me. Call me a recusant, but I have always harboured grievances at the actions of King Henry since no mortal may overturn the authority of God's chosen representative on earth, his Holiness the Pope in Rome. Meanwhile young Hardcastle preens himself with protestant liberties, dabbling with heresy when proclaiming distaste for the ceremonials of mass. Although outwardly unaffected by Calvinist extremes, he must be viewed with suspicion.*'

'*He claims that Anglican doctrine is a compromise, a means of uniting believers under one harmonious, if uninspiring banner.*'

'*I cannot refute your saying.*'

'*So you accept Charles as suitable?*'

'*That is far from certain. Marriage is a union of families, a social undertaking to promote stability, harmony and prosperity. Respect and affection increment with time whereas love, to use diplomatic terminology for your attraction towards our parson, is a*

110

manifestation that civilised gentlefolk should suppress. When initial ardour fades a union turns cold and conflicting, destined to foster regret for youthful impetuousness.'

'My feelings towards Charles differ greatly from your insinuations for he is a great friend and comfort to me. I have hardly considered matters of the flesh and, you may be surprised to learn, I acquiesce with your condemnation of marrying to satisfy biological instincts. Do not think I contemplate my current situation without misgiving for, above anything else, I desperately wish you to be proud of me.'

To her amazement her garrulously grumpy father took his only daughter into his arms and hugged her until she could hardly breathe.

She waited for morning prayers to end then, as family and servants disappeared to pursue their daily routines, she cornered the family's representative of God.

'May we speak together?'

She explained her predicament and boldly asked him outright.

'Do you return my sentiments?'

'Please do not insist that I respond.'

'In other words, you admit strong affections for me.'

'I have already advised that pursuing our relationship would be futile.'

'You pronounce unendingly on love. Surely, therefore, you believe that those promising allegiance before God should do so for reasons of sentiment, not commercial compatibility?'

'Of course, but my Lady Elizabeth, I do not merit such an honour.'

'That is und...'

A manservant knocked and entered.

'Your Ladyship, forgive my interruption but a Mr Cedric Tilworthy awaits your presence outside.'

She was surrounded by reels and rolls, bundles and bouquets, satin and silk, her wedding dress, ballroom gown, going away attire and everything imaginable in the realm of extravagant clothing.

111

She inspected a farthingale, its wooden frame allowing dresses to bustle in even wider abundance than with the pannier. A couturier then explained the virtues of leather corsets which compressed the stomach into oblivion and bosom into prominence, something she considered distasteful but which fashion and therefore her mother adopted without questioning.

The arguments became heated when discussing the wearing of petticoats. As her mother insisted, the best protection of modesty was not concealment but making believe that beneath the finery a woman's head, feet and hands were disconnected. Which, she thought to herself, was ridiculous for a bride about to marry a husband.

The couturier departed huffed because his promotion of linen stockings generated acrimonious retribution from her mother, who recanted the dictum that God created woman, the Devil immodest clothes. The courtier condemned his cause by responding that the Devil only complimented God's less than perfect achievements.

Alone, she could finally address her mother on a subject of great importance.

'Mother, please describe what will happen upon my wedding night.'

'You know such matters perturb me. Ask Chatterby to explain.'

'But she has never experienced a wedding night!'

'True, but she knows about such things.'

'How?'

As expected, there was no response because matters relating to her mother having become a mother played no part in her mother's role of educating a daughter.

'Chatterby, I marry in two weeks. I wish to be informed of what happens during the nuptials.'

'But I know not!'

'You surely know more than I.'

'That is my affair. Oh, I apologise, your Ladyship, I spoke hastily.'

'I will forgive you.'

'Thank you!'

'When you have finished explaining!'

Chatterby revealed that her knowledge had been acquired during confessionals. Like other mischievous maidens she enquired into the nature of sins as yet uncommitted so that, aware of the perils, she might circumnavigate misconduct. The priest had been overjoyed to instruct his pious charges, providing lurid details of every imaginable misdeed confessed by local practitioners.

She listened to Chatterby with growing interest, fascination, incredulity and repulsion as the older woman described a wife exposing, making available and finally submitting herself to a husband. So it had not been misplaced humour, humans really did comport themselves like rabbits in springtime.

'Does he enjoy doing it?'

'Apparently so.'

'Do I?'

'Not the first time, but with practice and patience the pleasure, so I am informed, can be significant.'

Which confirmed her suspicions, for when performing her most intimate toilette she had not infrequently experienced agreeable sensations.

'Must I perform something in return?'

'Nothing of which I know. You simply make it as pleasurable as possible for him.'

'By doing nothing?'

'I believe such is the practice amongst married couples.'

'Is not pleasure in a woman disallowed? In books I read of dire punishment for sinning ...'

'No longer. With the new religion a woman may receive satisfaction from her husband if he agrees to provide it.'

Although controlling her sobbing, she failed to repress the tears that bore witness to her destitution. Oh how she had tried to prove herself worthy of her husband's fervour by offering herself unconditionally. But to no avail. Had Chatterby told a nonsense? Why did her body *refuse to welcome him? Chatterby never mentioned torture, merely momentary discomfort. Her husband's virile member was enormous; she would haemorrhage until dying. How did he conceal such a monstrosity when wearing trousers? She was not a normal woman; she could never be a wife.*

Another thought further aggrieved her misery. After centuries of denial men now displayed cognisance of women belonging to society. Yet God, for it must be Him, evidently insisted otherwise because, to become with child, a woman must accept the most denigrating exposure whilst her husband demonstrated physical and personal domination. How could the father of Jesus adjudicate so unfairly against the dignity of women?

Sensing an arm around her shoulder she gazed longingly into her husband's eyes, wondering if he could possibly love her as passionately as she adored him. Then she hid amongst his embrace, seeking forgiveness and hoping for understanding. Should she have married Cedric, he who so nobly freed her from their betrothal, insisting he would never deny her the happiness of true love?

She felt her husband's mouth gently caress her forehead, then her cheeks and lips; it was so enjoyable, why had he not acted likewise before? He fondled her neck and then softly stroked lower down, much lower down, forever lower down until sensations emanating from her body overwhelmed the hesitations of her mind.

Eleventh encounter: Henrietta and Walter
1642   Plymouth, England

She descended the stairs, crossed the cavernous entrance hall and entered the drawing-room. A north-westerly gale was blowing, from her bedroom she had watched crests of waves being shredded into mists of sea-spray, yet generous expanses of blue sky intermingled with the scurrying clouds. Protected from the elements and warmed by the rays of the ascending sun, she could embroider in the conservatory without fear of catching a chill.

But only when the administering of her estate had been completed. Mrs Lowther, the housekeeper, had followed and was waiting to be instructed. They confirmed sleeping arrangements and finalised the evening menu, then debated the placing of guests at table. She authorised Barnam to purchase seafood in nearby Westchapel and Jessop to select twelve bottles of claret from the wine-cellar.

Mrs Lowther retired to be replaced by Ben Jarvis the property overseer. Hired by her father, Old Ben was a relic from Elizabethan times, withered in body and plodding in mind whose philosophy consisted of convincing himself that something unchanged for fifty years should not be replaced. Unfortunately society evolved with alarming rapidity; without adapting it was impossible to compete with competition. She realised crops could be rotated more efficiently, she knew sheep-farming should make way for cattle and horses, and she knew potatoes and turnips should be planted in their heavy clay, yet Old Ben remained impassive to her arguments. Her husband had imposed authority with forceful words and the occasional whipping, but a lady could not indulge in such

115

authoritarian behaviour. Consequently her farm buildings were dilapidated and agricultural inefficiency ruled supreme.

'Please ask Beth to attend me immediately.'

Old Ben retired, his modest list of demands accepted without discussion.

Beth arrived and followed her to the conservatory. Once inside, the maidservant waited until she had installed herself, then handed over her precious embroidery. The other artefacts necessary to intertwine coloured threads into intricate artistry were stored in a work-cabinet attainable without rising from her chair.

'I require my grey formal gown to be prepared for this evening; be in attendance at six o'clock in order to assist with my toilette. As you are aware, we have distinguished guests arriving for dinner, including my brother-in-law from Plymouth. Since being appointed Justice of the Peace he has become extremely sensitive to suspicions of social impropriety. Consequently every effort must be made to encourage the belief that this household comports itself with utmost decorum.'

The maid nodded, unperturbed; evidently the impending visit of a juridical dignitary had already been discussed in the servants' quarters.

'Otherwise you may retire.

The maid curtsied and departed, her forsaken expression no doubt caused by a cancelled evening at the local hostelry with the stable-lad who had stolen her heart.

Surrounded by sewing materials she envisioned the images she would create that morning, then painstakingly selected suitably coloured threads and absorbed herself in recreating the scene of the Immaculate Conception.

Violent gusts of wind distracted her concentration. She had instructed the head-gardener to plant shrubs but in winter their barren branches permitted glimpses of ocean. Somewhere beneath those heaving waves lay her husband, drowned when his clipper encountered a storm whose vicious intensity gave the Bay of Biscay its sinister reputation.

116

Nearly five years had passed since he failed to arrive in Devonport. She recalled how anxiety turned to despair when the captain of another vessel confirmed her husband leaving Santander as planned, sailing straight into the maelstrom that devastated vast tracts of Brittany coastline. Initially she had been too distracted by administrative formalities to sense the void resulting from his absence. She then anguished when widows of crew-members accused her husband of recklessly defying a marine holocaust to deliver his cargo on time; she alone had understood the reason for his foolhardiness for her birthday coincided with the clipper's scheduled date of berthing.

God had decreed her husband should perish. But for committing what crime? Had he been sacrificed in order to punish herself? Yet she loved her husband and had unswervingly respected her marital vows. There must have been a reason for such divine intervention, yet it was impossible to elucidate the mysterious ways of the Almighty. Yes, following her husband's drowning she questioned His wisdom, yes she failed to control her outrage at losing the man she loved. Yes once, in an uncontrollable fit, she blasphemed the Lord Almighty. In retribution He confiscated her children, William from drowning and Isabelle from smallpox.

Now, thirty-seven years old, her life advanced towards an uninviting future whose only certainty was death. Her embroidery permitted the dubious self-satisfaction of creating something artistic. She would have preferred painting, oils permitted greater scope for self-expression, but it was considered inappropriate for ladies to engage in such activities. Her brother joked this was to avoid the tableaux adorning their walls displaying naked males instead of the supine splendours of Botticellian women.

She returned to the Immaculate Conception. As she sewed she reflected upon the conception of her own children, which had been anything but immaculate.

Having a seafaring husband, was it an advantage or hindrance to harmonious marital existence? At least it replaced the mind-numbing routine imposed by contemporary rural society. During her youth the nation was still imbued with Elizabethan pomp and pageantry accompanied by a relaxing of religious prying into personal behaviour. Sadly the uninhibited exuberance of socialising and literary jubilation of poets like Donne and Shakespeare were now disdained in a nation increasingly dominated by Puritans overacting against everything papist. As they gained influence their interference became bolder; consequently England was retreating backwards towards a darker age. Surely fining worshippers for not attending church was incompatible with God's all-embracing generosity? Surely outlawing on the Sabbath any pastime not devoted to glorifying God was an overreaction to increased laxity of morals? The population deeply resented losing new-found freedoms; the likelihood of strife was omnipresent.

Admittedly local society could benefit from change. She resented its hypocritical artificiality, outshining neighbours with external trappings being more important than generosity of thought or expression of genuine emotion; in a country of intensive farming nobody dared call a spade a spade. How different from the irrepressible openness of her beloved Henry.

She remembered how the days after each return overflowed with exchanges of family news and the recounting of his adventures, the opening of presents and the reviewing of the children's scholastic progress; every moment was precious. At night, alone in their bed-chamber, the intensity of his lovemaking recalled their honeymoon. Then his rugged eagerness accentuated and tenderness intermingled with moments of mutual passion.

During those nights she became a woman as opposed to the Lady Henrietta. Hence she recalled them with gratitude: also longing, because most unbearable of all was sharing an empty bedchamber with the memory of someone who would never return.

As for remarrying, considered by her family the least calamitous denouement to her tragedy, no suitor had claimed her hand. Bachelors old enough to plight their troth remained single for reasons ominously evident and wives generally outlived husbands, limiting the number of widowers.

'Is Her Ladyship ready to be served?'

The maidservant, receiving a brief nod of approval, disappeared only to return almost immediately with liquid refreshment. As she sipped her eyes focused on the sea, its surface lashed by a violent squall blowing in from the Atlantic.

'Never! Never! Never!!'

The judge was incensed. His younger brother, Henry Fitzwarren, had vowed before God to respect the sanctity of holy matrimony. So had his bride. Even though his brother's body might repose at the bottom of the ocean, his soul was alive in Heaven preventing, nay prohibiting Henrietta from remarrying. Especially ignoble would be the wedding ceremony, the hypocrisy of a woman promising fidelity to another whilst her husband waited in paradise. Puritan lawyers, perverted secular purloiners of ecclesiastical morality, may decree the right to remarry by reducing matrimony to the level of a judicial codicil, but their ploys ignored the inviolability of sacramental oaths.

'But Robert, be reasonable! Henrietta, even if of mature age, is healthy and extremely lonely, she needs masculine company. It is hardly her fault her husband's clipper sank in that storm.'

'Fiddlesticks! Henry would not wish to welcome an adulteress back into his arms when she ascends to heaven.'

He, John Mascotte, protective sibling of his younger sister Henrietta and brother-in-law of the judge, slumped back into his seat. He realised Robert could be stubbornly irrational when it suited him. Yet solving his sister's sentimental problems, rather their absence, required the consensus of the judiciary, especially when his design was marrying her to Sir Walter Cheswell, a university friend grieving the tragic loss of his Jane. There was nothing material or self-seeking in his scheming; both his sister and friend were financially protected. And yet having Walter living near Plymouth would be most pleasurable. Also, Staddiscombe Manor was sorely suffering from lack of overseeing. Its daily running created few problems, but times evolved. Selective crop rotation increased yields, erecting silos to store animal feed during winter avoided slaughtering when prices were lowest, and London was ready to pay exaggerated prices for fruit syrups and medicinal herbs. Under his supervision Walter could revolutionise the agricultural exploitation of the estate before it deteriorated into rack and ruin.

However, before Henrietta tied the nuptial knot to Walter or anyone else, a vexing problem required his attentions. His father, furious at his son's departure to London to seek fortune in the world of mercantile finance, had placed the family lands in trust to be inherited by Henrietta's eldest son when he attained maturity. If she died childless the estate passed to her brother, himself; if she remarried property rights transferred to her husband unless pre-emptive measures were taken. In other words, Henrietta must sign a legal conveyance before remarrying, bequeathing the estate to him.

He must act without delay, for Walter was attending a congress in nearby Devonport, a major confrontation between maritime traders and the importers who acquired their cargoes. He had proposed accommodation at Staddiscombe Manor, praying his friend would appreciate an opportunity to become better acquainted with his sister. Since it was inconceivable for a lady to invite gentlemen to her abode, nor the latter to propose such indiscretion, he personally delivered the invitation to his friend before announcing to Henrietta that her brother plus university friend, not forgetting one extraneous fraternal judge-in-law, would be gracing her home with their presence.

Damn the judge! Notwithstanding, he would advance with his intrigues. If Henrietta and Walter proved to be more than just socially compatible he would overcome the condemnations of the profoundly pompous Robert when the moment was propitious.

Waves lapped the shoreline in friendly welcome, caressing rocks savaged several weeks previously. Birds flew in differing directions full of the urgencies of spring. She sat admiring the stirrings of Mother Nature, her embroidery lying abandoned inside the conservatory.

She reflected on her encounter with Sir Walter Chesnell, also his suggestion that she honour him with a visit to Clifton. In spite of the discordant formality of the Devonport congress she had felt especially close to him, an affinity remarked by local socialites who started speculating with varying degrees of inhibition. Meanwhile she was circumspect in her optimism, reluctant to accept that after years of unrelenting solitude a miracle might be unfolding before her very eyes.

And even if so, the situation was far from simple.

Her juridical brother-in-law had pontificated publicly upon the infinitely permanent covenant of holy matrimony that no man might set asunder, even after death, marriage being a holy sacrament and not a temporal convenience as claimed by infuriatingly disrespectful Protestants. The local bishop, philosophically in agreement with remarriage yet reluctant to confront the local Justice of the Peace, mumbled incoherently, neither supporting nor condemning.

So who was right? The judge or a woman's heart convinced otherwise? Hopefully the latter, because her brother, who acted as messenger between them, notified that the gentleman in question harboured no qualms at welcoming a second spouse into his life. One irritation was John's suggestion bordering on insistence that she convey the family estate to him; it was not the concept itself, retaining the estate in the family made sense, it was the awkward hesitating way he broached the matter that aroused her suspicions. What was he scheming?

Nevertheless, abandoning Staddiscombe Manor would be both a relief and pleasure. Attending social functions alongside a husband in a metropolis like Bristol would provide a welcome change from staid Devonshire decorum. It was the night-time that concerned her. She had only known one man, she had sworn to love and obey him forever. She had indeed loved him, been loved by him, still devotedly respected his memory. How could she share her bed with a stranger, however charming, the father of three children begotten with a woman he had equally sworn to love forever? And still loved for all she knew. How could she offer herself to Sir Walter Cheswell whilst her husband was watching from above?

121

'Mr Cheswell, I have the information you requested.'

The warehouse was impregnated by the fragrance of saffron and spice combined with the odours of folders mouldering as damp pervaded their parchment. The book-keepers smelled no different, as if they belonged to the building. Quill in hand, he tallied the inventory valuations; the margins from his latest voyage would be astronomical, vastly more than he needed. In fact, when considering his cumulated fortune, any profit surpassed his requirements.

His son was a trainee officer in the Royal Navy and his daughters were satisfactorily married, rendering his life devoid of challenge. Settling into a agricultural estate in Devon and revamping its activities conformed to his quest for a change in circumstance, something to reinvigorate his enthusiasm for existing. Furthermore, the estate came with the Lady Henrietta. She was lonely and delightful company, her external sadness reflecting a search for personal fulfilment.

How exactly like himself!

She was no longer young but he appreciated her simple and unaffected femininity, so unlike most ladies of standing who camouflaged physical deficiencies with cosmetics and deflected cultural insufficiencies with vestments of appalling extravagance. The Lady Henrietta, on the contrary, displayed a purity of character that permitted her natural self to dominate. Admittedly she was not beautiful but she should satisfy a husband. Yes, he desired her, during daytime as a companion, during night-time as a woman.

She had accepted his invitation to visit Clifton. Rather, her brother had accepted and, by strange pre-ordained coincidence, had suggested whether, by any unlikely means, it could conceivably be possible for his sister to accompany him. And then he had been convoked 'unexpectedly' to London when it was too late to cancel the Lady Henrietta's arrival.

During her stay they would visit the Roman ruins at Bath and explore the coastline if the weather was favourable. Most importantly, he would introduce her discreetly to his family. Although, with them, discretion was something gleefully sacrificed in the pursuit of gossiping during which they distended figments of the imagination into possibilities, then probabilities and finally into the certitude of forthcoming events. However, since there was little possibility of marrying without enduring such indignities, he would dutifully submit. Then he would reap the benefits.

To do this he must tread carefully. He understood from John that Lady Henrietta owned the estate. Since England's ever-changing laws no longer accorded automatic transfer of property to a husband, she must be influenced to sign a suitable conveyance before the wedding.

'Charles may be an even greater idiot than his father, but he is king.'

He and his brother-in-law were lunching during a break in the latter's court proceedings. After social inconsequentialities the conversation had turned to politics.

'He is a Calvinist infiltrator from Scotland who obtusely seeks confrontation with Parliament without foundation to his arguments. His trustworthy lieutenants Strafford and Laud are executed, his Star Chamber and Court of High Commission are abolished and now the Triennial Act imposes Parliament against the monarch's wishes. His situation is desperate.'

'Instead of defending his crown he supervises treason overseas, never has civilisation witnessed such butchery in the cause of expropriating a nation. Perhaps Charles will succeed in Ireland but he will lose mightily in England for the Puritans of Pym and Cromwell, fearing the same fate if the King turns against Parliament, will resist with cunning and determination.'

'Of greater import is the polarisation into religious divisions, Anglicans and remnants of Catholicism defending the king, Puritans and Presbyterians supporting Parliament. If the situation is not diffused I see much malevolence ahead of us. King he might be but Charles, stubborn and impervious to advice, is the worst person to extricate our country from its political quagmire.'

'I must concur, much as it causes me distress.'

'Then let us talk of happier matters; for example, how fare the fortunes of your sister?'

He could no longer conceal certain matters from his companion.

'Excellent, for she and Walter Creswell are possibly to marry.'

The expected explosion did not materialise; had Robert decided to accept the inevitable? He assumed so and broached the subject which had incited the luncheon appointment. 'Perhaps less for myself, for a problem exists that requires your expertise and influence to unravel.'

'How to transfer ownership of the estate to your good self?'

The judge may be irascible but he was far from simple-minded.

'Indeed!'

'The answer lies neither with writ, subpoena nor legal indivision, but tact, charm and subtle persuasion. To put things simply, rarely possible in my profession, if you cannot convince Henrietta to relinquish the landholdings, there is nothing you or the nation's most able lawyers can accomplish.'

Then something suspiciously strange occurred. The Justice of the Peace looked in his direction and smiled with undisguised affability.

'Such persuasion might be facilitated if certain arable lands, those bordering my holdings, were transferred to my good self as representative of her dearly departed husband.'

'Of course, your Ladyship, our Bristol Channel cannot compete with the magnificence of the Devonshire coastline.

'With respect to picturesque beauty, Sir Walter, may I be so impolite as to concur. Nevertheless, I must insist that your region possesses mud-flats vastly more extensive than those found within the coastal confines of Devon.'

Was she mocking him? Never mind, they were out of earshot of inquisitive ears. Custom denied raising the subjects he so wished to discuss, for their conversation must remain impeccably impersonal. Even so, here at last was an opportunity to partake in private conversation with a person who intrigued him immensely.

Out of earshot they might be, but they remained in view of the leering leeches that constituted his family entourage. The die was practically cast; he had effectively announced his matrimonial inclinations to the entire community. Notwithstanding, a minor obstacle of importance remained, presenting his candidature to Lady Henrietta Fitzwarren. How, when and where should he broach the matter? And would she concur? Damn English society, they were the only two persons officially unaware of their intentions to marry each other.

'Oooh, I pray beg your pardon, your Ladyship.'

Engrossed in his ruminations he had veered towards the object of his thoughts, not quite colliding with but certainly more than brushing her outer garments. Furious at his clumsiness, he apologised a second, then a third time.

Thankfully she appeared unconcerned, her lips having curled into an impish smile, lips he should soon embrace before turning his masculine intentions to elsewhere ...

Stop!! Do not jeopardise the future by failing to accommodate the present. One misguided meander into her trajectory was pardonable, a repeat performance assuredly not. He returned to safer subjects, explaining that dolphins were occasionally sighted in the channel, although not in early autumn. Which was most regrettable.

She smiled back at him, failing to dissimulate profound disinterest in the migrating habitudes of marine mammals.

The gala celebrating her final evening in Clifton rivalled London's more ostentatious festive occasions. For once, for the first time in years, sitting alongside her host in the banqueting-hall, she was an accompanied lady escorted with due deference by a beaming and obviously proud host. The orchestra played favourites from Henry VIII's court as guests dined, for example 'Hélas Madame' and 'En Vray Amure'. There was a short foray into the world of madrigals but their solemnity had caused a fall from favour. After dinner guests sang and danced to popular Elizabethan tunes, speculating whether they would play 'La Volta' following the scandal of their so-called virgin queen who, dancing with the Earl of Leicester, had twirled somewhat over-enthusiastically and revealed a highly censurable expanse of scrawny royal leg. Also, if 'La Volta' was played, would 'he' accompany 'her' on the dance floor?

It was not played, much to her disappointment. However, much to her delight, he invited her to dance 'Tower Hill' and 'Kemp's Jig'. As the evening metamorphosed into night attendees realised there would be no betrothal announcement. But only for the time being ...

Next morning, as she installed herself in her carriage, her host spoke through the open window, expressing some last-minute thoughts.

'I am so delighted, Lady Henrietta, that your visit was agreeable. However, do not become over-attached to the region. I am contemplating selling my business and moving to the South Coast, possibly nearby to Plymouth. I am of the opinion the region is splendid, the climate agreeable and the inhabitants charming!'

Had the shock of realising she would not be moving to Clifton registered on her face? If so, had he noticed? She quickly regained her composure and replied as if nothing untoward had been spoken.

'Sir Walter, I cannot form judgement upon my fellow Devonians but if you find yourself in the environs of Staddiscombe Manor I would be offended if you did not permit me to demonstrate how our hospitality matches our reputation!'

Amazing!! She, an unmarried lady, had invited him to visit her place of residence! He would contrive numerous excuses for finding himself in the vicinity of Staddiscombe Manor before choosing an opportune moment to request her hand in marriage, not forgetting the remainder of her delectable body.

How she differed from his Jane who had epitomised sweetness and fragility, both of body and mind. He had tended to her every need whilst guiding her though recurrent illnesses. In return she devoted herself to accommodating his every wish. She had been so pure in thought, so saddened when noticing imperfection in his comportment, that he attained her standards of altruistic perfection. His father's agonising death from syphilis only strengthened his resolve to resist terrestrial temptation; God's punishment may have been severe in view of his parent's refrained profligacy but His message was clear. Yes, the Puritans were right; morality and abstinence were the only paths to follow.

He realised Henrietta would be a challenge, not physically for he could handle women during intimacy; it was her independence of spirit that merited attention. He had been dismayed at the signs of loose living when visiting Plymouth; regrettably the enlightened teachings of Protestantism had not infiltrated the Devonshire country-side. Hopefully the days of submitting to a vain monarch married to a Catholic of dubious origin, in spite of her name, were numbered as Pym, Hampden, Hazelrigg and others prepared to defend the interests of the realm. Once installed at Staddiscombe Manor he would support their cause by introducing its ethics to the local community.

The late autumn gale was weakening although gusts of wind still whipped branches of exposed trees into frenzied fibrillation. She sewed steadily, her latest oeuvre depicting the Nativity. She now regretted the choice of subject, anyone espying images of a mother and her newly-born would jump to impure conclusions. Although, impure or otherwise, there would be foundation to such speculation.

She was to marry; he had asked and she had accepted with alacrity. Marriage implied a shared bedchamber, hence potential motherhood because, while not wishing to dwell upon despairingly disgusting matters, she understood that becoming with child still remained a possibility. But motherhood, after years of withering widowhood, was misplaced in the extreme. Walter (she dared refer to him informally in her thoughts) had not broached the subject, so she remained unaware of his intentions.

Mrs Lowther entered the conservatory, highly agitated.

'Madam, Beth is in labour and suffers greatly.'

She abandoned her embroidery. Collecting the medicine chest kept ready for emergencies she hurried outside to where Arthur was waiting with the carriage. She clambered in and they departed at a gallop towards the outlying cottages. Dear Beth, a delightful girl who had married a stable-lad the previous year. Nobody was better qualified to raise a family than her former maidservant.

Inside the simply furnished yet comfortable cottage Beth's stony-white face was dripping with sweat. However hard she pushed, the baby refused to exit. Was the mother's body too narrow or was her baby incorrectly positioned? It was evident that time was running out. Doctors in desperation cut open the mother's belly, as with Julius Caesar, but they used surgical instruments and not carving knives purchased from the local ironmonger.

She administered ergot to relieve the pain, ignoring the Church's admonishments that suffering during childbirth was the Lord's punishment for Eve's original sin and should be accepted with equanimity. Beth's condition worsened so she and Mrs Lowther practically sat on the distended stomach in a final effort to force out the infant. Then Beth haemorrhaged.

Back in the manor she steadied her nerves with a glass of port, then another. She had failed; was it incompetence or the unflinching brutality of nature? Then she gasped, almost dropping her half-empty glass: within a year she herself could be giving birth.

He sat at his desk sipping Madeira and contemplating life and love, living and loving, sharing the same bed as Lady Henrietta. He admitted her well-rounded body, at least compared to Jane's, stimulated reactions potentially sinful. Since, however, their realisation would only occur after the wedding, he decided against praying for forgiveness. Anyway, his intentions towards the Lady Henrietta covered domains beyond partaking of her flesh; she was to become his partner in life and not just a bed-companion. She would help him endure living on earth until he rejoined his beloved Jane in Heaven. Oh my Dearest, even in your dying moments you displayed magnanimity of character, insisting that I remarry to ease my solitude.

He was mentally exhausted but triumphant. Negotiations for the disposal of his business were completed, the conveyance signed. Competitors had fought for the honour of acquiring his fleet of ships because, with Negroes generating greater margins than spices, the slave market was expanding vigorously. His merchandise should be thankful; not only were they transposed from an animalistic jungle existence to the cultivated plains of North America but they were introduced to the teachings of our Lord Jesus. For once business interests coincided with social propriety.

Managing Henrietta's estate must now occupy his thoughts. Infuriatingly, his plans to contractually inherit her rolling pastures and accompanying manor house risked being thwarted. But only temporarily, for he intended outwitting John Mascotte not by legal subversion but by producing an heir. Yes, he had convinced Henrietta to retain the estate in trust; it would only be inherited by John Mascotte if no child was forthcoming from his union with Henrietta.

The church service would be in English, with readings from the Authorised Version of the Bible and hymns from the English Prayer Book, suitably non-papist although singularly lacking in conviction. He did not protest such variance from Puritan dogma, the service was a once-in-a-lifetime occasion, but Renaissance paintings desecrating the manor's walls would be disposed of forthwith, especially those portraying grotesque harlots posing as angels. They would be replaced with pastoral scenes and suitably sober portraits of family ancestors. A complete review of the library was another priority, he had already discerned such ingloriously subversive tomes as Ben Jonson's *Masque of the Metamorphosed Gipsies* and John Donne's *The Faerie Queene*. He assumed they were indications of her first husband's moral corruption and that Henrietta was unaware of their existence. Whatever her protestations unsuitable books would be burned, for tolerance was a weakness and not a virtue.

He sipped on the Madeira, smiled and returned to his reading.

The fire blazed in the hearth of her bedchamber. Their bedchamber. Alone at last, yet there was little possibility to relax, the moment of nuptial verity would shortly confront them. Thankfully soiled towels could be ignored; she had sufficient concerns without pandering to male predilection for maidenly sacrifice. What was he thinking? Why did society decry people communicating their closest concerns, even spouses committed to sharing their lives together? During her first nuptials, as an innocent maiden, nothing had been expected other than submission; tonight she could no longer claim ignorance of matters conjugal to explain an inability to recompense her husband. Knowing his expectations would ease fear of failure, promote the success of such an important event in their lives.

She was stressed and fatigued. Although the bishop had begrudgingly condescended to perform the church ceremony, he imposed a service of utmost conservatism; the sermon was more a condemnation of temporal temptation than a blessing of their union. The wedding feast had been a joyous occasion but being both bride and hostess had sapped her energies. As a daring counteraction to the bishop's fire and brimstone eulogy, she inserted 'La Volta' into the dance selections, planning to swirl and gyrate with impetuous derision at bigotry in all its forms, only to discover her husband had ordered its removal.

Just what was her husband contemplating as he prepared his toilette? If only they conversed, they could work in unison to succeed in their marital endeavours. But she was too awed at the presence of an unknown husband in her private quarters to take the initiative.

Just what was she thinking? How did she expect to be deflowered, at least within the context of her second marriage? She was presumably used to certain conventions, preferences initiated by her first husband which, based on the reading selection in the library, could be improper for dignified Englishmen. Her inclusion of 'La Volta' into the dance selections also warned of trouble. How to impose proper decorum without generating resentment? Although, if that was the consequence of refusing insalubrious practice, then let it be so.

He would proceed with caution. Of course she was no longer a maiden, but years of sexual solitude must have affected her physically. Should he proceed as if she were indeed unsullied? Or would that insult her womanly pride? Damnation, what he had been

130

eagerly anticipating was becoming a vexatious obstacle to his future happiness.

She exited her private boudoir attired in a flowing night-gown that covered her as effectively as day-time attire. He was looking elsewhere, so she removed the outer garment and climbed into her allotted side of the bed, their respective maid and manservant having resolved that practical hurdle. But now, as she sensed him alongside her, she realised no servant could help negotiate the forthcoming challenges.

He extinguished the candle, feeling relief as invisibility enveloped them. Then, as his eyes adjusted to the darkness, he noticed illumination shining through an inner window, permitting him to distinguish her form lying across the bed.

His consternation had been noticed.

'My husband ... Ooh, I beg your pardon, Sir Walter. My first husband preferred a suspicion of light.'

'For what purpose?'

'So I could be certain it was indeed him entering my bed, thereby preventing a stranger pre-empting his conjugal rights. He equally insisted that it prevented him confounding another woman with his wife and inadvertently committing adultery. But I never believed him!'

She laughed nervously.

He remained silent, shocked by her vulgar joviality. Tomorrow he would instruct Old Ben to cover the window before he replaced the semi-senile nincompoop with someone younger.

'Are your satisfied that the correct woman has entered your bed tonight?'

Was there no limit to her irreverence?

'Since you are my wife, the question is of little relevance.' He moved towards her in an attempt to prevent further verbal impudence. He hesitated as she tensed, then placed a hand between her thighs, ready to prepare her.

'Charles has lost his mind; his actions are equivalent to a declaration of war!'

They were in the library. The wedding guests had departed and the married couple were presumably indulging in what newly married couples were expected to indulge in. News from London had distracted them from the niceties of the occasion, even the playing of backgammon, for their country was lurching towards the unthinkable due to a lawfully crowned king's resolute stubbornness and a determined group of ambitious parliamentarians.

'Whilst Pym and Cromwell plot in London, the king raises an army and flies his standard in Nottingham. Something has taken his sanity, unless he yearns for martyrdom pursuing a lost cause.'

'Which poses a conundrum. Do we support our rightful yet deranged king or Puritan schemers seeking to impose their misguided religion on all free-thinking Englishmen?'

There was a long silence. Civil war was unthinkable, yet increasingly inevitable. In such circumstances neutrality was impossible, implying that father and brother, neighbour and servant would become allies or bitter enemies. Never would he, John Mascotte, swear allegiance to King Oliver and he fervently prayed those sipping brandy with him would decide likewise, which was all but certain. Then he recalled who was upstairs with his sister ...

The shock of physical contact made her recoil. She realised this was instinctive, also that it could be misinterpreted. Yet surely it was incorrect to move directly to her privy parts? Her sadly departed Henry caressed her generously whilst instructing how she could maximise his pleasure, but she knew from hearsay that husbands might consider such initiative misplaced. She took the risk, touched his arm, then his shoulder. His countenance confirmed surprise, then evident disapproval.

Confused, she lay immobile until, from his movements, she realised the moment of being taken had arrived. Bracing herself she waited for the inevitable, no longer with excited anticipation but with foreboding.

Twelfth encounter: Martin and Louisa
1723   Plampinet, France

Whoops of delight and thumping of feet accompanied the enthusiastic if somewhat erratic harmonies of the musicians. He sat and sweated, as much from the afternoon heat as from blowing into his instrument. But he was happy, as was every inhabitant of his village.

The summer had been excellent. July thunderstorms provided plentiful rainfall, resulting in an abundant harvest of rye which, less suited for baking bread than wheat, better resisted their uncertain climate. Some of the crop had been lost, both Radegonde Franchon and her daughter Edith suffered their monthly indisposition during the week of harvesting. Marcellin Franchon pleaded, dared raise his voice in anger, but Père Joseph, unmoved, repeated that the Book of Leviticus, although not actually speaking of labouring in fields, unequivocally decreed that women issuing blood rendered unclean everything they touched. Nobody was surprised when thunderstorms flattened the Franchon's unharvested crop before the women's week of exclusion expired – the Almighty was not adverse to wreaking revenge on those who questioned His wisdom.

Those same thunderstorms moistened mountain pastures, providing sheep and goats with nourishment; rarely had so few been lost to starvation. Vegetables growing in the valley had never been so succulent, broad beans and lentils adding consistency to their habitually insipid watery soups. Apples and pears, cooked and conserved to provide nourishment during winter, were still ripening. April frosts had damaged numerous trees, but sufficient blossoms survived to avoid a disaster.

That morning they thanked God for his mercy, generosity, love and protection. Then, after resting during the afternoon heat, everyone gathered for the annual village fête, a rare distraction from toiling in the fields or minding livestock.

He looked around as he played. Although the surrounding summits were not particularly high, they represented formidable barriers which isolated their valley from the rest of civilisation. However, it was the altitude, with its climatic extremes, that rendered their lives so precarious, an existence bordering between poverty in good years and famine most of the time. Instead of keeping livestock for breeding and selling excess grain to purchase farm machinery they sacrificed precious food to purchase essentials like salt and linseed oil. Their project to construct a watercourse to irrigate fields was eternally delayed due to lack of funds, exacerbating the vulnerability of their existence.

Politics caused further depletion of their meagre possessions. Following the Duc de Savoie's invasion in 1692 and pillaging further south, local authorities had obliged unscathed communes to contribute to reconstructing those of their less fortunate neighbours. With money they did not have. Shortly afterwards, two able-bodied villagers perished in the battle of Malplaquet and another returned to his family prone to nerve-wrenching nightmares. Poor Gaston explained that the French under Villars had been fighting the Dutch and English under Marlborough in the War of the Spanish Succession, which made no sense to anyone. Apparently the French army numbered over 90,000 and tens of thousands of gallant soldiers, vastly more than their combined flocks of sheep, had been annihilated in a single day. Why should they, impoverished peasants, pay the price for the incomprehensible ambitions of far-distant dignitaries?

He knew certain villagers hauled sack-loads of salt across the isolated Col de l'Ours, benefiting from excise tax exemptions which rendered its price in Briançon half that of Piedmonte. Since the smugglers were risking their lives to feed undernourished families and not accumulate unneeded riches, other villagers either assisted as lookouts or ignored their activities. Père Joseph heard them confess but never preached that they cease their activities.

As he blew into his cornet he observed the steep inclines of the Pointe de Péce and Massif du Guiau. Faint scars disfigured their natural beauty where winter avalanches descended. More vivid traces bore witness to recent mud-slides, reminders that summer thunderstorms may provide welcome moisture but also brought destruction. Nobody had perished that year, although the path winding up the valley towards Nevache had been washed away. Mountains were so beautiful yet they harboured destructive powers only the Devil could unleash. Just like certain women, as his father repeatedly warned, especially wenches of ill-repute living in the nearby garrison town of Briançon, women with whom he must never associate when visiting the market.

The leader of the orchestra announced a pause so musicians could quench their thirst and briefly socialise. The latter was becoming urgent because Martin, son of Mathieu Arduin the shepherd, had been dancing with the girl he adored, someone far from impartial to his own charms. Naturally Louisa had not invited Martin, the latter had imposed himself because their respective fathers were negotiating their betrothal, logical if you were the village stonemason with no heir to assume the family business and a shepherd with sons destitute since losing flocks to wolves. All that remained was the family dwelling, a building so dilapidated it was valueless. Last winter the youngest daughter perished from bronchitis; with no animals to warm the inside and gaping holes in the roof the building resembled an icy tomb.

Martin, with no prospects, had been hesitating between enlistment as a professional soldier until probably massacred in battle, working to construct army fortifications in Briançon or emigrating southwards to Provence where a highly uncertain future awaited him. Hence he enthusiastically supported marrying into a family with an established local business and beautiful daughter. Assuming the wedding bans were publicised Martin would become apprenticed to Antoine Salle, Louisa's father, an arrangement that satisfied everyone. Except him and Louisa.

Nearly twenty years old, he should also be marrying. He knew his father had been hobnobbing with Monsieur Rostollan who, apart from growing rye, painstakingly bred mules used for transporting charcoal. Combining these activities with his family's lumbering business made sense, especially due to barns and outhouses owned by the Rostollan family desperately needed by his father for winter storage. Monsieur Rostollan had a daughter, in fact three, and no sons apart from crippled Gaston.

Thérèse Rostollan was a kindly and hard-working daughter who tended her father's mules during summer. But that was all. He did not love her as he loved Louisa. He often wondered what love was. Logically it was God's way of convincing a man and woman to marry each other. But his father had ridiculed him, insisting that love was a manifestation inspired by the Devil; consequently choosing someone because she was pretty was a dangerous stupidity. Marriage was a practicality of survival; a wife must be sufficiently robust to assume domestic chores and toil in the fields, to be harnessed to the ploughshare when they had insufficient beasts. Of course a wife must also be fertile but this was never known until after the marriage. Also, if she did bear children, she raised them without slackening her other duties so the family could survive the rigours of living high in the mountains.

Love!! It was a dangerous pestilence that had nothing to do with marriage. In other words Thérèse Rostollan was the perfect wife.

So why did he have wonderful dreams about someone else? Was the Devil really rising up from hell to tempt him? Or was God sending him a message, urging him to marry Louisa?

His request to speak with Louisa was angrily rebuffed by Martin. He was about to grab her hand, lead her away, when the orchestra was called back to the podium. He reluctantly rejoined the other musicians, who launched into a lively rigodon. Unable to concentrate, his tempo diverged from the others, resulting in stony stares from their leader Monsieur Baudrand and a smirk from Martin.

He stared through the window as the blizzard raged around the village, the third since the beginning of the month. Numerous paths were blocked by avalanches, isolating villages further up their valley, and now the principal route to Briançon was impassable.

As was the custom they dug snow tunnels between their houses to facilitate visiting each other, to help pass the tedious months of winter in relative comfort. It allowed him to meet Louisa when, by strange coincidence, they sought water from the fountain at the same moment. They never dared embrace for, if discovered, she would be disavowed by her family and obliged to seek employment in Briançon as chambermaid or waitress. Poor Florence, the daughter of a neighbour evicted by an enraged father, had ended her life by jumping from the town's ramparts. She claimed to have been violated by a soldier billeted nearby but Père Joseph declared her becoming with child was the Lord's punishment for seeking pleasure and then telling falsehoods about being taken against her wishes.

Oh how he quivered with excitement when carrying his empty pails to the fountain, oh how he almost danced with joy when catching sight of Louisa. And how he dreamed of their encounter throughout the following night. Surely only God could be responsible for such bliss; blaming the Devil was ridiculous.

He interrupted his reveries, aware he should return to his wood-carving, when he heard a distant rumbling. Yet another avalanche was hurtling down the mountainside. But this was different; the reverberating was louder, advancing directly towards the village with terrifying speed. The ground began to shudder, someone screamed. Then it struck.

As soon as the thundering ceased he rushed outside into the swirling wilderness, heedless of the danger, anxious to understand what damage had been caused, learn whether anyone required assistance. Other villagers were struggling through the snow to where they thought the avalanche had passed, not far from the Pascallet dwelling. Except that it was no longer there, nothing remained other than compacted snow, rocks and splintered trees that had obliterated everything in their path. They searched in vain, rapidly concluding that neither the family nor its animals had survived; there was nothing to do except retrieve their bodies in the spring when the snow melted.

During the following night the Salle's house collapsed, its unstable structure no longer capable of withstanding the accumulated weight of snow on its roof. Villagers strove in the windswept darkness to locate survivors. Louisa and one of her younger sisters were pulled from the wreckage, neither seriously injured, then a terrible silence descended upon the ruins of what had been a happy family home.

The following morning, soon after daylight revealed the extent of the disaster, Marthe Salle was dragged from underneath piles of rubble. She died during the morning, thankfully unaware that four members of her family, including her husband, had perished amidst the ruins.

That evening villagers debated the situation.

The origin of the problem was climatic change; recent winters had been harsher and summers considerably wetter than in past decades. Nobody had forgotten the downpours of 1711 when the few crops not washed away by muddied torrents rotted in waterlogged fields. Yet the authoritarian, uncaring money-grabbing provincial governors had neither reduced taxes nor exonerated them from the burden of billeting troops guarding the frontier. To add insult to injury, soldiers complaining about inedible food had resulted in threats of fines and even imprisonment if they did not fulfil their 'patriotic duty'. If only the politicians would stop waging incessant wars; they were the culprits, their belligerence was the cause of centuries of deprivation and suffering inflicted upon those they were supposed to protect.

Nobody, however, blamed the politicians for the atrocious weather. Nor the increase in avalanches, for they themselves were partly to blame. Heavier snowfall contributed, but lumbering necessary to manufacture charcoal had levelled vast tracts of forest, natural barriers that halted if not prevented avalanches. The most recent disaster was linked to years of felling trees directly above their village. Alarmingly nobody proposed measures to stem future catastrophes. Why? Because they could not survive without supplies of local timber.

Their thoughts turned to the victims. The human corpses recovered from the Salle house were stored in an outlying barn; they would be buried next spring when the ground thawed. Monsieur Salle's beehives had been duly shrouded in black as a sign of mourning, as was the custom.

'Poor Louisa and Catherine, their parents are dead, they have neither home nor money. They will not survive the winter.'

'But what can we do?'

Marcellin Franchon, Mayor of the Commune, intervened. 'We must welcome them into our midst, integrate each daughter into a neighbouring family until they marry.'

'I offer to receive Catherine, she will replace my little Marie taken by the smallpox.' Auguste Corail had married the younger sister of the defunct Antoine Salle, it was normal he took the orphan under his wing.

Silence ensued. One did not invite unmarried adult women to live alongside husbands and growing sons.

When an impasse occurred it was for the village mayor to take the initiative.

'Louisa must marry without delay!'

He felt a surge of excitement, then deep foreboding. For Louisa was practically betrothed to another.

'Monsieur Arduin, is Martin ready to offer his hand in marriage?'

He gritted his teeth when Martin's father confirmed his son was indeed disposed. Not only was he losing his beloved Louisa but Martin would inevitably claim his rights as husband, despoiling the wondrous person who filled his dreams with longing and excitement. To add insult to injury, the expression on Martin's face revealed he was not only disposed but eagerly anticipating such an occurrence.

What could he do to prevent the wedding?

Nothing.

'Let us not waste unnecessary time. The poor girl has nowhere to live and no revenues to pay for her sustenance. They must marry immediately. I, as mayor, formally approve the union. Equally, out of respect for Louisa and to permit us to proceed as quickly as possible, I authorise a simplification of the marriage regulations pertaining to the publication of bans and obligation for an *isaumarande* to officially request her hand in marriage.'

Heads nodded in agreement.

'How about next Saturday?'

It was decided. In three days Louisa Salle would marry Martin Arduin. The church service would be officiated at three o'clock in the afternoon. Custom decreed that merrymaking occur in the bride's home; this being impossible a simple banquet would be organised in the Arduin residence. Yes, Marcellin Franchon insisted, there would be music and dancing because a man and woman were marrying before God, just like any other couple. The tragedy must not diminish the significance of the occasion.

There were murmurs of agreement. The die was cast; within days his beloved Louisa would be marrying Martin.

'I will announce the good news!' And Madame Carail rushed home to inform her niece.

'Now we should discuss the disposition of Antoine's fields and mountain pastures.'

'As his brother, it is I who automatically inherit everything.'

'As husband of his sister I know I have no rights, but I would appreciate receiving pastures near Les Savoyes, it would create a good sized field for my rye.'

'But you cannot expect me to give land for nothing!'

'No. But if we could negotiate an exchange.'

He sighed. The evening would be long, the negotiations arduous and probably embittered. And he had other things to contemplate.

Next time he fetched water Louisa was not there. Nor did she reappear on subsequent visits. Whereas Thérèse Rostollan just happened to be present when he visited Monsieur Vallier to discuss repairing bridges on the path leading to his summer pastures. He had smiled at her with due deference. But nothing more.

That evening, he prayed that God would intervene to halt the wedding, allow him and Louisa to consummate their love within the confines of holy matrimony.

'Please dear Almighty, send a sign, warn everyone of the terrible mistake being made.'

He committed himself to effacing thoughts of Louisa and courting Thérèse if no sign was forthcoming. He should become better acquainted with her for he had every interest to make their relationship as pleasurable as possible.

The sun shone brightly but without warmth as the bride and groom exited the church, only to hurriedly trample across the snow to the residence of the mayor who had kindly organised an aperitif. Then, as the all-embracing cold of a winter's night descended, guests congregated in the Arduin house for the wedding feast.

He was hardly surprised that the atmosphere was strained, the villagers' comportment during the confined months of winter contrasted starkly with the liberating freedom exhibited in summer. Gossip and childbearing kept the women reasonably occupied from November onwards, drink was the all-too-frequent solution chosen by their husbands, a scourge leading to drunken excesses and conjugal violence. Added to this, the groom's over-eagerness contrasted embarrassingly with the apathy of his bride, hardly surprising since Louisa was destined to enter her nuptial chamber with someone she hardly knew and who, by his expressions and actions, was having difficulty containing his marital ardour. What torments might she be suffering? Unfortunately, no fortunately, he could neither read her thoughts nor imagine precisely what experiences awaited her, for he had never lain with a woman nor discussed such indelicate matters with other villagers.

Members of the orchestra were invited to collect their instruments. Although unhappy at participating, he admitted that music would add gaiety and that he should perform with due decorum. Somewhat self-consciously, the musicians launched into the first tune.

Slowly the effects of music and generous quantities of genepy liquor distilled from flowers growing in the highest pastures helped everyone forget their troubles and dance away the evening. Then the time to separate arrived. He knew, everyone knew, that the highlight of marriage ceremonies was the jubilant teasing of newlyweds, the guests locating where the couple were spending their first night together and doing everything to prevent the groom from accomplishing his duties. If he displayed gracious humour he was rewarded by the departure of the guests, enabling him to achieve what must be accomplished. But the reaction was without appeal if he displayed aggravation; the entire night would be spent singing, dancing and drinking in his bedchamber as his bemused, trembling and still maidenly bride lay alongside her husband.

However, due to the tragic circumstances, consideration would be shown. The nuptials would proceed without risk of interruption.

Carrying his cornet, he returned home, prepared for bed and huddled underneath the freezing blankets. Lying alone, shivering, he thought about his Louisa.

She would already be installed in their bedchamber, a large room situated in the Arduin residence, for custom dictated that an eldest son's bride be received into his parents' home. They would be undressing, she probably in the small room overlooking the fountain where she fetched water, and he in the bedchamber.

As explained by his father whilst they watched a ram inseminate some ewes, a husband and wife must never expose their nakedness since this aroused bestial urges. Once in bed, their bodies must not touch except through the rough material of their night-garments, each of which had a slit conveniently placed to allow insertion without uncovering one's legs. A husband could kiss his wife on her lips, but mouths remained closed. The act itself should be performed without wasting energy because the following morning hard work would require their attentions.

By now Martin would be installed in the marriage bed. It was easy to guess his rival's excited emotions, he merely had to envisage himself waiting to be joined by Louisa. But the latter, soon to submit herself to the neighbour's son she loathed, what thoughts would be destroying her peace of mind? She would have espied the slit in her

142

night-gown whilst preparing her toilette, understood its implications. Had she sobbed silently, thinking about her truly beloved until her husband called to indicate he was ready?

By now she would be entering the bed. Martin, the candle extinguished, would be moving towards her, searching for the opening in the material.

He sobbed silently. God had allowed the wedding to proceed, He must therefore condone the union of his Louisa to another. But why? To punish him for sinning? If so, He was punishing Louisa even more greatly.

The deed would shortly be accomplished; possibly it was taking place at this precise moment.

Louisa was no longer his.

Thirteenth encounter: Rosie and Samuel
1848   Rochdale, England

Oldham.
> *Two more stations until Rochdale.*
> *Royton and Shaw.*
> *Then she would gather together her belongings, descend from the train and be greeted by Uncle Ben, short for Benjamin, who would be waiting on the platform.*

He had better be because she was alone, aching to visit the lavatory and sorely intimidated by the scruffy-looking passengers occupying her third-class compartment.

Added to that, she was lost. Well, not completely, she knew she was sitting in a train at Oldham station. Although, apart from being near Rochdale, she had no inkling where Oldham might be. Nor Rochdale. In his letter, Uncle Ben made reference to an important town in Lancashire with factories bigger than mountains, lots and lots of houses and, most importantly, jobs and therefore wages for buying food and clothes. But where was Lancashire?

For the umpteenth time her thoughts returned to Wrenbury, the village she had never left except for visiting Whitchurch market with her father. He, forced to abandon dairy farming when the remaining common lands were enclosed, now worked as field labourer for Sir Edmund Jefferies, somebody very important who lived in a modern castle and owned most of the countryside. Nobody protested the enclosures. Since 1830, when three farmhands were hanged and many deported to Australia after protesting wage reductions, agricultural labourers were too scared to defend their rights.

145

Her brother left home to seek employment in Stoke-on-Trent. He mailed a letter, a friend helped with the writing, complaining that the buildings in which they 'fired' bricks were hotter than hell; women were refused employment because everyone stripped to the waist. His next letter announced a pile of bricks had fallen on him, crushing a leg. He had been fired for carelessness, they assumed it was a different 'firing' from cooking bricks, and was living with injured and destitute men in a poorhouse. Another letter said his leg was hurting something awful, smelled and was turning black. Since then they had heard nothing.

Then the man who employed her elder sister Maggie closed down his workshop; his woollen shirts were twice as expensive as cotton garments woven on steam-powered machines. Poor Maggie! Engaged as a domestic by Sir Edmund, she became heavy with child after he imposed himself repeatedly upon her. Refusing an 'intervention' because others had succumbed to the well-meaning attentions of Betty Swaggart, she was dismissed from service when somebody remarked upon her expanding belly.

With insufficient money to feed everyone, her father sought somewhere to send his next-eldest daughter. Herself. Uncle Ben agreed she should come to Rochdale; there was plenty of room, they rented a complete house just for themselves, and the textile mills hired thirteen-year-old girls. She hardly remembered her uncle who had uprooted his family eight years previously, never returned to Wrenbury and, in spite of the penny post, never communicated because those left behind could not read with reliable accuracy. Thus it was with much misgiving she caught the express to Crewe where, in a bustle of scurrying people, she located platform three and clambered onto the slow train to Manchester and Rochdale.

The man sitting opposite stretched his limbs, yawned and closed his eyes, leaving his left leg resting against hers. Although not unpleasant, it worried her, it did not feel right. She moved slightly, but his leg followed. So, neither daring to remove it nor snooze in case she missed Rochdale, she stared at the sign announcing passengers without tickets would be arrested.

146

To her immense relief both the horrible man with the left leg and three other passengers descended at Royton, enabling her to occupy a window seat from which she observed the greeny-greyish countryside, however uninspiring it might be.

The train arrived in Rochdale. Wearing her straw bonnet as instructed and displaying a damp patch on her frock similar in size to that staining her window seat, she gingerly climbed down onto the platform, only to experience unimaginable relief when a man and boy rushed up to welcome her.

He sat in his office, his production schedules incomplete, all because harebrained parliamentarians had voted the Ten Hour Bill reducing working hours for women and children. How could one possibly run a factory under such conditions? Adding to his woes, the Public Health Act permitted government inspectors to verify that legislation, however idiotic, was actually being respected! Whatever next?

Admittedly lifting of the Corn Laws, with an immediate reduction in bread prices, had relieved pressure on wage demands. But only momentarily. Before long workers would be clamouring for further increases. Maybe their claims were justified. Notwithstanding, as representative of the owners he was obliged to block redistribution of economic wealth, relying on arguments as fallacious as his tactics were despicable.

With Louis-Philippe ousted in France, the Communist Party Manifesto circulating freely and a looming economic crisis making everyone jittery, the future of Britain indeed looked bleak.

Screams, followed by shouting from the factory floor, interrupted his ruminations. A foreman banged on his door and entered.

'Mr Brewster! Come quick! Bertie Shortman's trapped in a shredding machine and bleeding to death!'

Damnation. Damnation. And, once again, damnation.

He slid an index finger under his dog-collar in an attempt to relieve pressure on his Adam's apple. Having failed, he sighed, a habit formed since arriving in Rochdale, denominated as such because a sparkling stream called the Roch once meandered through a pleasant valley on its way to join the River Mersey. The stream now resembled a sluggish cesspool and the valley a sprawling smoke-infested labyrinth of factories, warehouses and waste disposal depositories.

He agreed the Church must follow its disciples. Infuriatingly, these were uprooting themselves in droves, moving from farming communities to manufacturing centres. Thus, instead of an idyllic rural parish, he had been nominated to a newly created ecclesiastical district with a brand new church as ugly as the surrounding ware-houses and a flock of impoverished and irreligious parishioners to supervise. No, not irreligious, just disinterested in his preaching. Although, to be perfectly honest, many of them were damnably irreligious as well.

He was caught in a trap. The workers and their families desperately ... No, start again. The workers desperately needed his guidance. That was better, adding 'families' was illogical because wives and children worked alongside their men-folk. In spite of recent legislation working conditions remained unchanged, as if implementing laws was an irrelevance, yet his hierarchy seemed blindly impervious to the resultant injustice.

In the countryside the Church's tithe was every tenth suckling pig, so people contributed from earnings. In contrast, the Church Rate levied on town dwellers ignored their pecuniary situation, causing resentment and riots, also alarming absenteeism from Sunday services. Many claimed they were too fatigued to visit his place of worship, something believable, for brothels were suffering similar sabbatical absenteeism. Instead, workers stayed at home and drank themselves unconscious, at least those without wives to confiscate offending bottles of ale and spirits. Meanwhile exhortations to bolster Sunday collections arrived with unfailing regularity from his bishop.

Relations with local industrialists were equally strained, partly his fault for proclaiming poverty was no longer considered God's

148

punishment for sinning but the consequence of unchristian actions by practitioners of capitalism. Ostracising him as the workman's vicar, mill-owners hobnobbed with ecclesiastical dignitaries scrounging from plush wallets in exchange for tacit maintenance of the status quo appertaining to social legislation.

Things, however, might possibly change. Whereas his Established Church warbled vacuously about saving the soul, 'In the Shadow of His Wings' and 'Praise My Soul, the King of Heaven' being standard fare at evensong, the mushrooming Nonconformists were allying themselves with social reformers to promote social justice. To further complicate matters, firebrand papist preachers who accompanied starving Irishmen immigrating to England in the aftermath of the 1845 potato famine were now seducing his parishioners with their flamboyant traditional trappings and wine served during mass. Consequently the Lord was being represented in Rochdale by theologically antagonistic factions more intent on spewing forth vindictive disrespect for each other than preaching brotherly love. No wonder the populace stayed at home on Sundays.

Thinking about seduction, Mrs Shortman was becoming ever more indiscreet with her insinuations. Since her husband's demise in a factory incident, his sectioned limbs being transported to the morgue in a wheelbarrow, she was living alone with two kiddies, one born shortly after the funeral. She needed help, financial and spiritual, but most of all physical, a shoulder to cry upon, a ... Well, no need to be vulgar. And he, available bachelor, had been selected to service her extremely feminine body. Which was not the problem. The problem was the temptation to accommodate her.

He sighed again. What message of hope should he pronounce on Sunday to his mostly empty pews? And to Mrs Shortman who would be gazing longingly in his direction?

Worries about reeking of urine were soon forgotten. The wind conveyed smells far more nauseating than ever experienced before, safely neutralising personal odours; before long her throat was irritated and eyes started watering. As for her damp patch, the driving drizzle soon rendered everything as sodden as where she had been sitting.

Uncle Ben lugged the wicker basket, the young lad accompanying him, introduced as Jimmy, carried the picnic remains and farm produce donated by her parents. She was interrogated about her family, whom in their village was still alive and whether recent harvests had been satisfactory. She gazed around the town centre whilst answering the flurry of questions. Not a tree was visible, nothing green was growing. Instead there were bricks, bricks and bricks, brick factories, brick warehouses, brick shops and brick walls, even a brick church. Houses were also built with bricks, aligned neatly in rows and miniature as if shrunken by the damp climate.

'Come on in.'

Back home people exuded a certain pride when welcoming guests; however humble, their cottages were bright and clean. Not so in Rochdale. Uncle Ben's absence of enthusiasm was understandable; his home consisted of a dingy downstairs parlour with a ladder ascending to the bedroom, plus a door leading to the garden. Except the garden was not a garden, being a small courtyard with the lavatory in one corner, identified as such by excrement trickling into an open sewer. There were no flowers, only weeds that sprouted enthusiastically amongst puddles of rainwater. A smashed hobbyhorse contributed the sole hint of colour.

She declined to use the 'facilities', puzzled by her aunt's consternation until realising she had supposedly not relieved herself since Manchester. She was led upstairs to the bedroom in which two double and three single beds covered the entire floor-space. She supposed the larger double bed was for her uncle and aunt, the other for their daughters Jenny and Patty, the single beds for Jimmy and her aunt's brother Herbert who lived with them, plus herself.

Aunt Ally crammed her belongings into a rickety chest-of drawers. She explained that visiting the outside lavatory was impossible once the downstairs hearth had been extinguished – it was pitch dark everywhere. A bucket was available for spending pennies during the

150

night, also 'number two' if absolutely necessary, although this was not appreciated because of the smell. Her aunt pointed to the store of special napkins for 'those days'; to avoid embarrassment they were immediately rinsed in a special enamel bucket and hung to dry behind the lavatory.

Shoes were removed before retiring, it being important that the bedroom floor and therefore bedclothes remain relatively clean; laundering was complicated, there being no local wash-house, only a fountain with running water carried home in buckets. They washed downstairs, a sluice in the wall permitting dirty water to evacuate.

Everyone admired her offerings.

'But do yer not find fresh food in Rochdale?'

Uncle Ben explained the 'truck' system whereby employers obliged workers to purchase goods from the company 'tommy-shop' for half their salary. Since the other half was deducted to pay rent, the company owned their house, they had no money to purchase anything else. The choice of food, clothes and household necessities at the shop was limited, the quality inferior and prices outrageous.

'Why yer not change employer?'

Uncle Ben explained that several years ago, when working at another factory, he joined the 'Chartists', a movement of disgruntled workers led by London intellectuals. The owners fired everyone associated with the movement, refused to pay outstanding wages and threatened transportation.

'What be that?'

'Instead of prison, yer be shipped to the colonies to work in quarries and mines. Hundreds of Tolpuddle marchers went to Australia, it being terrible for their wives and kiddies. Many workers volunteer 'cause they be promised a better life. I once considered it, but it too compillicated with a family.'

Hired at another factory, he subscribed to the Rochdale Pioneers, a group of workers who opened a shop called a 'co-operative' because they owned it. Staff were hired to run the business, profits being shared amongst everyone. When asked, his employer refused to release him from the 'truck' system, finally inventing a reason to *dismiss him. His current employer, informed of part misdeeds, offered a reduced wage and threatened blacklisting if there was the slightest troublemaking. Since then he worked hard and kept his political feelings to himself.*

'So you see,' he concluded, 'it ain't that simple ter change jobs willy-nilly.'

He remained silent, at a loss for words for the Aldermen had refused easing the proposed rates increase. Why? Because a town as important as Rochdale could not exist without a museum and library. If the workers were insufficiently educated to admire artistic exhibits or read the country's literary heritage that was their outlook. Furthermore, poor-rate annuities were crippling the town's finances; the moment was propitious for workers, following wage increases, to financially support out-of-work companions. The owners? Heavens above! Subsidising layabout labourers was not their concern; industrialists were the last to be taxed, their contributions to funding theatres and monuments were already amazingly generous.

Now, if the Church was willing to help solve the problem ...

Which it was not, because it had no money.

He left the town hall doubting the foundation of John Stuart Mill's dictum that 'one person with belief is a social power equal to ninety-nine only with interests'. He traversed the magnificent public gardens and made his way to Eastern Row, an especially insalubrious concentration of worker cottages.

'So how is Mrs Jenkins today?'

'Real worse than affore, her coughing be awful alarming.'

'Any stains on her pillow?'

He meant bloodstains, but discretion was recommended. In any case other symptoms sufficed to diagnose tuberculosis. The rest of her family risked contamination if Mrs Jenkins was not interned in a sanatorium, impossible because such institutions were reserved for the wealthy, those who did not succumb because they ate properly and lived in well-heated mansions.

The dying woman was lying in the middle of the bed; her husband

– not unwisely – was sleeping elsewhere. From the disposition of the pillows he was sharing with a daughter; from the agitated ruffling of the sheets he was not remaining his side of the bed. How could one expect healthy adults to live in suffocating intimacy without acceding to temptations of the flesh? How, therefore, could he condemn Mr Jenkins? In any case, bearing in mind the daughter's professional activities, she was used to 'welcoming' males into her bed.

London was supposed to have 50,000 full-time prostitutes, a realistic total since the nation's husbands indulged on average three times a week. The Church huffed and procrastinated, yet shared responsibility for the moral disorder by declaring female desire an aberration and sexual intercourse a degrading biological necessity. How many wives viewed pregnancy as a relief from sexual imposition rather than the joy of future motherhood? Had not the same ecclesiastical dignitaries pronounced male masturbation the cause of blindness, deafness and insanity? Did they not condone placing nail-encrusted metallic rings around adolescents so, if untoward swellings occurred, the puerile dreamers were awoken before discharge caused mental and physical malformation? It was only natural that husbands, aware of the distress they inflicted upon their spouses and the dangers of indulging in self-satisfaction, sought sexual release beyond the confines of their homes.

Nobody seemed to appreciate that pampered ladies surrounded by servants were just as female as the comely wenches catering to the most pernicious whims of their customers in the most abhorrent of circumstances. The absurdity and hypocrisy of the …

'Please, Reverend, if you give Mrs Jenkins proper medicines, Polly my daughter she pay you 'in kind', you see what I mean?'

He saw what Mr Jenkins meant. However, he would have desisted even if the sixteen-year-old overflowed with ladylike graces; bearing in mind the prolific number of her sexual partners she was surely infected. One cause of the mother's tuberculosis was weakness from syphilis or gonorrhoea, caught from her husband who had become infected following repeated liaisons with his daughter who had been

153

infected by one, if not several, of her paying customers. Yet whilst bishops lobbied politicians to outlaw medical treatment to ensure that sinners suffered for their misdemeanours, politicians postulated that preventing women from exploiting themselves commercially contradicted the philosophy of economic *laissez-faire*.

Mrs Jenkins bout of coughing ceased and she lay exhausted looking up at him. In spite of its hypocritical futility, he pronounced a hackneyed prayer of encouragement to calm the expression of frightened hopelessness in her eyes. He then bade farewell and returned to his luxurious by comparison but extremely modest vicarage.

Supper was finished, her hosts having greedily gobbled her farmyard goodies. She, although starving, only nibbled at their stew which smelled suspiciously of rotting weeds.

No evening entertainment was planned, no walking outside, no visiting friends, no nothing. Rumours abounded that in the residential area of New Lanark, where the owner treated his employees with utmost consideration, gas streetlights had been installed. As a result residents visited neighbours in the evening and a social club enabled employees to play darts and card games as well as engage in singsongs. Rochdale's mill-owners, to nobody's surprise, offhandedly scoffed at such ill-conceived 'radical' notions. So everybody stayed at home before going early to bed, especially in winter when it was dark and cold.

She remembered packing a game of spillikins and challenged everyone. For the first time since her arrival her foster family appeared to be enjoying themselves.

Before darkness fell, being Sunday, it was time for washing. A tub was dragged into the middle of the downstairs room and filled with hot water. Then, to her amazement, Aunt Ally enquired in front of everyone whether she was 'indisposed'. She blushed violently and shook her head.

'Normally Uncle Ben waits, he being dirtiest, but if a woman be bleeding she goes last.'

She watched as Aunt Ally and Patsy stripped and washed in front of the entire family, even Uncle Herbert. Then it was her turn.

'Dahna worry, yer'll soon become used to it!'

She turned away whilst undressing but eventually had to face the tub. Throughout the ordeal she sensed Uncle Ben and Jimmy observing her every movement. At first she was embarrassed but by the time she was standing in the middle of the room, dried and ready to pull on her nightdress, she was rather enjoying herself.

Then it was Jimmy's turn. She looked away until realising the stupidity of her gesture, for nobody bothered about his nakedness. It was exciting pretending not to watch, especially since he seemed as thrilled as she was. Uncle Ben, however, was big and hairy, most unpleasant, so she chatted to Aunt Ally.

Jenny stripped and stepped into the oily-brown water. This time everyone turned away, for she required privacy.

Exhausted from the long journey, retiring early was not difficult. Lying in bed she was amazed to hear noises coming from Aunt Ally and Uncle Ben proving they really were married. Then Jenny and Uncle Herbert started, it sounded as if they were enjoying themselves immensely! Did they have no modesty, no morals?

And then she fell asleep.

He entered the auditorium. Almost everyone of distinction was present, from the Mayor and factory owners to hospital governors and the newly appointed Chief Constable.

'Gentlemen, let us commence.'

A cholera epidemic had decimated town populations in 1832, the disease was again spreading across the country. Urgent measures were necessary because foreclosing the factories would be calamitous. He reiterated earlier speeches, insisting that without proper sanitation in residential areas it would be virtually impossible to prevent a serious outbreak if the disease reached Rochdale. So, once again, town dignitaries debated overcrowding and lack of hygiene, this time with positive results because lost production would cost more than adopting his recommendations.

There was one drawback. The cholera could arrive within weeks whereas it required months to entrench sewage pipes and construct a water-treatment plant. It was agreed that if the epidemic struck before completion of the projects residents would be confined to their homes, naturally without receiving wages.

A doctor propounded the notion of advising residents how to avoid infection, prevention being preferable to cure, but community bigwigs declared lecturing illiterate workers a foregone fiasco. Perhaps. He was reminded of Little Oliver whose parents died during the 1832 outbreak. Living in an orphanage, he remarked that his parents were not people, not even memories, just gravestones. He added they were lucky to be dead because they didn't have to work and could do nothing for ever.

The other hazard facing Rochdale emanated from the National Association of Operative Spinners, a form of anti-social organisation that had recently opened an office near the railway station. When the landlord attempted to evict them their lawyers found loopholes in the law preventing this. Then, the previous week, the Association asked permission to parade in the town. This had been denied, provoking protests that refusal was illegal. And they were right.

What could be done to remove such blight from the town precincts? How could duly elected authorities possibly prevent disorder pervading the green fields and chimney stacks of England if the country's laws protected anarchist organisations?

She wanted to cry. So she did, alone in their communal bedroom. After three severe warnings she had been dismissed for being too clumsy to work the machines. Since the value of damaged threads exceeded her wage, the difference would be deducted from Aunt Ally's earnings.

No employment meant no wage, which meant Uncle Ben received no money to feed her. Either she returned home in disgrace or was accepted into a workhouse. Then Jenny proposed another solution.

It was sunny and warm, which was worse than rain because of the flies. Farms had flies, but they preferred cows and pigs. However, in Rochdale, humans were the only livestock available.

Walking to the fountain managed to temporally allay the attackers.
'What yer gonna do now yer ain't no job?'

Jenny, raised in Lancashire, spoke with an accent more Rochdale than back home, but not quite either.

'I harrf not an idea.'

'Yer karn do like me.'

'But yer work for Beaminsters, an they downe wanna me no more.'
After one week she was speaking more pseudo-Lancashire than her cousin.

Jenny announced she had a special occupation on Sundays, something done since her fourteenth birthday. Mr Brewster, the factory manager, had proposed it. She sold her virginity to rich gentlemen who loved bedding maidens – 'deflowering' was the term used. Her father accepted because if he refused Mr Brewster would probably evict them. Her mother had sobbed for hours, which was silly because everything had worked out fine.

'But yer canner do it only once?!'

'Mr Brewster, he explained whatter do!'

Her cousin described how she pushed a blood-soaked sponge inside prior to each assignment. Her outside was then doused with vinegar, which tightened the skin. When alone with each gentleman, always a different one, she made a terrible fuss about undressing, saying she was terribly shy. Then, lying in bed, she pleaded not to be touched which excited the gentlemen incredibly. Afterwards she moaned with pain as blood oozed everywhere; of course it came from the sponge but the customers were fooled. Apparently the sponge prevented becoming with child; either it did or she had been lucky. As Mr Brewster said laughingly, they did not wish her belly to become bow-windowed because juices spent by customers had taken firm hold.

She herself was getting too old to pass as a maiden; in any case there were no new customers. She would have to work normally, serving ten different males to obtain the same earnings unless, as proposed by Mr Brewster, she learned special 'tricks' which paid more. Mr Brewster, whose brother owned a butcher's shop in the town centre, everything happened in a room above, was looking for someone younger and unknown to replace her.

'Are you still intact?'

She admitted she was, not knowing whether to be proud or ashamed. Her parents would he horrified but Uncle Ben and Aunt Ally obviously thought differently. In any case, she must earn some money and pretending to be a maiden sounded much more amusing than working in a horrible factory.

'Good afternoon, Mrs Jackson, how are you today?'

As expected she was unwell, his parishioners usually were. But his question permitted them to launch into a much-needed dissection of their miseries, and Mrs Jackson was no exception. Her husband no longer attended church because clergymen repeated ad nauseam that God was kind and loving, which was a dastardly untruth. If there was a God, He was Robert Owen who ran the textile mill where everyone was treated well or John Doherty who organised the Association for Protecting Workers. They and others like them were doing God's job, not Him lazing around in heaven.

He muttered his standard response that the Almighty's ways were difficult to interpret but that He loved everybody whatever they might think about Him.

He left Mrs Jackson to her miseries and continued his walk, wondering why he served an unfeeling master who ignored the miseries of those He had created. It was pomp and circumstance for some, poverty and prostitution for the vast majority. Perhaps, in the larger scheme of things, one must suffer before meriting a place in Heaven. But, if so, why? And why only the workers?

Back at the vicarage he learned a father of young children had been maimed at work, yet another family was destined for the poorhouse because the wife was too feeble to work or prostitute herself. He was unable to decide whether the latter was a relief or disaster; traditional theology no longer coped with the deprivations of modern industrial society.

'So we visit Mr Brewster Sunday. If yer be good and please him, then yer be starting following Sunday.'

Uncle Ben seemed pleased with himself. She hoped Mr Brewster would treat her kindly; certainly the wage was generous, more than at the factory.

Uncle Ben had other matters on his mind.

'Rosie, the first time be special like, pity to be doing it with stranger. If yer like, I'll show how, being very careful not to stretch yer too wide.'

She declined the kind offer, convinced Mr Brewster couldn't possibly be more hairy and foul-smelling than her uncle. Also, if she was too 'stretched', she might be refused.

Jimmy sidled up to her.

'So yer gorna do same as Jenny?'

'Yes, I see Mr Brewster next Sunday.'

'Please, why donna yer do it first with me? Someone yer know. I be very gentle.'

'Have yer done it affore?'

'Nay, I'm only fourteen.'

'Then how'll yer know whatter do?'

Silence.

'After my first customer, then yer can do it. I'll show how!'

The grin on Jimmy's face indicated he did not mind waiting.

Sometime later Jenny wished to converse with her cousin.

'Rosie, I hope everything be good with Mr Brewster. Yerl probbalee get same customers so we can compare!'

She smiled at Jenny, her new job was going to be fun.

'Mr Brewster, he teases sumphin' awful, calling me his "bowl of cherries"! But he takes good care of me.'

The look on Jenny's face became serious.

'But Rosie, if Uncle Herbert wanna you, yer say not.'

'You in love with him?'

'Nay, but he good in bed and keep me warm in winter. Yer go with Jimmy an' leave Uncle Herbert fer me.'

She agreed, delighted at the arrangement.

159

'Mrs Shortman.'

'Yes, Reverend?'

'Please come and have dinner on Saturday evening, we can discuss your problems and how the Church might possibly help.'

The two Mr Brewsters were neither tall nor short, thin nor fat. They were just men. They greeted her in a formal manner, neither nasty nor friendly, introducing themselves as Robert and Samuel. The latter stared at her intently, then addressed Uncle Ben.

'Seems a good choice. If she passes the "interview", since she has no weekday job I'll use her Rochdale Sundays, Manchester Tuesdays and Huddersfield Fridays. Two days between customers is sufficient to restrict and be ready for the next deflowering.'

Uncle Ben nodded, smiling broadly. The arrangement obviously suited him.

'Alright, Rosie, you come upstairs whilst your uncle waits here.' She followed her new employer up the deep, narrow stairs into a spacious room with a large washbasin and double bed.

'Place your clothes on the chair and climb onto the bed.'

'Shouldna I fuss and complain, say I'm shy?'

Mr Brewster smiled, in fact he almost laughed.

'Only when pretending, not when actually being deflowered.'

Fourteenth encounter: *Winston and Rosalie*
1886   Wiltshire, England

Having escorted the ladies to the drawing-room, the men entered the library where after-dinner drinks would be served.

'Please be seated, gentlemen.'

He, Cedric Hamersham, waited until his guests had installed themselves before settling into his preferred armchair. Hawkins, Senior Butler, arrived carrying freshly brewed coffee. Whilst pouring he inquired whether the guests would partake of port, brandy or whisky.

The drinks and cigars served, Hawkins withdrew to supervise the other domestics as they cleared away the vestiges of a copious meal.

'So, Archibald, what is happening in the rarefied monetary atmosphere of Threadneedle Street?'

All three relaxed. Relieved of the company of their wives they could forgo inconsequential small-talk about latest fashions, how longer Queen Victoria would reign and whether she would outlive her corpulent son and heir Edward, and whether Gilbert and Sullivan's latest operetta *The Mikado* was superior to its predecessor *Princess Ida*. Admittedly the conversation had become animated when debating the impropriety of grown daughters prancing around tennis courts, in spite of wearing skirts that descended to their ankles. Of even greater concern was the increasing tendency for ladies to accompany men on beaches, parading in hideously scanty bathing suits that exposed ankles and forearms. Everyone agreed whole-heartedly that females should refrain from involving themselves in male pursuits and concentrate on being decorative, domesticated and

161

ladylike. Equally unanimous was the fear that halting proliferation of such behaviour would be well nigh impossible.

Closeted in the library amongst themselves, the serious discussions could commence, discussions that constituted the real reason for organising the dinner in the first place.

Archibald Standsley, second son of Lord Hardcastle, condemned to work unless his elder brother died precipitously, had transferred from Oxford to a merchant bank before accepting a governorship at the Bank of England. As such, he worked closely with those defining British economic policy, knowing in advance what the public would learn sometime later, or not at all.

'Nothing dramatic. The change of government is welcomed, monetary stability seems assured. Our latest Treasury Bonds were issued without mishap; nobody is talking about crises waiting in the sidelines. Although the depression continues it would appear to have attained its apogee; we expect a rapid return to normality barring further wars, always a possibility bearing in mind the hot-headed idiots ruling nations south of the Channel and east of the Baltic.'

Pausing, the distinguished guest sipped his port and puffed on his cigar before continuing his dissertation.

'My chief worry is the Boer War. Although ultimate victory seems certain, military costs are emptying government vaults already depleted from the debacle of Crimea. It may be anathema to the Conservatives, but raising taxes could become the only means of balancing the budget.'

'So there are insufficient funds to finance an expansion of our navy, enabling it to contain Kaiser Wilhelm's growing fleet of warships.'

'Yes.'

'But he is nephew to our queen, he would never make mischief!'

'According to my reports, making mischief in order to expand Germany's frontiers is his over-riding passion.'

'At least the Liberals lost the election. The Conservatives will inject sense into Britain's defence policy and, even more importantly, refute Gladstone's crackpot ideas about giving workers voting rights simply because they own a house, gerrymandering poppycock liable to undermine democratic stability. Can you imagine a radicalised government under the influence of trade unions? Wage increases and reduced working hours would rapidly bankrupt the nation!'

'What is the future for agriculture?'

His other guest had remained silent until then. Richard Sandershurst, Lord Welyn, owned vast tracts of land upon which he cultivated wheat, barley and hops. The financial security of Treasury Bonds was of little interest to him whereas price trends of agricultural commodities were infinitely more relevant to the continued success, or ultimate failure, of his agricultural interests. If trends continued, the fault of cheap imports from North America and wage increases negotiated by British farm-workers, his financial well-being would suffer seriously. However, for the moment Lord Welyn was outstandingly wealthy, hence his presence that evening.

'I believe the worst is behind us. Disraeli was almost right when predicting that repealing the Corn Laws would sink English agriculture. However, to prove him wrong, landowners like yourself must digest unpleasant realities, for example that grain production has been irretrievably lost to the Americans. Your future lies with fruit, vegetables and dairy products that cannot be transported across the ocean.

'Regrettably my soil is unsuited for market gardening and breeding cattle.'

He almost rubbed his hands in glee; Lord Welyn's admission was precisely what he wished to hear.

'Then you should seek other solutions. The nation's population continues to increase; we should exceed fifteen million before long, and there will always be plenty of hungry mouths to feed. Some scaremonger university professor estimates a population of eighty million by 1960!'

'Balderdash, we would asphyxiate from lack of oxygen!'

'If you require populations to grow you should banish that deranged American Annie Besant, she who published *The Laws of Population* prescribing contraception for women. Even Alice, during

163

her troubled sojourn in Wonderland, never encountered such social cretinism. Upon my word, encouraging wives to consider matrimonial responsibilities as a distraction akin to croquet instead of God's gift of procreation! No more children would be born and the moral fabric of society would collapse!'

'And, with no children to rear, what in heaven's name would our wives do with themselves?!'

He recalled a Limerick published recently in a political review, an oeuvre not written by Edward Lear.

> *An American woman of misguided perception*
> *Promoted the use of female contraception*
> *An idea misconceived and sadly forlorn*
> *Unless preventing her from ever being born*
> *And saving mankind from feminist contention.*

He rejoined the discussion.

'You should subscribe to the Catholic Church, their philosophy of "copulate to procreate" should ensure soaring prices for your produce!'

His guests laughed at his humour.

All seemed relatively plain-sailing for Archibald, his guest from Threadneedle Street, likewise for Lord Welyn whose problems, although potentially alarming, were far from immediate. Whereas his industrial empire was already in dire straits. His factories manufactured gaslights and steam-powered turbines. Their profitability depended upon totalitarian exploitation of his workers; either they accepted his meagre wages or starved. The distant locations of his factories north of Bolton increased transport costs and delivery times, resulting in orders lost to forever more aggressive competition. He had unwisely 'invested' recent profits in horses that arrived last at the post, rebuilding his country abode Ecclestone Manor and acquiring the lavish Mayfair town-house in which he was currently entertaining his guests. As a consequence his factories were antiquated, reeked of inefficiency and no longer conformed to current legislation. Recent strikes had petered out ineffectively but he would not escape worker retribution much longer.

Even worse, at least in the longer term, were Faraday's weird inventions of fifty years ago, laughable gimmicks called electric currents. Who would have thought they would replace steam and gas as sources of power and lighting? Well, he certainly had not. He knew he must invest in research, construct modern factories to exploit new opportunities before his existing products became redundant. But he had no money to provide the necessary funding.

Which is exactly why Lord Welyn was invited to dinner.

Rich his guest might be, but for not much longer unless he revamped his agricultural activities. His land may not be suited to dairy farming, nor growing fruit and vegetables, but it had enormous potential for industrial expansion thanks to bordering the Severn-Thames Canal and railways linking Bristol to London and the Midlands.

Combining his manufacturing ambitions with Lord Welyn's disgracefully underexploited family fortune was strategically brilliant for both of them, but how to broach the subject, convince his Lordship?

Archibald Standsley did it on his behalf by launching into a discourse on the dramatic need to reduce agricultural costs by mechanising tasks such as baling hay and milking cows. Steam-powered horseless ploughing machines could revolutionise farming if they were made more efficient. A fortune was waiting to be made!

'I have the terrains and funds to finance research and production, but no industrial know-how.'

'I have the expertise but insufficient available funds.'

Lord Welyn glanced at him with piercing eyes, external symptoms of a brain working furiously.

It was not the moment to hesitate.

'Richard, that delightful daughter of yours, how old is she now?'

'All my daughters are delightful. I presume you mean Rosalie, the second eldest? The unmarried one?'

Of course he did.

'Indeed I do. Married daughters are of little consequence whereas their unwed sisters are of constant concern to their parents.'

Richard, Seventeenth Lord Welyn, nodded in agreement.

'My son Winston needs to settle down. He is thirty-seven and has achieved wonders in my factories.' A falsehood, but in business one resorted to truth only when necessary. 'He needs revolutionary products to develop in order to overcome frustration at the lack of challenges in our somewhat static industrial environment.'

Lord Welyn nodded, barely disguising his enthusiasm. 'I propose a weekend for our respective families at Warrington Manor, the hunting season starts shortly. We can discuss your ideas, my own ambitions. Bring that delectable wife of yours. Oh, and why not your son Winston. It would be a pleasure to make his acquaintance.'

A month had been dedicated to deciding what to wear and writing letters to ascertain who would be attending and, of the unmarried guests, who was courting whom and who, consequently, was still 'available'. The whole neighbourhood had been in social turmoil since receiving their invitations to the Regimental Homecoming Ball.

The ball had been organised to welcome home officers fighting in the Boer War. Her mother had obliged her to come, her ultimate argument being that both Captain Heathcote and Lieutenant Llewelyn-Jones would be in attendance. Whereas, having finally received the sheet music of Franz Liszt's latest piano solos, 'Die Trauergondel II' and 'Trauermarsch', written in 1885 only months before his death, she had better things to do than watch local society flaunt its inner self-satisfaction. But to no avail.

And now the moment she dreaded had arrived.

'Please, Dearest Rosalie, at least pretend to be of good humour; do not disappoint our valiant soldiers in their moment of glory.'

Her mother was endowed with persistence, but not tact.

'I promise to try.'

Her father was endowed with comparable persistence and even less tact.

'No, Rosalie, you will promise to succeed.'

Their carriage pulled up in front of the Regimental Headquarters. The next thirty minutes were devoted to executing the fastidious social formalities fundamental to maintaining the exclusiveness of upper-class British society, preordained rituals more important than religion, political allegiances or democratic rights. She curtsied in the correct manner, held out her hand at the pre-ordained angle, remembered each person's appellation and titles, also the names and ages of their respective children, well-nigh impossible with families exceeding a dozen or more, and complemented female acquaintances on their magnificent attire.

'Greetings, my dearest Rosalie.'

'How delightful to encounter you, Lady Rosalie, after such an interminable time.'

Lieutenant Llewelyn-Jones was not as intimately acquainted as Captain Heathcote. However, neither wasted much time in claiming at least two waltzes.

'Rosalie!!'

Her younger sister Adelaide embraced her with habitually flowering false affection. Poor Adelaide. After falling madly in love with Horatio, whose family owned much of Buckinghamshire, and enduring two years day-dreaming, scheming and longing until he proposed, she married and discovered the realities of life. She was installed in a country mansion with instructions to avoid activities that could be construed as practical, women belonging to Britain's highest nobility affirming their superiority through aloofness to ordinary living. Elevated to a social status where exterior beauty avoided the necessity of possessing a brain, even Adelaide soon realised her existence lacked substance. During his fleeting visits her husband must have performed his conjugal duties because two children had been born of the union. She met them briefly for meals and family occasions such as birthday parties, could remember their names but had difficulty in confirming their precise ages. To while away the time she painted aquarelles and embroidered tea-cosies.

How typical of upper-crust British society.

Her elder sister Patience greeted her without emotion, not because affection was lacking but because she was unable to combat the wretchedness of her life. Her Foreign Office husband lost interest before the honeymoon was over, two maid-servants were dismissed discreetly and rumours abounded of lurid affairs with wives of foreign diplomats. Involving herself in charitable and other unladylike activities to counter the triviality of her life, she had been taken to task by a spouse who resorted with increasing frequency to verbal and physical aggression as an expression of contempt for her lack of social delicacy. She had mentioned divorce to her mother, who immediately told her father, who threatened disinheritance if another word was mentioned on the subject.

Judging by the blotched countenance of her otherwise beautiful face, drink had become her companion in life, supporting her through the empty periods until the next dispute and probable beating.

How typical of upper-crust British society.

All of which did not prevent her parents lamenting their daughter Rosalie's inability to find a husband and explaining her mother's excitement at the presence of Captain Heathcote and Lieutenant Llewelyn-Jones.

'Rosalie!!'

Uncle George greeted her affably. Brainless buffoon he might be, but he was hilarious company.

'So what has my favourite niece been up to since we last met?'

'I have been mastering several piano works, traditional classics by Chopin and Beethoven and more recent fugues and fantasies by Felix Mendelssohn. I have given private recitals to family friends, also public performances sponsored by Wiltshire County Council.'

'Yes, your mother was mentioning your political involvements.'

'I prefer that my interventions be referred to as social as opposed to political, bearing in mind that I avoid making empty promises and cultivating my own interests.'

'What are your current preoccupations?'

'Following the repeal of the Contagious Diseases Act last year, I am working with the Salvation Army and representatives of the

medical profession to protect the country's vast numbers of prostitutes from disease now that the Government has abandoned attempts to regulate their profession. I helped organise the rally in London that urged our country's males to replace vice with virtue.'

As expected, her uncle showed signs of embarrassment.

'But, my dear, someone like you should not become involved in such sordid matters.'

'Why not?'

'Because ladies should avoid exposing themselves to the more indelicate aspects of our society.'

'Dear Uncle, would you say that the majority of prostitutes are male or female?'

'I beg ... I mean ...'

'Every single one of them is a woman, all exploited and often battered by their male consorts. When being treated for venereal diseases, endemic to their profession, they are forced to submit to intimate examinations by male doctors.'

'Because doctors are exclusively male!'

'Why?'

Receiving no reply she pursued her diatribe. 'How would you like to have your naked nether regions examined by women who cared little for your personal feelings?'

'Rosalie, that is uncalled for!'

'So what measures do you propose?'

As expected, her uncle found an excuse to withdraw.

He was replaced by Lieutenant Llewelyn-Jones.

'So, Lady Rosalie, how have you been occupying yourself since we last met?'

'Not in ways likely to interest your worthy self.' Which was true; however passionate, her involvement in social affairs was unlikely to interest the lieutenant.

'Tell me, that I might prove the inaccuracy of your statement.'

'I am involved in a project to provide free contraceptive advice to working class wives. Inadequate diets, exhaustion from extended working hours, insufficient medical attention and nobody to help

169

raise their children all contribute to high infant mortality and jeopardise the mother's survival. With no income to feed extra mouths, no space for unwanted family members and no time to educate their children, large working-class families represent one of the nation's major calamities. The goal of my project is to match the number of children with the parents' ability to raise them.'

'Since your efforts reduce the working class population, they should be encouraged.'

'But your methods are even more effective.'

'I beg your pardon?'

'The thousands of soldiers slain in battle during your campaigns in Africa, did they not originate from the lower classes?'

'Yes, but ...'

Captain Heathcote's arrival terminated the conversation. She pre-empted his inevitable questions about her activities by asking one of her own.

'Tell me of your experiences in Africa, especially the courage shown whilst slaughtering the Afrikaans.'

'My dear Lady Rosalie, I hardly think military matters are suited for the ears of a lady.'

'You have been fighting for Britain; I am a citizen of that country, so I fail to see the logic of your argument.'

'War and its resultant horrors are the affairs of men.'

'Since men instigate wars, I accept your reasoning. Instead, dear lieutenant, tell me more of Africa and its inhabitants.'

'Negroes are proof that societies evolve at differing rates. Homo Britannicus *is by far the most advanced, with other European nations following at a respectable distance, whereas our African cousins trail by thousands of years. Although, and this is a major consideration overlooked by Darwin, the state of evolution is far from homogeneous within individual societies, the gentry and bourgeoisie being significantly more evolved than the workers, validating recent warnings against intermarriages.'*

'What about Femina Britannica?'

'As certain religious leaders have recently pronounced, God

170

decided males should be 'active, progressive and doers' and females 'sweet, adoring and domestic', making men's lives enjoyable by looking beautiful for their benefit. Like yourself, my dearest Lady Rosalie!'

She smiled sweetly in his direction.

'Regretfully the physical effort of motherhood saps a woman's energy, drains her physical and mental capabilities; males should be grateful for the sacrifices made!'

'How about your good self?'

The fatuous fool insisted he harboured infinite appreciation for the self-effacement of the weaker sex. Did he not realise that his pronouncements, made whilst ostentatiously courting her, were hardly likely to make her swoon from romantic adoration? She shuddered inwardly as thoughts of being impregnated by the lieutenant flashed across her mind, especially the injection of his sperm, that 'reeking trace of male victory', into the deepest recesses of her physical being.

Ugh!

Sadly the lieutenant was far from alone in his attitudes. Had not Havelock Ellis written that menstruation was debilitating and disqualified women from pursuing higher education?

The lieutenant excused himself.

Her eldest sister Florence had been waiting to replace him.

She listened to how her sibling was at the forefront of latest fashions, how she outshone her entourage at charades and amateur theatrics, and how her collection of pressed flowers was the envy of the neighbourhood.

'How do you involve yourself with community affairs?'

Florence looked at her blankly. 'But I have just been telling you.'

'No, that is how you occupy yourself. How do you help less fortunate members of your neighbourhood overcome their difficulties?'

'But that is not my concern!'

'Why not?'

'Because we engage other people to handle such matters.'

171

Not wanting to embitter her sister, create a family feud, she changed the subject.

He added an extra bank-note to those already placed on the table.

'An indication of my appreciation for your devotions, sweetest Maisy!'

And he exited the room, the room he rented so her body would be at his disposal whenever he wished.

She had earned that extra ten shillings. It was her fault for allowing him to drink too much. Too sober and he had difficulty performing, which resulted in frustrated brutality and vivid bruises. Too inebriated and he lost control of his emotions, rendering her almost unconscious with the force of his passion. Just right and she was consumed in every way imaginable until prostrate from the physical effort.

She stumbled to the washbasin and doused her face with cold water before gently soaping where her skin was chafed. She then picked up the bank-notes; yes; they more than compensated for the moral mistreatment she endured. All but one would be deposited in the savings bank, adding to the steadily cumulating balance. Another couple of years and she would purchase a modest house far from Bolton and those who knew her as a slut, then find employment as a barmaid. In the meantime she must not sustain permanent injury from her benefactor, nor catch any of the debilitating diseases prevalent amongst her fellow workers.

He emptied his glass of cider and sat contemplating his lot as the setting sun slid majestically behind the hillside. He was fit, forty years of labouring in the fields for Lord Welyn had toughened his body; consequently he should continue working several more years, no more because each evening his muscles ached more than the day before. As he joked to himself, would he die before or after retiring? He hoped the latter but knew this to be the exception.

His children had married, leaving him alone with Amelia, his wife of thirty-five years. Alone, but only between visits from the family;

172

being a grandfather was a time-consuming occupation, especially when introducing the youngsters to the magic of Mother Nature. He knew every nook and cranny of the surrounding countryside, knew where birds nested, otters could be seen swimming in the river, foxes and ferrets hunted for food. Other areas of Britain were possibly more beautiful, but this was home, this is where he would live contentedly until the Lord Almighty decided otherwise.

He wished his fellow drinkers farewell and wandered slowly down the lane towards his friendly little cottage where the missus would be waiting to serve supper. His mouth watered at the thought of consuming freshly picked beetroot and turnips from his garden accompanied by poached eggs laid that very morning by Hettie, Amanda and Elfreda.

'Bang! Bang!' The pheasant fluttered in mid-flight and sank to earth.

'Bravo, Sir!'

He was seething inside. Not only had he been commandeered for the weekend, sacrificing rumbustious debauchery with Maisy and other music-hall *habitués*, he had not hit a single bird all morning. He could have refused, but his father had issued an ultimatum: if he wished to retain his allowance he had better marry Lady Rosalie Sandershurst, daughter of Lord Welyn. His indignation had mollified when promised vast sums of money to spend on new industrial complexes and a transfer to Wiltshire, an area with a superabundance of rowdy nocturnal entertainment. He was aware his own family fortune was no longer shrinking; it had already shrunk. The coffers were empty. Without someone else's generosity his existence was doomed to become less convivial. So he had cancelled his weekend engagements and caught a southbound train.

He supposed marriage was not the end of living, so long as his wife remained at home and cared for the children. And while his spouse performed her duties he would run an industrial empire by day and indulge in pleasures of the flesh by night. There was a recent tendency towards combining sex and marriage; younger husbands were limiting sexual experience to their wives, another symptom of

Victorian insistence at attempting everything at least once, however half-brained. Surely William Acton was right when declaring 'The best mothers, wives and managers of households know little of sexual indulgence.'

Having met Lady Rosalie the previous evening, Mr Acton's intuition had been proven only partly sound; his intended wife was far from unattractive, possessing an alluring face and body ample enough to accommodate a husband in comfort. Another enticement was of equal weighting: respected and educated his family might be, but they were industrial upstarts, members of the bourgeoisie, whereas Lord Welyn's title signified the landed gentry, the only thoroughly thoroughbred breed of Englishmen. Ignoring class distinctions in Britain was akin to being colour-blind; both he and his father might treat their workers like scum but it did not prevent nobility from treating them as unpolished traders. Nobody, however, would dare disparage the impeccable social standing of Lady Rosalie's husband.

He had charmed Lord Welyn and his wife Lady Kathyrn, plus the latter's mother who resided with them; you never knew what fortunes decrepit old widows might bequeath to unsuspecting beneficiaries.

As for Rosalie, well there was little point in submitting to the indignities of courtship. He had been extremely courteous; after all she had to be convinced to accept him. In return she had pointedly under-enthused at making his acquaintance, displaying a predilection for the company of household pets. There was no laugh, no smile, no sense of amusement, nor ambition to familiarise herself with a possible husband, although she refrained from the sarcastic tirades he had been warned to expect. Without doubt there was breeding and intelligence, most relevant now that medical researchers had proven that the female 'egg' contributed to the physical characteristics of children, a biological aberration that insulted the dignity of the male.

He committed himself to conversing with her, soften the invisible armour protecting her personality, before instigating a formalisation of their betrothal. In the meantime he needed to regain some of the pride misplaced when failing to hit those damnably acrobatic pheasants.

174

'No thanks, Luv!'

She was used to being solicited; after all she was gorgeously good-looking and sitting unaccompanied with other women was an open invitation to males visiting the music-hall in search of more than singing. However, in exchange for being taken care of financially, she was obliged to be faithful.

Her 'benefactor' had travelled south that week-end to attend an important business meeting, so after 'Auld Lang Syne' she would be returning home alone. Bearing in mind the amount of her weekly earnings, she was not going to take any risks by committing extra-marital adultery.

An owl hooted somewhere in the distance. He smiled, was his feathered neighbour jealous or sending a friendly message of encouragement? The hooting stopped and his thoughts returned to his love-making. In the dark he imagined Amelia as she had looked at the time of their marriage; in all probability she was doing likewise. Never mind, they still loved each other after thirty-five years.

Her heavy breathing indicated his efforts were being appreciated. Then sensations from down below confirmed his moment would shortly be arriving.

He proposed a walk in the grounds. Her expression indicated distaste for an activity of advanced asininity, but she could hardly refuse in front of those attending Sunday luncheon.

He led her down the staircase onto the forecourt leading from the mansion towards the resplendent summer garden. They walked in silence whilst he gathered together his thoughts into something approaching coherency.

Failing, he spoke of something different.

'I am most impressed by the gardens. Is his Lordship interested in horticulture as opposed to agriculture?'

'Not particularly.'

Silence.

'Of course the climate must be more clement in Wiltshire than Lancashire, where our family resides.'

'I would not know.'

'We are a mere fifteen miles from the coast; it rains with excessive frequency.'

Silence. Apparently remarks pertaining to a propensity for rainfall did not merit a response.

'You must surely appreciate your good fortune, living in such surroundings.'

'No.'

Surprised silence.

'I would much prefer to reside in London. There are numerous concert halls where one can listen to excellent music.'

'Excellent music' presumably implied solemnous classical composers, not happy-go-lucky songs sung at glee-clubs and public houses.

'Music is not my sole consolation in life. London has numerous other distractions.'

Uncertain as to the gist of her conversation, he negotiated a return to safer subjects.

'I understand your family possesses a town-house near Piccadilly; do you accompany your parents on visits?'

'My father will not entertain the idea of his daughter travelling with him unless my mother is in attendance, whereas she disapproves of large cities and remains resident here.'

So far so bad. Because, if he were to visit London, the last company he would wish would be that of his spouse. He recalled that Bristol was nearby; he would invent business commitments that retained him overnight.

'You spoke of music, who might be your preferred composers?'

'I appreciate Brahms and Chopin, even more so Lizst and Franck whose works attain the finesse of perfection. Although cognisant with the oeuvres of other writers, these habitually display flawed structural content, especially those of Strauss and Verdi whose paucity of concept renders them suited for the lower classes. The only modern composer who compares favourably to the great classicists is a young Englishman, Edward Elgar, someone little known outside his native Worcester.'

They walked in silence. He knew she was informed of the nature of his intentions, more pointedly their fathers' intentions. Thus he was in a quandary. Should he broach the subject as if everything was settled or should he enquire what inclinations she might have, if any, with relation to becoming his wife? And, having sought her opinion, how to react if she displayed antagonism?

'Do you paint or engage in needlework?'

'No.'

He was running out of subjects before attaining the limit of the trees, where they would commence their return journey.

'I presume you read; who might be your preferred authors?'

'I particularly relish the novels of Dickens and Thomas Hardy, also translations of Victor Hugo, for they describe the hardships of normal people and do not hesitate to condemn the iniquities of society. I also read *The Times* and *Punch* in order to keep myself informed of current events.'

The authors mentioned had strongly leftist leanings and riddled their publications with absurd attacks on capitalistic society. *Punch* was hardly less provocative. Presumably she knew his family ran one of the country's largest industrial empires?

Little was said as they retraced their steps until she suddenly turned to face him.

'I have been given to understand that our respective fathers are promoting our betrothal. Is this correct?'

Regaining his composure required several moments, during which time she waited impatiently, almost insolently, for a reply.

'I believe that is correct.'

'You only believe so? Have you not been consulted?'

'Of course, but ...'

'I would very much appreciate you speaking plainly since the matter is of great concern to me.'

'It is factual that our fathers have formed an understanding ...'

'An *understanding* or formal agreement?'

Things were getting out of hand. Yet her questions were hardly unwarranted.

'An agreement.'

'And you are party to this agreement?'

'I believe so. I mean, well, yes I am.'

'So you committed yourself to marriage before being introduced to my person.'

'I believe so. No!! Of course not.'

'So you are against the idea?'

'No. I, having heard about you, agreed to become acquainted and determine whether such a possibility would be advisable.'

'So, having become acquainted, what are your observations?'

'I find you a most fascinating and cultured person who, if I might be so bold, is considerably more attractive than I had been led to believe. Although I cannot commit myself in such a short space of time, my initial impressions are most comforting.'

'Would my opinions on the matter be of interest?'

'No. I mean, of course, yes.'

'I am fervently opposed to our union. Please do not construe that as a personal affront; I simply do not wish to associate myself with a husband. Instead, my ambition is to devote myself to something worthwhile; I would especially hope to practise as a doctor helping ease the misery of the less fortunate sectors of our society.'

'But women ...'

'Elizabeth Garrett qualified in 1865, six other women have graduated from the Edinburgh School of Medicine in spite of attempts to sabotage their studies. Women have practised medicine for centuries in Italy.'

'But Queen Victoria is adamantly against, she intervened to forbid women attending a medical congress in London because it implied male patients being required to abase themselves in front of ladies.'

'You have heard of Florence Nightingale?'

'But she was a nurse!'

'So what? The principle is the same. The ballyhoo is a smokescreen to avoid admitting the real reason for defying women candidates: males frightened of losing their superiority in the medical profession.'

He was about to say 'balderdash', then realised his interlocutor was a lady.

'You might be familiar with the Contagious Diseases Act, rescinded by Parliament earlier this year. For information, such legislation had become necessary to prevent millions of women from becoming infected with venereal diseases caught when providing sexual favours to licentious males. Repealing the legislation removed what little protection the nation once offered. Other women, their numbers are unknown but substantial, suffer physical and mental abuse from their husbands, violence that male doctors refuse to testify. All these women need access to affordable medical care and legal protection, both to be provided by understanding women, not unfeeling males. It is in this particular realm that I wish to devote my life.'

'But that would mean intermingling with unpolished individuals!'

Something, he reflected, he was not averse to doing.

'Prostitutes are human beings created in God's image, just like you and me.'

'But your music?'

'Is a means of overcoming the uselessness of my current life.'

She had clenched her fists whilst speaking; the Lady Rosalie certainly had a fiery temperament.

She continued speaking. 'Enough procrastinating on the subject most concerning us, our supposed yet not quite distinctly possible betrothal. Even though indicating my distaste, I do accept the inevitability of marriage and motherhood. My only concern is to ally myself with a husband who, even if not actively supportive, at least accepts my career ambitions. The rest is of little importance.'

Reeling from her loquacious onslaughts, he managed to attain the drawing-room without further verbal peccadilloes, leaving him in the uncomfortable position of being neither engaged nor betrothed, yet more than somewhat committed to marrying the Lady Rosalie.

She was missing him. No, not him, but the satisfaction of giving pleasure to a male however little appreciation she might receive in return. Winston's company was better than no company.

It was becoming increasingly difficult to rebuff music-hall patrons clamouring for access to her bounteous and financially exploitable charms.

Before dinner they entertained themselves. His father played sonatas on the violin, then the Lady Kathryn delighted with her renditions of songs by Franz Schubert and Fredrik Handel. The Lady Rosalie played Beethoven and Liszt in a languid style that either stimulated the musical senses or surmounted insomnia depending upon one's musical inclinations. He accompanied himself on the piano as he warbled modern ballads including 'Home Sweet Home' and 'Once Again', sensing reprobation as if such simplistic melodies were better confined to the working classes.

Dinner passed as pleasantly as possible, the only debate of note being whether photography was a scientific process or visual art akin to lithography. The majority believed that the movement towards 'Impressionist' painting was a reaction to the mechanical fidelity of photographic reproduction, contemporary artists being obliged to explore fantasy styles where the camera could not compete. After all, they had a living to make.

It being Sunday evening, a day of reposing and resting with one's family, everyone congregated in the drawing-room after supper.

'Well, my boy, have you made the acquaintance of my daughter Rosalie?'

'Indeed, Sir. A most fascinating, intelligent and delightful young lady, if I might be permitted to say.'

'You are permitted!'

All those in the study laughed, except the delightful young lady in question.

'I was also wondering if I might be allowed to consider marrying your daughter. I may not have known her for long, but I hold her in high esteem and I am anxious not to delay. I am of the opinion that "he who hesitates is lost" is a saying of unequivocal veracity.'

Again everyone laughed; even a certain delightful young lady managed the suspicion of a smile.

'I hope that you are not merely "considering" marriage to Rosalie.'

'Of course not! However, before proceeding further, I would insist upon hearing the Lady Rosalie's views, for her opinion is of great relevance.'

Her erstwhile pretender had sought a meeting after the game of croquet. She had accepted, abandoning plans to walk her dogs, and was awaiting his arrival in her private chambers.

Religious aristocracy declared that God created women to be dominated by males, submitting to their physical needs in order to procreate. Giving liberty to women, theologians insisted, would result in diluting women's morals. Perhaps so, but she refused to accept current claims that 'women belonged to nature and men to culture', nor that intellectual study rendered women infertile. Elizabeth Blackwell had written in The Human Element of Sex *that 'Sex is an immense spiritual force of attraction. The impulse towards maternity is an exorable but beneficial law of woman's nature and is a law of sex. She must subject herself to the almost ungovernable lust of men even though chastity, the highest law, is one natural to women.' She agreed that the impulse towards maternity was inexorable; she longed to raise her own children but could not endorse succumbing to the 'ungovernable lust of men'. Yet, infuriatingly, chastity and motherhood were incompatible.*

Was her defiance well-founded but premature, society not being ready to accord equal status to women, or was she a mentally imbalanced aberration who should be incarcerated?

Her thoughts were interrupted by a knock on the door; her 'suitor' had arrived.

'Lady Rosalie, during our walk I made a fool of myself. Although unprepared for your questions there is no excuse for the crassness of

my comportment. Since our walk I have been feverishly considering your questions, which explains why I lost so disastrously at croquet.'

He smiled at her in an extremely embarrassed yet amused way that, for the first time, generated feelings other than cold dislike.

'First, let me reiterate my comments about finding you a fascinating person. Your insistence on forging a career is indeed worthy of respect. If we marry, I would in no way hinder your ambitions. I do, however, question the advisability of following a medical career which appears incompatible with raising children. Involvement in the social and political realms of health care is, on the contrary, a worthy and practical ambition. As an entrepreneur concerned about the increasing complexity of worker skills and the scarcity of suitably trained young people, I would be especially supportive of your involvement to improve the equilibrium between industry's requirements and educational training. I admire you immensely, although I cannot claim to be romantically infatuated. Such emotions may develop with time: who knows. However, I am keen to form a partnership based on mutual respect, although on one condition.'

'Yes?'

'You occasionally let me win when playing croquet!'

She had burst out laughing, stupefied by his openness, amazed at his condoning her career ambitions and delighted by his sense of humour.

'Lady Rosalie, before asking your father I would insist upon receiving your verdict.'

He may not have won her heart, she reflected, but he had certainly conquered her head.

And now, in the drawing-room, everyone was waiting for her reply; was she, or was she not, willing to marry Winston Hamersham?

What would she say? He had used every seductive skill imaginable to convince her, being astute enough to realise that making her abandon a career would be disastrous; also, if she was absorbed in her own affairs he would be freer to indulge in his preferred pastimes.

In her private chambers she had offered her hand as a sign of acceptance. Had she had second thoughts? How was she going to reply?

'I am in favour of the proposal made by Mr Hamersham.'

Her mother rushed up to embrace her daughter, her father announced that, bearing in mind the close relationship bonding the two families, the usual 'enquiries' into a suitor's moral and financial well-being would be misplaced.

The bailiff arrived to announce three days' notice. She was being turfed out of his life, ejected without being informed of the reasons.

Accepting Jessie's offer to share would save money, but prevent bringing home 'business', so she chose an expensive flat near the centre of town whose rent would only be affordable if she found replacement customers. However, remembering the animated jostling of eager males last time she attended the music-hall, ensuring a steady income was going to be the least of her worries.

He surveyed the surrounding countryside. The architect was gesticulating excitedly as he exposed his plans for the industrial site, proudly explaining how warehouses would be placed alongside the railway siding which linked the factory to the Swindon-Bristol mainline. The power unit would be constructed alongside the river so coal-barges could unload directly into the boiler-room and waste products could be disposed of with minimum cost.

The site would initially specialise in hydraulic pumps for steamships and railway locomotives. A research laboratory would develop designs for machine tools and mechanised farm equipment. Also, heartened by reports that Edison's 'talking machine' actually worked, they were committed to reviewing the feasibility of producing under licence the contraptions for listening to wax cylinders.

After a final exchange of estimates he bid farewell to his visitors and mounted his horse. It was time to return home to his wife. His wife of four months. His virgin wife of four months.

Their relationship had been relatively harmonious, he devoting his time to developing the industrial site and she lobbying politicians to introduce health-care for prostitutes and legal protection for battered wives. She had, against his advice, associated herself with troublesome agitators fighting for the extension of voting rights to all adults regardless of sex and property ownership qualifications. They were even claiming votes for married women, as if being represented by their husbands was insufficient!

When they met, they spent their time exchanging information on each other's activities, obviating discussion of more private considerations. When he broached the fact that, being his wife, perhaps she might accord him the right to nocturnal visits, she had pleaded for time, insisting she was too occupied with other matters to risk becoming pregnant.

However, after four months waiting, his patience had run out; he would no longer accept pleas for postponement. That night he would consummate their marriage.

He sat on the porch of his brick bungalow trying to remember how his stone cottage had looked. Oh, how he missed the sound of the hooting owl and chirruping chaffinches, watching herons fishing where they were now building wharfs, and foxes stealing stealthily through the undergrowth towards their lair over which turbines were being installed. Brand-new 'extremely pleasant' houses had been built to lodge those displaced by the factory development; they would be more comfortably installed than before. Which was not true; comfort meant pottering around your garden and living amidst the miracles of nature with no neighbours breathing down your neck.

Dismissed farm workers were employed building the factory and would eventually help operate it. But how would he, after a lifetime of hoeing and scything by hand, learn to handle complicated machines?

Mr and Mrs Pollock were arguing again, Ben Fordham was having a smoke in his yard and a member of the Sykes family had just been

184

to the lavatory. Damnation to Lord Welyn; nobody had asked him to abandon his home, Warrington Manor, to make way for a warehouse or railway siding.

She knew it was inevitable, so she had committed herself to being brave, be taken by her husband in as dignified manner as possible. And now she knew it would be tonight. She had considered inventing a 'headache', but ruled out falsifying facts to her husband. In any case, the sooner the deed was accomplished the better.

Medical books dealt with sexual disorders, not normal conjugal comportment. She was too proud to ask her mother or sisters for advice, so her knowledge of marital matters was based on listening to prostitutes, watching bitches on heat and her vivid imagination. In any case, how could a wife enquire about sexual initiation four months after the wedding?

Having accepted her destiny, she vowed two things. Firstly he would never see her naked, nothing was more private than her body. And secondly, she would not suffer the indignity of being taken, she would offer herself. Always assuming she had the courage.

One deed could be accomplished in advance. After having taken a bath she removed, with the handle of a hairbrush, an object that could cause pain when she was least ready to endure it, would unnecessarily prolong her initial coupling and might stain her sheets, an embarrassment impossible to hide from her maid.

Her toilette completed, she waited for her husband, desperately hoping that he would prove to be a gentleman.

He walked across the landing, knocked, entered her bedroom, placed his candle on the commode and was about to commence undressing when she insisted his candle be extinguished, having no desire to witness the object that was to impregnate her. Furthermore, he was absolutely not permitted to see her without night-clothes.

He agreed; after all her requests implied acceptance of the marriage being consummated.

Fumbling in the darkness, he climbed in alongside her. He was about to lift the hem of her night-dress when she hissed 'no' and grabbed his hand. This was ridiculous, surely she realised he must access her private regions which, in the dark, would remain invisible. He heard sounds; she was lifting the material on her own accord! Then, to his utter amazement, she spread her legs.

Her maidenhood ceded without pressure. Within minutes he ejaculated, hopefully ensuring the Welyn-Hamersham dynasty would be blessed with an heir.

With nothing left to accomplish he stumbled back to his bedroom, leaving his companion in life to contemplate the duties of a married woman. Oh how different impregnating her had been to the gloriously energetic erotically sinful tussles he used to have with Maisy.

Fifteenth encounter: Brian and Ethel
1905   Warrington, England

'Two pounds, eleven shillings and seven pence three farthings.'

'Here's three guineas.'

He pulled out a pencil from a drawer, sharpened it, and proceeded to calculate how much change he owed Mr Munsford.

'There you are, sir; eleven shillings, four pence and a farthing.'

He watched as the customer exited the shop, only to notice another enter. It was Johnny Smith, who worked for Barston & Johnstone, Plumbing Contractors, situated in the town's Riverside Industrial Estate. He and Johnny were friends; they played football Saturday afternoons and chased girls together the rest of the time. That evening would be no exception; after the match they would meet at the Warrington Workmen's Recreational Club before seeking more sophisticated entertainment in less respectable establishments.

'Afternoon, Brian! Sorry ter innerrupt yer daydreaming; wondr'in' which young lady'll fall for yer charms th'ssevening!?'

'Get on with yer! The customers never stop coming, everyone wants ironmongery Saturday morning as if they'll be spending whole weekend fixing houses. Daydreaming, indeed!'

'I need this lot for Mr Johnstone real quick, they be in a fine old tizzy at municipal theatre, water leaking all over and nothing to stop it.'

He studied the crumpled sheet of paper and started gathering together the various goods requested. Whilst doing so, he noticed Johnny placing some of smaller items in a straight line. When the last bit of hardware had been unearthed, an inch spanner, Johnny had a question for him.

'Study these closely; they tell a story about a madman who escaped from his cell in a lunatic asylum. On the way out he encountered two cleaning women, imposed himself upon them and then scarpered.'

'Has he been caught?'

'That's not part of story. Explain how these bits and pieces tell what happened.'

He studied the objects aligned on the counter, totally mystified; how could bits of ironmongery relate to an escaped madman? Johnny couldn't wait any longer, so he explained.

'Nut screws washers and bolts!!!'

Johnny had long left the shop before he unravelled the conundrum, leaving him to charge Mr Johnstone's account with thirteen shillings and thruppence halfpenny.

After having updated the sales register he wondered whether, by any chance, he would be doing some 'screwing' that night. If so, it would be the first time for six months, all because of Molly, sweetly delightful and extremely extroverted Molly Saunders, someone stubbornly introverted when it came to petting. He had proceeded upwards, almost reaching a stocking-covered knee, had extended downwards towards her bosom, although only outside her blouse and whatever else she wore underneath it, but had progressed no further for over a month.

When she hinted a band of gold would remove remaining hindrances to attaining the ultimate target, he decided enough was enough. No, not enough was enough. Or should that be not enough was too much? Anyway, Molly, refusing to prove her love by offering herself to him, had been ditched the previous Sunday, twenty-two being far too young to commence running a home and raising kiddies. Tonight he would be seeking a replacement for the girl encountered the previous November during one of the club's social evenings.

He sat waiting for his friends. The club was filling up, it was usually jam-packed by five o'clock now that factory employees only worked

Saturday mornings following introduction of the fifty-four hour week.

Mothers with children congregated in an area cluttered with games and toys; a rocking-horse was in constant use and the pile of teddy-bears and golliwogs was swarming with excited youngsters. Some husbands were drinking tea with their wives, placating children with cream cakes whilst their womenfolk chatted to each other. Other husbands were playing darts or billiards, smoking cigarettes and pipes, their bodies almost indistinguishable behind clouds of tobacco fumes. One of his uncles was reading the *Daily Mail*, waiting until a billiards table became free.

Bachelors like himself were sitting alone, eyeing nothing in particular except the adolescent girls and younger unmarried women. During which time the lasses in question, whose attractiveness ranged from physically uninspiring to bordering on outright ugly, were sitting in the furthest corner pretending to ignore their potential dates for the evening.

His uncle, having finished, handed over the newspaper. With nothing to do until his chums arrived, he turned to the front page and commenced reading.

Juan Franco had been nominated Prime Minister of Spain with exceptional powers, almost dictatorial powers, which had given rise to speculation over the future of the monarchy. New legislation forbade women working nightshifts although, as the paper commented, it presumably did not apply to prostitutes. King Edward VII would attend Ascot Races with Queen Alexandra and the Prince of Wales. Aston Villa had beaten Newcastle United 3–1 in the Cup Final, preventing Newcastle, who had already won the Top Division championship, from achieving the 'double'. Alf Common, the footballer, was transferred from Sunderland to Middlesbrough for the incredible amount of £1,000. Another article speculated with foreboding that Mary Sutton might become the first foreigner to win a Wimbledon title in next July's championships; she had recently beaten Britain's Miss D.K. Douglas who won the title in 1903 and 1904. He commented to himself that the obvious solution was to stop foreigners entering the competition in the first place.

In Westminster, the twenty-nine Labour Party MPs were battling to increase pension rights and extend annual vacations for workers. Kaiser Wilhelm of Germany was threatening to annexe neighbouring countries like Belgium, how dare he! He read carefully, however, an article describing how members of the newly-formed Women's Freedom League had interrupted political meetings and smashed windows; they insisted upon universal voting rights for women and were part of the 'Suffragette' movement. In his opinion, anyone smashing windows should have no rights whatsoever. On the other hand, if the League passed a law obliging attractive young girls to offer their charms whenever he asked, he would support anything they wanted however many windows were smashed.

Bernard and Johnny arrived, grinning broadly. He returned the newspaper to its appointed cubby-hole and greeted them.

'Been waiting long?'

'Nah, fifteen minutes. Not much to look at, though.'

Which did not prevent them from studying that evening's selection, a couple of whom stared back hopefully, the sort you would least want to be lumbered with when it was time to get serious.

'You win the match?'

'Nah, three-all. They were leading three-one at half time, but got overconfident. Another five minutes an' we woudda smashed 'em.'

His two chums 'aaaahed' consolingly.

'Better luck next week!'

Abandoning the world of football, he enquired after Bernard's afternoon activities.

'How was the rehearsal?'

His friend played trombone in the Fisher-Talbert Joinery Works Brass Band, one of thousands of amateur 'orchestras' created by employees working in the same company, one of the few that had gained national recognition.

'As usual, we thought we were brilliant an' Mr Simpson, the bandleader, never stopped moaning. We spent ten minutes trying to convince him to play "I Love a Lassie" and "After the Ball", instead of his endless marches and classical things.'

'D'yer succed?'

'Nah!'

'What about yer recording?'

The band had been asked to perform pointing towards an outsized horn, thereby engraving their music onto a discus-shaped platter made from shellac. The platter was then spun at seventy-eight revolutions per minute on a mechanical machine and you heard yourself playing.

'Nothing has been decided with the phonographic company, it's called His Master's Voice because a dog can listen to his master talking or singing!'

'But I thought yer was gonna record so *people* can hear you?'

''Course we are! Records being double-sided, Mr Simpson has selected the Sousa march "Liberty Belle" and a good old English favourite "A Life on the Ocean Wave".'

'Do you realise yer won't need to appear on bandstand Sunday afternoons, yer just play the record!!'

'Wow! We could even sit in the audience and applaud when it's over!'

'What if yer have several records and different machines to play them, can yer perform to different audiences at same time?'

Tommy had not considered the implications.

'Gee! If you can play music when yer not there, whattabout when yer be dead? You can listen in heaven whilst those still living applaud!'

'Blimey, it's weird!'

'Like magic!'

Duncan arrived and they repeated their amazing theories to the eldest member of the group, twenty-nine years old and a machine maintenance repairman at the shoe factory.

'That'll mean you only need one brass-band in the whole country!'

Which meant recording was not such a good idea after all.

They ordered a pint of ale each, it was pay-day and one did foolish things on pay-day.

'Brian, yer truly finished with Molly?'

'Yers!! Waste of time. But why yer ask?'

''Cos my brother Jimmy, heeze taken a fancy.'

'Good luck to him. She may be smashing ter look at but whatser use if yer can't touch?'

'She's never done it?'

'Nah, saving up for wedding night.'

'Perhaps Jimmy'll persuade her, he managed with Glad!'

'Glad?'

'Yes, Gladys Atkins.'

'Ain't she the one awfully pregnant only three months after marrying Dickie Allenworth?'

A silence ensued as they contemplated the implications. Duncan, however, had other matters on his mind.

'Let's eat here! It's sausages an' mashed potatoes followed by apple crumble. And I get four sausages, instead of three!'

'How yer manage that?'

'Well, I says to Daisy, if she gives me an extra one, she receives a kiss.'

'An' …'

'And she tells me to get lost if I want any sausages at all. So, I says to her, how about an extra sausage if I promise never to kiss yer? She thought abawt it, then agreed. Which is why I get a fourth sausage!'

'She's too fat, not worth kissing anyway.'

'Plump girls be great kissers and be extra warm and cuddlesome when yer start proper business.'

'Yer ne'er done it with her?'

'Ner! I'm already "walkin' out" with Emily Ellis and Janie Frickness.'

'Both of them?'

'You bet!'

'Which be the best?'

'Emily, she be great at kissing and cuddling, but Janie she caresses better, including "down there", making it real exciting. However, she insists on using a rubber whilst Emily don't bother.'

A silence ensued as the others contemplated Duncan 'screwing around' with two gals whilst they had none.

It was time to order their food and another pint of ale. After all, it was pay-day.

Duncan hadn't been joking; four sausages accompanied his mashed potatoes and gravy.

'Whatzyer gonna do for summer holidays?'

'The family'll probably return to Blackpool, to Mrs Jossop's guest house. We had a smashing time last year what with the amusement arcades, donkey rides and bicycling along the sea-front. Believe it or not, lots of women now ride bicycles, some even dress different, wearing baggy trousers that look like a skirt when their legs are together. However, for those who insist on wearing real skirts, they've invented a special woman's bicycle.'

'How's it different?'

'The bar in middle is lower so it don't get in way of their skirts. Also, when climbing on, they don't show their stockings.'

'That don't seem a good idea! What else didja do?'

'In the arcades, some of the machines were called "What the Butler Saw!". You pay a farthing, turn a handle, and you see photographs of women in their petticoats and drawers. For a halfpenny she removes her petticoat and you can see both her breasts! Then, for a whole penny, she removes everything, but it's a cheat 'cos her hand covers where you most wanter see!'

'What was they like, pretty, fat or thin?'

'Mostly plump, dark hair and beautiful!! Even better are the naughty postcards, some are real photographs of women in bathing costumes, others are drawings with witty comments written underneath, mostly rude! One shopkeeper has a drawer of special cards, completely naked women with enormous bare bottoms!'

'Did yer purchase any?'

'If yer promise never to tell, one evening next week I'll let yer see the ones I bought!'

'Buy lots more this summer, I'll pay for them!'

'What about real alive girls?'

'No such luck, my parents were there.'

'Did you swim in the sea?'

'Far too cold and wet, though we rolled up trousers and paddled.'

'What about the theatre?'

'Amazing! There was a music-hall with comics, acrobats and performing dogs, plus famous singers. At beginning of week there was Gus Elen, who sang "Wait Till the World Comes Round" and "Two Lovely Black Eyes". Midweek it was Florrie Ford singing "Anona" and "It's a Long way to Tipperary", then on Friday Vesta Victoria was the star and sang "Riding On A Motor Car".'

'You mean they sing songs about motor vehicles?'

'Yes, especially when they break down and the driver must repair them!'

'Have you ever ridden in one?'

'Nah. But I've nearly been run over twice!!'

'My brother's gonna work in a garage, says you make lotsa money fixing them.'

'When it rained, we visited a picture house. There was a comedy film, *Raffles, the Amateur Cracksman* and an adventure feature called *The Great Train Robbery* starring G. M. Anderson.'

A silence descended whilst they attacked Daisy's solidly consistent culinary masterpieces, the occasional appreciative burp discernible above the babble made by the club's numerous other members.

'Tommy, are yer going away this summer?'

'Nah. The band plays extra concerts during summer, so I'm stuck in Warrington.'

'Tell your bandmaster to play records so you can visit seaside like everyone else!'

'How about you, Johnny?'

'No, my Dad's bought a house on outskirts of town; its got three bedrooms, a scullery and garden! It's near new secondary school where my younger sisters study. Thanks to Dad's pay rise, Mum's salary as cleaner at Farrington's Dairies an' the two eldest children both working, also a whopping bank loan, Dad just scraped up enough money. But there still be plenty of painting and carpentry to finish. Even if there weren't, we ain't got money fer holidays.'

They drained their glasses, the evening's serious entertainment was about to commence.

'And now, ladies an' gentlemen, for the very first time in Warrington, the fabulous Bluebelle Girls!!!'

The orchestra launched into can-can music from Paris, the dancers swirled onto the stage, lifting their skirts to expose frilly bloomers and black stockings. No actual skin was visible, only normal since ladies were sitting in the audience. Which was stupid, because it was women who were dancing.

He gazed longingly at their undergarments, trying to imagine what was hidden underneath. Was every woman different 'down there', just like they had pretty or ugly faces? And how to find out? Presumably this was possible at Madame Suzanne's, but each visit cost a week's wages. Perhaps Bernard's naughty postcards from Blackpool would solve the mystery.

The juggler and magician were amusing, but not as exciting as the dancing girls. Then Albert Chevalier, the star of the show, walked onto the stage to wild cheers and bravos. He sang "My Old Dutch", "Two Lovely Black Eyes", "The Preacher and the Bear" and "Percy from Pimlico". Everyone joined in the choruses, thumping their jugs of ale on the tables and stamping their feet. You could hardly hear the singer. Then the show was over, but drinks continued to be served for another half-hour.

'Duncan!!'

'Ethel!!'

'Can we join you?'

''Course yer can.'

Duncan whispered in his ear. 'You can have Ethel, she's great fun and does anything yer want. I'm getting bored with her; well, if you must know, she no longer fancies me.'

So he found himself sitting next to the flamboyantly dressed and, when sitting in certain positions, flamboyantly undressed, glamorous and vivacious Ethel. Once he caught sight of a scarlet garter wrapped around her leg far above her knee, a very long way above her knee where drawers should normally be seen, or not be seen, depending upon one's opinion of the matter. He was surprised at not being intimidated by the older woman, probably because several pints of ale helped him forget whom he normally was. He made some daring comments, which resulted in hoots of laughter and some even more risqué remarks in return; in fact the innuendoes were not innuendoes at all.

Without warning, as the band started playing a waltz, he was grabbed and led onto the dance-floor. During the second waltz her hand slipped downwards onto his left buttock; in exchange his hand sought one of her breasts. She squeezed closer, so nobody could see what was happening, not that the other couples cared for they were also trying to prevent people from seeing what they were doing.

Then it was "God save The King" and back outside into the rainy real world.

'Brian, yer wanna come back for a drink, I've got a bottle of whisky stored away!'

Never in his life had he been invited home by a woman except to have high-tea with Molly and her family. By the time he decided to accept she supposed his silence implied willingness, placed an arm around his waist and her head on his shoulder, and was leading him down Milford Road shouting a rollicking 'goodnight' to the others.

She led him upstairs and into her drawing room, which also served as kitchen and dining room. Having gingerly turned on the light, she explained she was terrified of being frizzled by the electric current, she hung their coats, hats and umbrellas on a stand, bade him sit on the sofa, then fetched two empty glasses and the bottle of whisky.

'You pour, but not too generous. It's not that I'm stingy but we've already consumed more'n a fair share.'

He poured half a glass each, pushed the cork back in the bottle, placed the bottle on the table, held out her glass and, waiting politely until she took a sip, drank some of the scorching liquid. Still holding her glass she cuddled up and kissed him on the cheek.

'Where's Duncan been hiding you all this time?'

'Nowhere, you ain't been looking hard enough!'

'Who cares, I've found you.'

'No; I found you.'

'We found each other, so stop quibbling.'

She moved even closer, swallowed the remainder of the whisky, stretched to place her empty glass on the table, turned so she was facing him, cuddled as closely as her outstandingly oversized breasts would permit and sighed in a way that expressed contentment. He felt her tongue exploring where the tongues of rampantly eager females could be expected to explore, but he pushed her away. She looked hurt and puzzled.

He smiled.

She stared at him, perplexed.

He smiled again, swallowed the remains of his drink, placed the empty glass next to hers, lay back on the sofa and pulled her down onto him, feeling her breasts squashed against his blazer lapels. This time her tongue almost reached his tonsils.

Returning from the toilet she stood gazing down at her reclining guest.

'You wanna stay longer?'

'You bet!'

'Then follow me.'

And follow her he did. Lying alongside her in bed, he learned her husband had been killed in a mine explosion and that she still loved him very much. Getting drunk and inviting men home helped her forget, at least until after breakfast the next morning. She insisted she only spent nights with men she liked and had been attracted to him immediately. However, he shouldn't get any ideas about marriage, she wasn't ready for that.

Which suited him perfectly.

She was in a communicative frame of mind. She related how she had started work in a millinery factory as seamstress, making scarves and bonnets. She had been promoted supervisor, then transferred to the design department. Her superior, Mr Ralston, on leaving the company to open a clothing store in the town centre, suggested she follow; she could handle suppliers and the retouching of customer orders. Her speciality was lingerie, explaining the eye-popping spectacle that greeted his eyes when she undressed; her corset was one of the most beautifully exquisite things he had ever seen.

She cuddled up closer, this time practically clinging to him.

Her younger sister had attended secondary school and was training to be a hospital worker, the nurse's entrance examination proving too difficult. After her husband's death, she herself had attempted to enrol, but was considered too old. So she decided to remain in the clothing business. Mr Ralston was hoping to open a second shop in Wigan or Salford, which she would manage by herself.

The time for talking was over, she was sleepy and feeling very loving.

'Please be gentle, just like my Robert.'

He moved in, ready, in fact extremely ready, to prove how very much he liked her. Which was genuinely true, not just invented so she would allow him.

'And if I cry, don't be alarmed. It's just 'cause I'm feeling happy.'

He kissed her very gently on the mouth, on each nipple, then moved further downwards to take his pleasure. No, they both moved downwards to take each other's pleasure.

Sixteenth encounter: Tommy and Edith
1916   Abbeville, France

They ran forward in the squelching mud, stumbling over the twisted wreckage of war machinery whilst side-stepping mutilated corpses from the previous assault. The enemy positions faded and then disappeared from view as smoke from the artillery barrage thickened. Without slackening their pace, they proceeded haphazardly towards where the enemy should be, fervently hoping he would no longer be there when they arrived. Then, uncertain whether they were still advancing or inadvertently retreating towards their waterlogged trenches and a court-martial for cowardice, they momentarily wavered.

They had been longing for this moment since embarking for France, dreading it since understanding the similarities between modern warfare and industrialised slaughterhouses. Admittedly differences existed; an abattoir provided meat to consume whereas war produced corpses to bury, and abattoir employees ensured the animals died swiftly and painlessly.

Their mission was simple: scramble out of their trenches, run towards the enemy, destroy his positions, claim the conquered land for Britain and celebrate their victory. Annoyingly the military strategists had overlooked one minor detail – that the enemy might not entirely agree with the morning's agenda and resist attempts to dislodge him. And, whilst doing so, massacre every British soldier in the vicinity.

Something he would be doing at any moment.

The smoke cleared. They distinguished enemy emplacements a

hundred yards ahead, then realised they had veered off-course and were advancing along an exposed ridge instead of a shallow decline.

'Tommy! Ewan!!'

'Yes, Sarge!'

'Follow me!!'

The raucous staccato of machine-gun fire ended the brief silence. Maxie Helms, running several yards ahead, received bullets in his abdomen that emerged from his back accompanied by most of his guts. Jimmy Thompson flung his arms in the air as his head disintegrated. Piercing screams bore witness to the accuracy of the enemy marksmen; before long he, Tommy Atkins, was the only unscathed soldier out of eighty who had clambered from their trenches fifteen minutes earlier. In other words, he was the only target offering himself to those manning machine-guns seventy yards away. The smoke swirled around him again, delaying his annihilation until it drifted elsewhere, which it would at any moment.

He sank to his knees, lungs wheezing from the sustained effort of running. What should he do? Advance to be shredded, or retreat and be branded a coward?

He had an idea. If he found a wounded comrade and carried him back to safety he might escape both the enemy bullets and a court-martial. He turned, searching for a suitably wounded compatriot. The first two were dead, the third's entrails slurped from within as he was pulled upright. Then he heard moans from his left. Not only were the wounds relatively mild, bullets had smashed both legs, but the soldier's slender frame would be relatively easy to carry.

Straining under the weight, he swung the man over his shoulders, causing him to scream in agony. He then staggered towards where he hoped the British trenches might be. The smoke remained resolutely dense, screening him from both safety and danger; then he recognised a stunted bush visible from where he was billeted.

The smoke lifted and he heard shouts of encouragement from comrades who had wisely stayed behind. Two forms ran towards him, ready to grasp his human burden, when the shell landed.

She sat alone, trying to forget where she was and why she was there, remember who she had been before the world went insane.

Back home she had been Edith Craven, twenty-six-year-old daughter of John and Margaret Craven, bank manager and housewife. Denied professional training because her parents refused to allow their daughter to pursue a career, most improper for a respectable middle-class woman, she involved herself in charitable activities – for example, running errands for old people in Bognor Regis and providing blanket-baths for residents of a local alms-house. In the evenings she visited music-halls with girlfriends until, following a series of lethal fires, such establishments had been forbidden to serve meals, which radically altered their friendly family atmosphere. Instead they frequented public ballrooms, but watching rows of males goggling at you was nerve-wracking and a complete waste of time because those you wanted to dance with inevitably invited someone else. So she stayed at home, knitting and reading.

Yes, that's who she had been once upon a while ago; nobody in particular, neither happy nor miserable, just as bored as hell.

Matters improved marginally when she became the girlfriend of Michael Jones, articled clerk in a firm of estate agents. However, almost immediately afterwards, on the fifth of August 1914, King George V declared war on Germany for invading Belgium. Nobody thought much about it until Lord Kitchener stuck posters everywhere proclaiming, 'Your country needs YOU'. Mickey, as Michael was known, decided a paid trip to Paris with the boys would be more amusing than filing legal documents dedicated to the construction, selling, renting and occasional demolition of buildings. So he volunteered and was integrated into the 2nd Corps, spending several months marching round holding a stick pretending to be a rifle, cultivating blisters from ill-fitting boots and backache from feeding horses.

He had commenced cajoling her, pleading that she prove her love, give him courage to depart for foreign lands. Shocked, she refused. Yet some of her girlfriends had surely 'given into temptation' as the vicar would say. Also, it was now patriotic to support the country's *brave young soldiers. Furthermore, a woman's reputation was now increasingly based, however belatedly, on what she achieved instead of what she refrained from doing, at least until her wedding night. Women finally had the right to lead their own lives. Except her. And she loved Mickey very much. So she allowed him, and spent the entire night regretting her stupidity. The next evening she again metamorphosed into a willing and wanton woman, only to endure another night of remorse and regret. The third time her willingness attained new heights of wantonness and she experienced no remorse whatsoever. Then, a couple of weeks later, well what should have occurred did not. Mickey hadn't a 'rubber' nor she a douche with syringe like her mother, but he had promised to be careful. Obviously not careful enough.*

Convinced that God was punishing her, she swore never again to stray from the path of righteousness. And then, when she had resigned herself to motherhood and was about to inform her parents, what should have occurred, did occur. God, if He existed and she assumed He did, had been most lenient.

By then Mickey, unaware of his brief encounter with fatherhood, had departed to France with the British Expeditionary Force, not to Paris as expected, enabling him to explore Montmartre and the Quartier Latin, but Maubeuge surrounded by beetroot fields which transformed into quagmires when it rained, which it rarely ceased doing. Then, after months of talking about wreaking havoc upon the Germans, the Allied forces inadvertently bumped into them at Le Cateau. From what she had been told, which was not much, they had brilliantly outmanoeuvred the enemy. Except that, a minor inconsequentiality, they sacrificed 8,000 soldiers whilst doing so, including Mickey.

With hundreds of thousands of working men volunteering for the armed forces it was inevitable that problems would arise. Who would replace Britain's heroes? Her father surmised that, due to a shortage of mentally viable geriatrics, pre-adolescent schoolboys and trained chimpanzees, the country would have to rely on the next best source of manpower: women.

He was right. A harassed government called for the nation's ladies to work in the armaments industry and anywhere they could be useful, even as 'policewomen' and bus 'conductorettes'. They would even be paid, although less than men. Her father persuaded his bank director to engage his daughter as a cashier, then informed her of the marvellous news. But she had other ambitions. Newspapers and newsreels mentioned hordes of injured soldiers, many more than those killed, suffering dreadfully because nobody had foreseen the need to transport them to suitable hospitals. Not that the hospitals existed, nor the staff to manage them. It was a national disgrace.

If she could change bedpans for crotchety old folk, she could comfort wounded soldiers. So she applied to the Nursing Auxiliary Services and discovered that amidst the mayhem of modern warfare nurses, however inexperienced and squeamish, did not change the occasional bandage and banter with patients over a cup of tea. Instead they were thrust into the epicentre of a military hospital with its horror and hopelessness, ineffectual attempts to stitch together bodies torn apart by shrapnel, amputations that sometimes removed more than remained, and the immorality of assuring soldiers their injuries were minor as they died before your eyes.

Someone screaming in prolonged agony brought her back to reality. She struggled to her feet and returned to her daytime nightmare.

He heard muffled sounds, sensed a shaking and shuddering, and briefly half-visualised a reddish incandescence. Then the pain engulfed him until everything merged into nothingness.

The periods of torment became longer, more specific, more frequent; he started detecting sounds and smelling antiseptic cleanliness. Sleep intermingled with unconsciousness, waking was synonymous with suffering. He had liquids forced down his throat, medicines or nourishment? Nobody bothered to inform him. Someone changed his dressings, somebody else washed where his body was not enveloped in bandages, somebody else dealt with the embarrassment of not being able to visit the toilet. Or was it the same person? Whoever he or she might be, they were always in a hurry, rough to the extent of being aggressive and indisposed to socialising.

Once he fought against the pain, attempted to ask where he was. Even he failed to understand his malformed croaking. Not surprisingly, no one responded. So he abandoned his attempts and waited for sleep or unconsciousness to provide relief.

'Nurse, you must stop the pain. Cut off my leg if you must, but please, for God's sake, stop the pain!'

She knew the surgeon had decided against such an operation; the patient was going to die within forty-eight hours so it would be a waste of hospital resources.

'But there is no need, Captain Fitzgerald; your leg is recovering remarkably well. Just be patient a little bit longer.'

'Corporal Jenkins?'

Had he been asleep? In a world of permanent blackout it was impossible to know.

'Corporal Jenkins? Can you hear me?'

He tried to reply, abandoned the attempt, nodded his head, moaned as pain reactivated within his body, and finally managed to emit a rasping wheeze.

'Eahrrsssss.'

'Corporal Jenkins, I am Doctor Jameston. I have been looking after you since your arrival three weeks ago.'

Three weeks ago!!!

'Firstly I would like to be the first to congratulate you on your exemplary bravery, saving your comrade whilst under enemy fire. You have been awarded the Military Medal!'

Three weeks, what the blazes had he been doing during the last three weeks?

'Thanks to your fighting spirit the British won a major battle!'

But we never reached their defences, everyone was killed. How could there have been a victory?

'We are all extremely upset about your injuries, but I can assure you that everything is being done to accelerate your recovery.'

His Company, probably the entire Battalion, had been massacred, torn to shreds by machine-guns. What does he mean by 'victory'?

'Due to the improvement of your condition we have decided to transfer you to a hospital near Abbeville where you can continue your rehabilitation in more suitable surroundings.'

Abbeville? Where the damnation was that? Certainly not in England.

'The journey will not be very comfortable. But you have already demonstrated extreme courage so I know we can count on your understanding.'

I want to return home to England. And I want my bandages removed so I can see what is happening.

'You leave tomorrow.'

'Nurse Craven, we are in the midst of a war. I would appreciate a little more action and a lot less dawdling.'

Without waiting for a reply Matron departed to confront some other crisis, fail to save another life. Damn the woman, she was as arrogant as the average male.

She knew what was required, and dreaded it. He had arrived that afternoon from a front-line hospital, from the middle of the conflagration. The lower half of his youthful body contrasted sharply with the stained bandages binding together what remained above the waist. Apparently he was a hero, the sole survivor of four persons caught in a mortar blast. Based on the extent of his injuries the shell must have landed practically on top of him; his face had been partly blown away, he was blinded, probably permanently, and his arms were nothing more than shortened stumps. In all likelihood he had clutched his face to protect himself, possibly saving his life but at a terrible cost.

As the medical staff said all too frequently when talking amongst themselves, it would have been kinder if he had been killed outright. However, the hospital's job was to nurse him back to health. No, not exactly. Help him recover from the worst of his wounds so he could suffer a living death until he died.

He had not been told. And Matron had ordered her to change his bandages without creating suspicion and without dawdling. To hell with 'thunder-guts', she herself refused to treat patients as assorted livestock. So she slowly and carefully unwound his bandages, knowing it would hurt as the final layer of pus-impregnated protection was pulled from his face. She instinctively sniffed the wounds; there was no tell-tale stench of gangrene. Unable to wipe his burned flesh without removing what remained, she poured the antiseptic directly onto his raw flesh then delicately draped clean bandages around his head and upper torso, hiding but not healing his deformities.

'Why 'oo ayne 'annnagees 'n darrrk?'

He had managed to speak and she had understood.

'Sorry, I am unable to answer your question. I must attend another patient. I'll be back tomorrow morning.'

She exited the room aware that someone, preferably someone else, would have to tell him.

The reddish haze that distinguished daytime had faded into blackness. He heard clattering from the corridor, the sounds of plates and cutlery, the paraphernalia of eating. Soon his dinner would be served by the woman responsible for feeding him. Once again it was vegetable soup, although he suspected there were more weeds than vegetables. He sniffed again; yes mincemeat, or rather mince-best-not-to know-what followed by apple purée, not that his heightened nasal senses smelt his pudding but they served apple purée every evening.

She arrived. It was 'fat, middle-aged schoolteacher from Huddersfield'. Not that the person entering his room was necessarily plump and elderly nor an academic from northern England but, unable to see and unaware of her origins, he was reduced to imagining who might be tending him.

He obediently opened his mouth and the first spoonful of soup was poured inside.

She undressed and carefully folded her clothes before placing them in the wardrobe; she would not be requiring them for a very long time. She shivered from the cold; even so it took courage to climb into her uniform, transform from Edith to Nurse Craven.

'Good morning, Corporal Jenkins!'

She was back, 'friendly, motherly but not very pretty blonde from Surrey'.

'Good morning! Where have you been for so long?'

'I was allowed home on leave.'

'Having returned, are you going to remain for long?'

'I hope so!'

'Liar!'

'I beg your pardon?'

'You are lying. Nobody would willingly stay here; the thing you most want is to return home. Consequently your statement about hoping to remain is false.'

She did not respond.

'Come on, admit it. I won't tittle-tattle!'

'I admit it. Please do not be insulted, it is nothing personal.'

'Of course I am not insulted. On the contrary I am delighted; for the first time since being injured someone has treated me like a person and not a rotting half-dead corpse.'

'A corpse cannot be half-dead, by definition it is totally dead.'

'How about half-alive?'

'I will have to consider your proposal. No, I overrule your presumption; you are considerably more than half-alive.'

'You might think otherwise if you were me.'

'Rubbish!'

'Now you are speaking like a blasted doctor.'

'Sorry.'

'I forgive you, but only if…'

'Yes?'

'You never talk to me again like a doctor.'

'I promise.'

'In exchange, I am prepared to consider myself more than half-alive, but only in your company.'

He sensed her uneasiness. Not unexpectedly she excused herself, mumbling that other patients required her attentions.

She breathed in the late autumn air, so different from the oppressively overheated atmosphere inside the building. She was off-duty, fleeting freedom graciously granted for relaxing and enjoying oneself. Initially she had driven round the countryside and visited bistros with colleagues, but cumulating fatigue, mental and physical, soon dispelled any incitation to explore the nation they had come to defend. Precious free time was now spent sleeping or reading popular books such as Ian Hay's The First Hundred Thousand, *a satire on life in the British trenches, and John Buchan's* Thirty-Nine Steps, *a new kind of novel called a mystery thriller.*

A gramophone found hidden in the cellar initially played patriotic numbers such as "Pack Up Your Troubles In Your Old Kit Bag", "Keep Right on to the End of the Road" and a military band's version of "Land of Hope and Glory". However these were discarded when a selection of music-hall songs arrived from England; patriotism was replaced by "If You Were the Only Girl in the World" and "Sister Susie Sewing Shirts for Soldiers".

A blackbird twittered angrily and rose into the sky, proving that some vestiges of the outside world, the one she lived in before war was declared, had miraculously escaped the folly of mankind.

Oh how she longed to return home to normality. Except that during her leave she had been introduced to toothpaste squeezed from a tube, liquid nail varnish and safety razor-blades, and the absurdity of advancing clocks one hour during summer. Women in uniforms bossed everyone around as if they were men and her socially snooty mother proudly donned overalls when working in a munitions factory whose final product, as her father said half-jokingly, was not weapons but widows and orphans. So little remained unchanged, it was as if tradition and conformity had been put in cold-storage until the end of the war.

She wandered back towards the building in which they struggled to refurbish the human wreckage of war. Rumours were circulating that 400,000 Allied troops had perished in the Battle of the Somme; nearly half the population of London! All brave men. At least they were dead. Then she realised the obscenity of her thoughts, before remembering that almost two soldiers were injured for every one killed. They would never cope. A few beds were empty thanks to patients they had failed to save, but the hospital would never absorb an invasion of newcomers. Her thoughts returned to some of those she would no longer be tending. On arrival in heaven, had St Peter restored their health and missing limbs? Did they remain forever young or continue growing older until it was time to die normally?

Back in her empty dormitory she lay on her bed unable to write home because her pencil-lead was broken and the nurse who borrowed her sharpener had not returned it. A voice with an upper-class accent was heard moaning about something. Wounded officers were obnoxious in the extreme, their ingrained superiority convincing them they could treat nurses like maid-servants. At least Matron defended her staff when complaints were made about lack of servility.

The ordinary soldiers were either too seriously afflicted to speak, had no conversation or denigrated themselves by making misplaced references to her femininity. She bore her disconcertment with equanimity, assuming that making such remarks provided relief. There was one notable exception, the arm-less corporal, who actually talked to her, bravely overcoming his tragedy in order to render their lives more enjoyable. Less insupportable. She recognised his mind needed healing as much as his body. No, not healing; it required saving from contemplating the purgatory that awaited him for the rest of his life. She must help. The previous day they had argued over the words of a music-hall ditty, she had promised to listen to the record.

How long had he lain there since somebody took his temperature? How long would it be until something else happened? Normally it would be supper but with good fortune a member of the maintenance staff may come to repair something.

He had remembered the names of England's cricket team, the one that lost the Ashes. How about trying to list the names of England's monarchs, starting with Edward and working backwards? That should keep him busy until dinner was served.

'Corporal Jenkins, I confirm with great delight that your interpretation of the third verse corresponds to the recorded version as sung by Mr George Robey.'

'Fibber! You must be flipping furious at having to admit you were wrong.'

'If you wish.'

He remained silent, not certain whether or not he wished.

'Yikes! Where's your uniform?'

She had played the record and rushed to inform him of the good news, forgetting she was off-duty.

'It's my day of rest.'

'So why visit me instead of having fun with normal people?'

'Wait a minute! How do you know I am not wearing my uniform?'

'Because it rustles differently and emits a starched hospital smell as opposed to the scent of a human being.'

'In other words I stink.'

'No, you smell very sweet.'

She changed the subject.

'Please do not assume us medical folk socialise during our rest periods, we are too exhausted.'

'Oh, I am sorry.'

'No! It's not your fault.'

'Whose fault is it?'

'Kaiser Wilhelm, Sir John French who sits back home whilst his soldiers are slaughtered, the generals who issue the orders, the soldiers for accepting to carry them out. Probably the whole

blooming lot of them. My Dad says the politicians spend more time arguing amongst themselves than fighting the war.'

'They should go over the trenches like us; that would make them declare everlasting peace.'

'Someone mentioned forming a "League of Nations" so all countries could sit down together and discuss solutions instead of fighting each other.'

'If only they would. But it's too late for me.'

'You must not talk like that.'

'Why not?'

'Because ... Because I say so.'

'You are the only reason I have for not talking "like that".'

'I am simply doing my job.'

Which she knew was not true.

'I know. I am merely one of the many invalids you look after.'

'No. Yes. But you are different, I enjoy talking to you.'

Silence ensued. Was he aware her comment effectively admitted that they had crossed the invisible barrier that separated nurse from patient? He squirmed in his bed, his head wounds were hurting. She instinctively placed her hands over the bandages, hoping to allay the pain.

'Thanks. From now onwards I'll only itch when you are present.'

'I won't believe you!'

He sagged on the bed, saddened by her implied rejection.

'All right, I promise to believe you.'

'Even if I fib?'

'That is enough tomfoolery, Corporal Jenkins.'

'Don't you mean "Tommy-foolery"?'

She burst out laughing. However, in spite of the jesting, things were getting out of hand. It was time to leave.

'I must leave you now.'

'Please nurse. No, you are off-duty so I cannot call you nurse. What is your name?'

'Miss Craven.'

'Miss what Craven?'

211

'That is my concern.'

'If you tell, I promise never to divulge the information to anyone.'

'Edith.'

'Thank you Miss Craven.'

As she was leaving she placed her hand gently on his head where it had been itching, felt the urge to stroke him as a sign of affection, regretted her initial gesture, bid him goodbye and made her escape.

The nights were just as eternally long, but now he had something to dream about. He had fallen in love before, until realising the person living inside the body that so thrilled him was not to his liking. Nurse Edith Craven was different because he had never seen her. He had formulated vague images in his mind, but was she blonde, tall, thin or plump, and how old was she? She sounded young, but … No, her age and looks were irrelevant, he was falling in love with a person, not a woman. If she was pretty she would have boyfriends, it was better she be ugly. Like Jane Eyre and Rochester. Except that Rochester had arms. No woman, however ugly, could possibly consider him a suitor, someone with whom she could start a relationship.

He returned to his dreams, romantic fantasy was more enjoyable than reality.

She rushed through her patients, gaining several minutes on her schedule so she could spend a few extra moments with him.

'Good morning, Nurse Craven. I trust you are well.'

'It is for me to enquire after your state of health, Corporal Jenkins.'

'Are patients not permitted to show concern for those tending to our needs?'

'Not really.'

I humbly apologise for disrespecting the rules, which I declare ridiculous. Also, I would wish to confirm that you have not answered my question.'

'What question'

'As to the state of your well-being.'

'Not over-brilliant but less worse for seeing you!'

He smiled, proving such action was possible without lips. She smiled in return, secure in the knowledge her gesture would remain unnoticed.

'And you, Corporal Jenkins, how are you this sunny morning?'

'All the better for seeing you. I mean hearing you.'

She commenced her professional duties, content his wounds had healed sufficiently to allay the risk of gangrene. He writhed silently as she wrapped the clean bandage around his head.

'Sorry, did I hurt you?'

'No, I was trembling from the pleasure of your touch.'

She remained silent, she must not encourage him.

'Please relax, Nurse Craven, I assure you that I am perfectly "arm-less"!'

She shuddered at his cynicism.

'If I were to invent an itch, would you rub my chest?'

'Why not your head?'

'Because I will only feel your hand through the bandages.'

'Your request is out of the question.'

'Why?'

There were thousands of reasons but her brain failed to register a single one.

'Since I am unable to offer a suitable explanation, I will respect your request.'

She gently caressed his upper torso, only to witness stirrings from his loins.

'Sorry, but there is little I can do to hide my immense gratitude for your kindness.'

'I consider it an honour.'

'Really?'

'No.'

'Oh.'

'From a medical standpoint it provides evidence of your continued recovery.'

'A somewhat useless recovery since there is no possibility of benefiting from my renewed interest in life.'

What on earth could she say? It was entirely her fault he had achieved an erection. Yet he had obviously enjoyed the experience.

So had she.

'Tomorrow is my birthday, Nurse Craven. You have twenty-four hours to think of a suitable gift.'

Sensing her disapprobation, he regretted his indiscretion. She would shun him if he continued imposing excessive familiarity, ask to be transferred to another patient. Meanwhile he was already paying for his impetuousness; the erection may have deflated but the desire for release remained.

He lay immobile, until his foot started itching. Oh, the pleasure of scratching with his other foot, for once behaving like a human being. Other sensations abruptly ended his euphoria: normally he would have asked Nurse Craven for the bedpan but one does not urinate in front of friends. So he wet the diaper she had wrapped around him a mere twenty minutes earlier.

She tossed and turned as she felt the tension within her body. She must control herself; the other nurses desperately required sleep and tomorrow was not their day of rest. Oh how she missed Mickey, more specifically the satisfaction of joining her body with his. Although Mickey, she now realised, was a debonair, self-centred authoritarian cad who had exploited her innocence and affections. How at variance with Corporal Jenkins. No, even he managed to manipulate her sentiments, proof that she needed his companionship.

Was she metamorphosing into a slut, or had she been conceived as one? Had the Devil organised the war to deviate humans from the path of righteousness or was it God's way of testing the moral fibre of his human flock? Bastards, both of them. When the war ended she would presumably be condemned by the Almighty as a sinner, even if British society had become broader-minded about such matters. But to hell with the future, her yearnings claimed more immediate solutions; better be a sane sinner than a deranged puritan. She placed her hands on her lower stomach, the resultant sensations left no doubt as to the path to follow.

After breakfast she walked in the teeming rain, the Atlantic gale tearing at her raincoat and reducing her hairdo to a bedraggled tangle. Thankfully he had a single room, not out of generosity but because the original owners of the chateau had constructed individual bedrooms for their guests and not dormitories for wounded soldiers. She carefully protected the book from the rain, proud of her subterfuge; if accosted entering his room in everyday clothes she would explain she was lending her patient a book.

Lending a book to a blind patient!

Damnation! Damn, damn, damnation to those responsible for this ghastly war, the unthinking, arrogant, power-crazy, senseless blasted lot of them. Millions of decent citizens around Europe were sacrificing everything because of their leaders' despotic egotism; they should rise up, impose everlasting peace upon mankind. But they never would. Instead, she would show them, yes she would flaunt their damnable rules, provide pleasure to that poor corporal whose distress meant nothing to politicians and generals.

The corridor was empty. A batch of wounded arriving from the front had been deposited at the main entrance; carrying them up the marble staircase and installing them in their rooms would keep everyone occupied for hours. Matron haranguing some well-meaning yet clumsy auxiliary worker only hardened her resolve to flout their inhuman imperviousness.

She entered his room without knocking.

'Good morning, Corporal Jenkins. Happy birthday!'

'Why are you whispering?'

'Because I am not supposed to be here, I'm off-duty.'

'So why are you here?'

'To give you your birthday present. But first, let me look at your bandages.'

Whilst feigning to verify his various dressings she watched, waited and before long was rewarded; a stirring, a swelling, a rising confirmed her attentions had achieved their objective. She kissed him

215

on the head then, uncertain that he had noticed, placed her lips on the exposed skin of his chest.

He writhed in pleasure. Dare he ask that she provide the ultimate release? No, he must respect her professional situation by refusing to impose his uselessness upon her. But why was she exciting him, stimulating his already oversensitive virility? It was almost as if she was doing it on purpose, taunting him, benefiting from his immobility to humiliate him.

He heard a rustle of material as if she was adjusting her clothing, then she sat down on the side of his bed. Without warning her hand surrounded his manhood, oh so gently, oh so differently from his morning wash. He felt ready to explode, what was happening?

There was more rustling of material, movements as if she was climbing onto the bed. Then, where he had recently felt the gentleness of her hand, he felt the roughness of hair, then sweet softness as he slid inwards and upwards towards infinite ecstasy.

At the precise moment of his release she whispered something in the hole where his ear had been.

'Happy nineteenth birthday, Corporal Jenkins.'

Seventeenth encounter: Maggie and André
1925   Mayfair, England

'*Damn!*'

'*Tut, tut! Such language! A refined young lady articulating masculine vulgarities, most terribly shocking!*'

'*I protest slurs upon my personality, commencing with accusations of being "refined". Sugar is refined, whereas I am not susceptible to bouts of sweetness. As for "young", twenty-six is stretching youth beyond acceptable limitations. Finally...*'

'*I say, you two, have we gathered together to prattle or play tennis?*'

'*Both!!*'

'*Agreed. But tennis first, then the chit-chat.*'

'*Love-thirty.*'

And five games to two in the final set. Alice and Betsy were thrashing them. What on earth was distracting Elsie? Her backhands normally scorched along the side-lines with devastating precision but that afternoon she was flunking even the easiest volleys.

Gritting her teeth, determined not to be beaten, she served with such force that Betsy ducked in self-preservation. In the ensuing confusion nobody remembered where the ball had landed.

'*Fifteen-thirty!*'

'*Love-forty.*'

'*First serve.*'

This time her ball thudded into the protective netting surrounding the court before Betsy commenced contemplating how to return the serve.

'Fifteen-thirty.'

Thffffyyswiiissh.

Thffwaaapp.

Alice's return span helplessly into the net.

'Thirty-all.'

The next serve practically knocked Betsy's racquet out of her hand.

'Forty-thirty.'

That was the last point she and Elsie won.

With ten minutes remaining of their allotted two hours they changed partners and launched into the best of three games. The first two demonstrated their prowess, the last became a shambles from the moment those booking the court after them arrived and stood watching.

They returned to the changing-rooms avoiding eye-contact with the four males. Each modestly disappeared into her cubicle carrying a towel and change of underclothes to emerge fifteen minutes later encased in London's most fashionable lingerie, apart from Elsie whose indisputably plump contours were squeezed into one of yesteryear's frumpish all-in-one corsets worn over a thick cotton petticoat and bloomers that descended to her knees.

Elsie sensed their disapproving looks.

'Do not expect me to wear imprudently revealing undergarments just to follow fashion. Their purpose, may I remind you, is to conceal and protect, not attract public attention.'

'Our undergarments are not imprudent; they are practical and comfortable and reflect our natural selves. Why should we struggle into ugly restrictive clothes imagined by men who, may I point out, never suffer the ignominy of wearing their sadistic creations. Finished are the days when a woman, having dressed, is so encumbered she can hardly breathe, let alone engage in anything energetic.'

'Your bodies are shamefully revealed, not only can the shape of Alice's bosom be visualised, anyone with voyeuristic predilections could observe her knees if carefully positioning himself.'

218

'For goodness sake! We are contemporary women leading liberated lives, which means rejecting Victorian attitudes.'

'Including Victorian morals?'

'Some of them!!'

'Remember that women who dilly-dally before marriage are rarely faithful to their husbands.'

'Stop bickering! Let's continue the debate in a friendlier manner as we sip tea and munch scones.'

She, Maggie Asquith, walked to the clubhouse with her long-standing friends and perennial tennis partners. There was Alice who owned a boutique in Knightsbridge, an establishment acquired with money wheedled from her father. With two female staff (males refused to work for a woman), she was building a faithful clientele by identifying yesterday what women would want to wear tomorrow. Tallish with cropped hair and a lithesome frame, she was the most successfully masculine of the quartet. Not that she wasn't feminine, ask those who hovered around her, but the time had come to narrow the inferiority gap that separated women from men. Alice's particular strategy was to metamorphose into a man. She failed. Why? Probably because women should concentrate on asserting their natural selves and not become something they were not.

Betsy attempted but failed to follow Alice's lead, possessing neither the gumption nor determination to fight the ingrained arrogance of male superiority. So she dressed like a 'flapper', the term coined by an American magazine to describe post-war unfeminine females, and oscillated between social liberation and play-acting a virtuous daughter in search of her prince charming. Like many others she worked as a typist-stenographer, in other words administrative maidservant to a dictatorial male boss.

Elsie, in spite of her thumping serves, represented the previous generation. Docile, fawning and convinced of her inferiority, she quoted Church dogma to justify opting out of the fight for equality. She even obliged her friends to read extracts from Sigmund Freud's treatise on sexuality, where he equated females to hapless castrated males for whom motherhood was a social necessity and sole reason *for their existence. Males had a penis and females breasts; what further proof of women's subordinate status did they require?*

So Elsie dressed as if King Edward was still reigning although, admittedly, with her muscular frame she could never have worn 'flapper' fashions without causing embarrassment.

Her own particular situation hardly abounded with social or sexual satisfaction. True, her career was flourishing; another year and she qualified as a solicitor specialising in divorce proceedings. Olive Clapham had become Britain's first barrister in 1921, paving the way for university graduates like herself to infiltrate the all-male bastions of society. She had expected sexist retribution from colleagues, but even judges were selected for their incapacity to make decisions without recourse to biblical prejudices. How many times had a client been condemned for 'incompatibility' with her husband who, in understandable desperation, sought comfort in another woman's arms? Husbands, of course, were never incompatible with their wives. The battle would be long and embittered; it would take generations to infuse sexual equality into the British judicial system.

It was ironic that someone dealing with the vestiges of passionate love should have never known a man. She had been approached by women, those amongst the 750,000 maidens, spinsters and widows whose soldier sweetheart never returned from Flanders, who decided that another woman's affection was better than none. She was tempted, had allowed herself to be undressed, caressed and kissed, but manipulating a hairbrush persuaded her that love was strictly heterosexual. So she played the part of a 'bright young thing' and waited with increasing pessimism to encounter the man of her dreams.

She had overlooked Muriel, fifth member of their quartet. After allowing for several days 'indisposition' each month, five females were necessary to ensure a quartet capable of playing. Even then they were occasionally reduced to three. Although perhaps for not much longer.

Forgetting Muriel, she pulled a small packet from her handbag.

'What's that?'

She blushed from a mixture of embarrassment and pride.

'My aunt brought it from America, it's called a sanitary towel, recently invented by a company called Kotex. They are light and simple to wear, invisible under flimsy summer dresses.'

'You mean you have been playing tennis wearing one?'

'Yes! Admittedly we lost, but that was Elsie's fault!!'

Alice and Betsy 'ooohed' and 'aaahed' at yet another support to surviving as a woman. Elsie was thunderstruck.

'You have acted against God's will, for women must desist from normal activities when indisposed. How could you!!'

They were sipping tea surrounded by members of Putney Tennis and Bowls Club. After their violent dispute in the changing-room, three against one, Elsie had promised to consult her vicar before condemning her friend's behaviour. However, even though calmed, she was far from mollified.

It was time to change the subject.

'So what have you been reading?'

Alice was wading through Virginia Woolf's Jacob's Room, feminist drama somewhat strenuous on the intellect. Betsy had enjoyed T.S. Elliot's The Wasteland but was disappointed by F. Scott Fitzgerald's The Jazz Age. Elsie, as expected, had abandoned Dorothy L. Sayers Whose Body, a literary revelation that had enthralled the other three. Despairing at the perversity of recent publications, she sought comfort in If Winter Comes, A.S.M. Hutchinson's unrealistically romantic novel set in a once-upon-a-time period when idyllic love and reality co-existed.

'Have they arrived?'

She had asked a cousin holidaying in Paris to return with unexpurgated copies of James Joyce's Ulysses and D.H. Laurence's Lady Chatterly's Lover.

'Next week! And I read them first!'

'Who will accompany me to Marie Stopes' meeting on birth control techniques?'

Alice agreed, Betsy had an appointment and Elsie could not contain her disapproval.

'Women make love to procreate; contraptions to prevent conception are against God's teachings.'

'But surely you do not want to become pregnant every time you have intercourse?'

'When I am married…'

'If you marry.'

'… my husband and I will lie together in the hope of having many children.'

'How many children do you wish to have?'

'That is for my husband to decide.'

Their conversation turned into a cacophony of opinions pitting backward bigotry against forward-thinking feminism.

'And if you never find a husband?'

'I will remain childless.'

'What, I wonder, have the Suffragettes been striving for these last decades?'

Alice changed the subject.

'The BBC's weather forecast was correct for a change.'

'It's really topping knowing if it will rain; no need to wear a raincoat or carry an umbrella on a sunny day, nor water your garden prior to a downpour.'

'Anything else of interest?'

'Programmes on needlework, the benefits of free trade and today's religious thought.'

'The Government is using radio as a propaganda tool to promote conservative idealism. If only they would exploit its potential to broaden people's minds, provide a real debate on social issues.'

'It's stupid, radio has sounds but no images and the cinema images but no sounds. They should combine the two.'

'But how?'

Silence.

'The theatre provides both. I saw the musical comedy No No Nanette *and plan to see* Lady Be Good *next week. Anyone want to come?'*

'I wish I could, but without male chaperones to pay for tickets, taxis and restaurants, I must sadly decline.'

'That's too too awful, old thing.'

'Dashed bad form.'

'Utterly foul!'

'But you are coming to Henley?'

'You bet!'

Thank heavens the car had a windscreen; if not she would have choked. Admittedly authorities were progressively paving roads but they had given priority to town centres and trunk routes; most of the country remained unchanged from the era of horse-driven carriages. Thus, having left the Great West Road at Hounslow, they were churning their way along country lanes in clouds of dust.

Upon arriving they parked the Bentley in a field reserved for those attending the regatta, gathered together their picnic, parasols and, with great care, the gramophone and selection of records. The men were vaguely interested in the rowing, two competitors being university friends, but the ladies had come for a day in the country that permitted them to wear their latest clothes, not the retrograde extravaganzas of Ascot but simple garments ideally suited for summer.

They rented two boats, four persons in each, so they could row to a secluded spot to picnic before returning to watch the races. Bertie was in charge of winding up the gramophone and putting on the records whilst the women prepared the picnic. He chose melodies played by popular 'jazz bands' including Jack Hylton's Kit-Cat Band, Billy Arnold's Novelty Band and Paul Whiteman and his Orchestra, America's top attraction, all of whom recorded gently swinging melodies that captured the mood of the moment.

Oh the joy of wearing a simple blouse and shorts. The men were jovial and relaxed, gone was the exaggerated courtesy of past ages which insidiously symptomised male superiority over helpless females. Yet films at the cinema continued to represented women as love-struck halfwits unable to fend for themselves, inevitably falling

223

into the arms of a gallant hero who whisked them away into the sunset. Rudolph Valentino could not be genuine, in real life he was probably a woman-baiting cad, yet millions of women were infatuated by him.

'On reflection, I decree that the young ladies present are more delectable than those on show in the Picasso and Chagal exhibitions.'

Bernie was a terrible tease, but a regular sport. If only he had not married her sister...

'The way fashions are going the country's young ladies and Picasso's cubic shapes could well resemble each other before long!'

'So what type of clothes should we wear?'

They concluded that clothes should be comfortable, highlight each person's natural form and, most important, women should be allowed to decide what they wore. How wonderful that educated men could agree with such straightforward logic. The only argument involved the height of hemlines, the men insisting they should be higher, outrageously much higher, than considered decent by the women.

After watching the races it was time to return to London. She rode with her brother, James and Elsie, the others were in Bernie's spanking new Humber. She may not have found a man, she may have lost her latest court case, but life was wonderful. Then the horse and cart emerged from a field just as Bernie rounded a bend at high speed.

Four funerals in three days. She had no more tears to shed. Bernie, swerving to miss the farmer, had careered headlong into a tree-trunk and crushed his ribcage out of existence against the steering wheel; Alice's neck was broken when she hit a wall after being ejected; Betsy's skull was crushed when the car, having somersaulted, landed on top of her; and Roger bled to death whilst waiting for the ambulance to arrive.

The farmer said his family had used the lane for generations; if idiot town-dwellers drove along it in unstable machines, it was their fault if they caused accidents.

It was time to prepare for the evening's entertainment. Her Uncle, the British Consul in Paris, was accompanying civic dignitaries from Lille on a trip to study how the British Government was solving post-war housing shortages. Her affable and long-suffering father, persuaded to host a dinner-party in honour of the visitors, requisitioned his daughter and two of her female friends to counterbalance the all-male French delegation. Elsie and Muriel, still in shock following the accident, took some convincing but eventually agreed an evening socialising, however boring, would take their minds off more distressing matters.

She gazed at herself in the mirror. Her family had always relied upon maids to advise what to wear and assist when struggling into the chosen garments. Economy measures had reduced their domestic staff from seven to a cook and part-time cleaning lady. Thank heavens clothes had become more practical. Also more flattering, of great importance when the country had a dire shortage of unmarried gentlemen. Nowadays a woman was obliged to entice, seduce and convince, using her physical and any other charms she might possess to ensnare a husband. On the other hand, at least she had a say in the matter.

She returned to studying her breasts in the mirror. Current fashion dictated a woman being the same shape from the neck downwards – impossible with her twin monsters that refused to be squeezed into oblivion against her ribs. Woman she was, like it or not. So, bearing in mind they were merely visiting French bureaucrats, she accepted the situation and donned a flimsy chemise and cami-knickers over which she pulled a waist-less dress that just about covered her knees. She painted her lips, powdered her nose and dabbed on her uncle's gift from Paris, Chanel No. 5 perfume.

Waiting downstairs for the guests to arrive she lit a cigarette, there being no law against women smokers, she poured a gin and tonic, there being no law against women drinking, and picked up The Times, *there being no legislation restricting newspaper readership to males. There had been rioting in Munich organised by the National*

Socialist Party whose leader was creating quite a name for himself. Ramsey MacDonald's speech implied his continuing enthusiasm for attempting nothing as a means of accomplishing something which, he claimed, would achieve more than the opposition's insistence on doing everything. Politicians were still furiously debating universal suffrage, the more conservative moaning that women, even at thirty, were insufficiently educated to cast an intelligent vote. Nobody mentioned the fundamental problem; British politics, run by males, was a disgrace and the only way to introduce some sense was to replace men with women. To add insult to injury, Cambridge had reaffirmed its refusal to accept female undergraduates contrary to Oxford's vote to integrate a small number each year.

The literary section reviewed George Gershwin's A Rhapsody in Blue *whose failed attempt to merge jazz and classical music reaffirmed that Negro rhythms emanating from the red-light districts of New Orleans were not proper music. Instead, one was advised to listen to Igor Stravinsky's ballet music,* Les Noces.

A recent government study had identified twenty-three different kinds of electric plug commercialised in Britain, each manufacturer imposing his own design. A national standard was urged but industrial leaders rejected the idea as undue interference into their affairs.

The telephone ringing interrupted her trying to elucidate an economist's opinion on the dangers of out-of-control national debts.

She was sweating in spite of her lightweight clothes. Having played three Charlestons, Carrol Gibbons, bandleader of the Savoy Hotel's resident band, announced an even more energetic dance sensation from America called the 'Black Bottom', presumably because Negroes swung their posteriors lewdly to the music. Which is exactly what she intended to do.

And did.

Whilst doing it she caught sight of a rip-roaring selection of garters, stocking tops and petticoats as London's ladies enthusiastically embraced the Jazz Age, before calming her own

226

particular enthusiasm; she doubted her brassiere straps would stand the strain much longer.

The visitors from France had been younger than expected, seriously middle-aged instead of despairingly elderly, but they were gay company especially when speaking with their adorable French accents. During dinner their flattery had been almost convincing; they knew how to rub ladies up the right way. Or should that be 'rub up ladies the right way'? Colloquial speech was drifting further and further apart from school grammar texts.

So, instead of sneaking away from the dinner-table with Elsie and Muriel as soon as considered polite, she proposed introducing the visitors to London's nightlife. Three accepted the offer.

They departed for the Savoy, leaving the others debating whether to build thousands of cheap prefabricated homes, which would collapse within several years, or hundreds of solidly constructed brick houses that would survive for centuries.

Having finished the Black Bottom, she decided a rest was called for; three sets of tennis with Elsie, Muriel and newcomer Prudence plus an hour's dancing had whacked her. Also, discussing French social customs with Monsieur Pantin was terribly enjoyable. He was a practising Catholic and married, neither of which were preventing him from attempting to seduce his hostesses. Was he teasing, having no intention to progress from words to deeds, or did he seriously intend to bed somebody? Whilst awaiting developments she returned his ripostes with counters of her own. Never would he have imagined she was a virgin.

What should she do if Monsieur Pantin became serious? She thought hard, only half-listening as he explained that Lille had more in common with Brussels, another Flemish city, than either Paris or Lyon. Her Kotex towels at tennis had been a necessary precaution, tightening of muscles confirmed its imminence, but until now nothing had started. Consequently, as Marie Stopes announced during her lecture, there was no risk of becoming pregnant. So she decided to finally discover what being a woman really meant, always assuming she was given the chance.

Monsieur Pantin invited Muriel to dance, before long they were
smooching rather enthusiastically; the die was anything but cast.
Then it was her turn to be invited. The band launched into 'Valencia'
and they gyrated around the dance-floor until the opening chords of
'Give Me a Little Kiss, Will Ya' reduced the tempo to a sensual
slowness and she found herself being drawn inexorably into the arms
of her partner. Each time her blouse rubbed against his blazer she
imagined her nipples had been inserted into an electric socket.

Then the familiar chords of 'Auld Lang Syne' announced the end
of the evening.

She was still scheming how to be invited to his room when the
limousine pulled up outside the hotel. She was seated next to the
kerb, it was normal she descend first. So she did. It was equally
normal she climb back into the car. But she did not.

Reports from Paris lauded British Government efforts to solve the
post-war housing shortage. The efforts must have been remarkably
successful because French bureaucrats normally ridiculed anything
English. Lille, seriously damaged during the war and experiencing a
population explosion, desperately needed to accommodate its working-
class homeless. Authorisation to send a delegation of architects and
town planners England was approved without hesitation.

The first three days were spent visiting as many housing projects
as possible, those finished, those under way and those in the planning
stages. On Friday they summarised their findings with Whitehall
officialdom and negotiated the acquisition of technical specifications
for the manufacture of prefabricated housing units. Their work
completed, everyone agreed they should benefit from visiting the
world's greatest metropolis. The following day they would sightsee
before attending a farewell dinner kindly organised by Sir Robert
Asquith, brother of the British Consul in Paris who coordinated the
project.

On learning that several young ladies had been requisitioned for
the occasion his colleagues expressed polite gratitude whilst considering the gesture inappropriate. However, their assumption was

based on the sexually anorexic demoiselles of Lille and not the flamboyant misses inhabiting London. Reluctance transformed into enthusiasm. Being invited out to dance was, however, more than most of his straight-laced companions could handle. He hesitated and then relented, because declining would be impolite.

He had endured twenty years of marriage to a churchgoing wife whose principal proof of femininity was a lack of penis. Having produced five children, the minimum acceptable for a bourgeois Catholic family, all physical contact ceased. Sneaking into a brothel was rejected, he needed affection and not anonymous sex, and no suitable mistress presented herself. The Misses Maggie and Muriel were perfect candidates to end a decade of sexual penury; they were liberated, experienced in the pursuit of immorality and hardly bothering to disguise their availability. The third one, Elsie, seemed afflicted with the same sensual suffocation as women back home, and was best left alone.

As the evening advanced he decided to commit himself, choose one before both abandoned him for somebody else. Miss Muriel was delectable but her way of dressing, mannerisms and attitudes were totally alien to anything he had known. Miss Maggie, apart from a horrendously bobbed hairstyle, could not disguise traditional roundness protruding from underneath her dress.

The choice was made.

He commenced by flirting outrageously with the others to render Miss Maggie jealous and determined to outmanoeuvre the competition. His stratagem worked perfectly because several hours later they were together in the lift mounting to the sixth floor where his room was situated. Inside was the photo album he had mentioned in the limousine; apart from the impressive town centre there were snapshots of his local tennis club. Would she like to study them, compare the facilities of the *Club de Tennis de Lille et Tourcoing* with those of Putney Tennis and Bowls Club?

As they walked down the corridor he was still deciding whether he should 'discover' before or after serving champagne that the photo album had been forgotten in Lille.

Eighteenth encounter: *Cedric and Joyce*
1928   Guildford, England

The summer sun warmed his face. Resisting the temptation to snooze, he watched as she requested of the ladies their preference for coffee or lemonade. Whenever she leaned forward his gaze focused on buttocks highlighted to perfection by a simple black and white uniform. Members of his family might be endowed with intellect, not that their level of conversation was correspondingly elevated, but the maid's simple sexuality stimulated more erotic emotions than the rest of the ladies combined. Paradise would be spending the evening with family and friends knowing she would be waiting in his bedroom wearing ...

'Coffee or lemonade, sir?'

'Gracie, have I ever drunk lemonade after lunch?'

'No, sir.'

'Then why ask?'

'Because ... because it is my duty to before pouring.'

'As instructed by Hughes, I suppose?'

'Yes, sir.'

'Coffee, please.'

'Milk and sugar, sir?'

'Gracie!'

'Please, sir, do not embarrass me in front of the guests'.

A most impertinent remark from a domestic, which only heightened his admiration, his longing to caress those thighs standing mere inches from his trembling hands.

'Milk, but no sugar, if you please.'

Her blouse was buttoned up to her neck; there was no point in looking as she leaned forward to place his cup on the table. But he did, just in case.

She stood up, her duties accomplished.

He contemplated requesting sugar in order to benefit from an encore, but sweetened coffee was undrinkable.

'Thank you, Gracie.'

When she disappeared from view, returning to the kitchen, he addressed the person sitting next to him.

'So, Malcolm, ready for a game of croquet with Joyce and Adela, we have a score to settle!!'

Yesterday, much to their surprise, the ladies suggested a male versus female competition instead of the usual mixed foursome. And thrashed them. Yet a return match was fraught with danger, what if they lost again to his impetuous sister and her chubby friend?

Malcolm had matters on his mind other than croquet.

'Do you suppose, dear chum, that the Treaty of Locarno will guarantee permanent peace?'

He knew his friend's concern was the stability of stock markets, not the possibility of war. In other words, would already astronomically inflated share prices continue to rise, confirming his status as millionaire, or should he sell his portfolio?

'French and British leaders are well-meaning in their quest for peace but they treat Stalin, Hitler, Franco and Mussolini as misbehaved public schoolboys. Fascists and communists think in vastly different terms from us; they seek absolute power incompatible with democracy. Although none have yet shown imperialistic ambitions, I consider them extremely threatening, especially since our Government fails to recognise the implications.'

'Does protectionism relieve the pressure by reducing trading disputes?'

'Heavens, no! It creates artificial trade barriers and inhibits economic growth.'

'Surely, with unemployment rising towards two million, we must protect workers in the mining and textile industries.'

He launched into an animated defence of free trade.

When he finished his friend sat silently, ruminating.

He placed his empty cup of coffee on the wicker-frame table, fondly recalling who had served it.

'Returning to your concerns about inflated stock markets, I recommend selling every share you own. Today's prices bear no relation to the economic value of the companies issuing them; market quotations cannot but drop to less insane levels. But sell discreetly; the last thing is to create a panic, the bubble must ...'

His words became inaudible as a tractor engine roared into life. Heads turned towards the fracas; the farmer who rented their lands was harvesting his wheat.

'I'll go!'

He climbed over the turnstile and stood waving his hands at the driver. After a bitter argument (harvesting was way behind schedule), a five-pound note exchanged hands as a means of convincing the disgruntled agriculturalist to occupy himself elsewhere.

The world was indeed a stressful place to inhabit, to raise a family. Not that he had a family to raise, nor a wife to do the raising.

It was time to defend his honour on the croquet lawn.

The cutlery and other utensils necessary to organise a formal English luncheon were spread around the kitchen in a cluttered mess. Whilst she, Mabel Winters, washed the dishes, Angela dried and Gracie tidied away, and Mr Hughes fetched the remaining dirty dishes from above, tut-tutting as he searched for somewhere to place them when entering the kitchen. Thank heavens Sunday lunch only occurred once a week.

Mr Hughes noticed some cutlery that was slightly damp, imperfectly dried.

'Gracie.'

'Yes, Mr Hughes.'

'Fetch clean tea-towels from the airing-cupboard.'

'Yes, Mr Hughes.'

He arrived with the last tray, placed it next to Mrs Winters, accorded himself a brief respite and sat down. He studied Angela as she performed her duties, his mind contemplating matters other than drying dishes. The badly-dressed, uncouth and dim-witted kitchen-help had strong muscles, ideal for scrubbing floors and carrying coal scuttles, which explained why she had been hired. She possessed all the requisites to satisfy a man but she left him unmoved. Why? After much contemplation he concluded it was her absence of personality. For, in the post-war world where girls attended school until fifteen and pursued a career until marriage, sexual intercourse had become a subordinate expression of love, not the overriding reason for males and females to co-inhabit. So, if there was no personality, as in the case of Angela, there was no desire to become physically intimate.

Explaining why he was so enamoured by Gracie.

The object of his fantasising entered the kitchen having finished serving after-lunch drinks in the garden.

'Everything satisfactory?'

'Yes, Mrs Winters. Mr Hughes, might I have a drink before tidying away the napkins?'

'Of course.'

He tried not to gaze, but failed. Luckily, engrossed with filling her glass from the tap, she did not notice.

'Mr Cedric not too over-friendly today?'

Mrs Winters' question may have been indiscreet, disrespectful of her employer's son, but the latter's predilection for maidservants was common knowledge. Two had been dismissed, one because she refused his advances and the other because she ceded to promises of greater prospects only to be disposed of when Mr Cedric's mother, Mrs Vaughan-Carstairs, discovered soiled underwear in a most unusual place. And now Mr Cedric's attentions were concentrating upon the girl of his own dreams.

'Nothing unusual.'

Which hardly allayed his fears. Although, he admitted to himself, he was part of the problem for never having announced his attachment. Why? Because he dreaded a rebuttal, something distinctly possible if not probable for four reasons: firstly he was her boss, they must respect professional decorum; secondly, the young woman was good-looking and displayed intelligence and temperament, she might consider a modest butler like himself beneath her station; thirdly, she had never indicated interest in him; and finally, her reaction to Mr Cedric's portending indelicacies was strangely ambiguous and not altogether disapproving.

He arose from the table; the tidying away accomplished they were free until afternoon tea. Angela planned to rest in her room; having no interests she occupied herself doing nothing or reading one of those awful picture comics. Mrs Winters would knit her niece's jumper whilst listening to the wireless. Gracie would read in the garden, concealing her book inside a magazine. Once he managed to catch sight of the title before it disappeared between the pages of *Illustrated London News*. Much to his surprise, instead of some paperback novel, her choice was a textbook on international commerce. What in damnation could possess her to study such an uninspiring subject?

He himself would be tending to Mr Cedric's Bugatti, checking the oil level, lovingly cleaning its bodywork. In exchange, he was allowed to drive around the grounds, occasionally visiting Guildford when running errands. One day he dreamed of owning his own motor vehicle, perhaps an Austin 'Seven' whose price was most reasonable.

She knew he was watching her as she served Mrs Vaughan-Carstairs. There was no way she could prevent it, her tight-fitting uniform had been selected by her employers and wearing it was obligatory.

She supposed any woman should feel exhilarated, however base the motives behind the admiring stares. But she wanted to captivate her employers by other means; with her personality and knowledge. So far she had made no progress, her uniform acting as a barrier separating upper-class bankers from commonplace servants. Admittedly Mr Cedric eyed her as a woman, obviating class distinctions, but his interest was purely biological. Oh how she longed to leave the servants' quarters, mingle with her employers on equal terms. She had the requisite grace and intellect, she scrutinised textbooks on subjects that concerned them, but she had never been permitted to demonstrate her mettle, prove she was their equal in every way except pecuniary inheritance and social upbringing.

When downstairs with the other domestics she felt distinct from their mundane existence, although she was sufficiently astute to disguise her feelings. She would have appreciated the opportunity to converse informally with Mr Hughes, who displayed more than an inkling of intelligence, but social distinctions between servants were as rigid as between lower and upper classes. In any case, mingling with colleagues would reduce her chances of acceding to the social spheres of the Vaughan-Carstairs.

The tidying away of coffee cups and sugar-bowls completed, she could retire to her room, collect her copy of George Bernard Shaw's The Intelligent Woman's Guide to Capitalism and Socialism, *and read in the grounds far away from prying eyes.*

Temporarily abandoning her knitting, she sat pondering the scraps of paper spread across her bedcover. There was no doubt about it, the dates matched, also the names and the places. Was the young girl aware of the scandal that would erupt if matters proceeded to their logical conclusion?

Having thrashed the ladies at croquet, restoring a semblance of honour, they punted on the lake. Now they were installed on the south lawn waiting for tea to be served.

He chatted to his sister Anthea, relieved her friend Joyce had been commandeered by his father who was waffling on about how socialist death duties would oblige Britain's wealthy to migrate to Switzerland, charming her in the puerile voice he reserved for attractive young ladies. Not that Joyce was appealing but at his father's age one wisely set standards at attainable levels. Why was he relieved about Joyce? Because, ensnared by his father, she could not continue glancing repeatedly in his direction. With Gracie in the offing, the last thing was to be caught flirting with another woman.

'So, dearest sister, what is happening in the world of show-jumping?'

He half-listened as she lauded the latest models of saddle, bemoaned difficulties of hiring competent stable-lads and protested aggressive antics of the Germans who acted as if sporting competitions were tests of national superiority. For once the British had stopped denigrating the French, both uniting against the obsessive onslaught of the Germans.

He ceased listening altogether when Gracie arrived with tea and cakes.

'I say, young chap, what's all this about outlawing war, making it a criminal offence?'

Uncle Rudolph was too indolent to read newspapers; instead he interrogated his entourage, Malcolm being his latest victim.

His friend had only the faintest notion; his forte being the medical applications of penicillin. Yet he obviously thought he should feign some knowledge, expound upon something.

'It's a plan to constitute an international police force so that people will stop fighting before the police intervene to break it up.'

If the response lacked conviction it was because his friend had commenced replying before deciding how to conclude.

'You, young lady, can you elucidate the matter?'

Espying Gracie standing before them, the rays of the sun rendering her servant's uniform indistinguishable, his uncle had mistaken her for a guest.

'Nothing has been validated, although the official signing of the Peace Treaty is scheduled to take place in Paris on August twenty-seventh. The American Secretary of State, F.B. Kellogg, has submitted proposals to the Locarno powers. In parallel, Aristide Briand of France has prepared a treatise recommending how to prevent the outbreak of war. The concept is to impose a formal negotiation procedure upon belligerent nations in the hope a settlement can be reached. If not, then the League of Nations has powers to arbitrate and, if necessary, enforce its decision.'

'Sounds wonderful, but will it work?'

'I sincerely hope so, after all Russia is a signatory. However, a mere decade after the cessation of hostilities, the world has rarely been more unstable and riddled with potential conflagrations.'

'Thank you, young lady, for your remarkable elucidation of the situation.'

'Sir, would you wish milk and sugar in your tea?'

There she was again, that vulgar servant chatting to him as if she was a family friend. What the hell was the hussy up to? Or Cedric, for it took two to concoct a complot, especially if immorality constituted part of the programme.

She, Joyce Selchester, was twenty-nine years old, the daughter of wealthy parents, obscenely wealthy parents, a modern-day socialite who consecrated her life to enjoying herself. Her favourite distractions were patronising the arts and theatre, and travelling around Europe to visit museums and art galleries by day, gambling casinos in the evening. Talentless, she specialised in being jolly good fun, a social drone, the life and soul of every party; posh plump Joyce, the girl everyone liked but no one loved.

She must have commenced being aware of 'getting married' when sixteen, assumed it would happen, did nothing about it, and now found herself sitting on the shelf gathering dust with other spinsters. Yes, as her eyesight weakened, the moustache above her lip darkened and her waistline thickened in contradiction to fashion's obsession with starvation-level skinniness, acquiring a husband, already far from evident, had become fraught with imponderables.

She supposed she wanted to have children, so long as a governess looked after them. She enjoyed sex, something those present were unaware of, for she limited her escapades to overseas encounters.

With no suitors in the offing her attentions focused on Cedric who overcame not being particularly handsome by entertaining himself lavishly. Nearly forty, he was approaching the age when bachelorhood no longer symbolised freedom but failure to acquire a wife.

238

So far so good.

So what the blazes did he see in that tart of a maid apart from rampant sexuality compensating an absent brain? The moment had come to act, attract his attention, something impossible with the skittish little bitch hovering like a hornet on heat. She realised that if she achieved her ambition to marry Cedric his interest in beddable domestics was unlikely to cease, but she supposed an unfaithful husband was better than none.

He watched as Gracie entered the kitchen carrying a tray loaded with teapots and sugar bowls, looking hot and flushed. The sun had indeed been shining but the temperature was not abnormally warm. There was an unusual air about her, she was vibrating with emotion and looked even more ravishing than ever. He must absolutely and definitely find a means of approaching her, prove that underneath his rigid professional exterior lurked a kind-hearted and passionate man. But, damn it all, how?

It was raining outside; eight o'clock was chiming. The caviar had been served and they were waiting for the fish course, probably carp from nearby Pendip Ponds accompanied by creamed potatoes.

'Cedric, where is that extraordinary girl who knew about peace treaties. I have more questions for her!'

Damn his uncle, now everyone would become aware of Gracie's extraordinary knowledge. Knowledge? Yes, undoubtedly. Yet she disgorged the information like a parrot, presenting facts but offering no opinions. For example, she duly explained the Conservative Party position on re-armament, at least Winston Churchill's zealously alarmist stance, but was unable to confirm its validity. Did she have no political opinions, or was she too discreet to share them with representatives of the upper classes?

'Uncle Rudolph, as I explained during tea, she is one of our maids.'

'Balderdash!! Maids do not understand politics and economics!'

Which was true.

'What is this all about?'

239

His mother had decided to involve herself.

'Gracie explained certain things to Uncle Rudolph. It's nothing to worry about.'

'What things?'

If the Olympics included inquisitiveness as a competitive sport, his mother would walk away with the gold medal.

'The menace of re-armament and protecting the Dominions.'

'Stop pulling my leg, maids do not understand politics!'

Nor did his mother.

Uncle Rudolph had other matters on his mind

'Bright young thing, although most unattractive; no sense of fashion.'

He could have embraced his uncle; with one phrase he had drawn away attention from the girl he was committed to bedding.

'Bring her here, my latest questions remain unanswered!'

Damn his uncle.

'No, Rudolph, she's occupied in the kitchen.'

Good old Mother.

And then she entered with the carp and creamed potatoes.

'Goodnight Gracie, Angela.'

'Goodnight Mrs Winters, Mr Hughes.'

The girls exited the scrupulously tidy kitchen, leaving him in the company of an exhausted cook. They sipped the vintage claret. As usual, when a meal was drawing to a close, he enquired whether anyone desired a final glass of wine. Mr Cedric always replied in the affirmative. The previous bottle secreted away, he uncorked an untamed one and poured as little as possible because, in accordance with household rules, unconsumed wine could be shared amongst the servants.

He described the day's events to Mrs Winters.

'She'll have to leave.'

Which was the last outcome he wished.

'For what reason? She works well and has wooed the "hierarchy" with her knowledge.'

'That is the problem.'

'You are correct, Mrs Winters; such intimacy is unacceptable and can only but result in trouble. Furthermore, Mr Cedric has her in his sights; his intentions are evident.'

'Does she encourage him?'

'It is difficult to tell.'

Mrs Winters was ill-at-ease, something was bothering her.

'Mr Hughes, there is information I must divulge to you, suspicions I have been harbouring but never mentioned due to lack of certainty. Many years ago, shortly after my arrival, there was a similar scandal, although it was Sir Humphrey, Mr Cedric's father, who was the guilty party, bedding a maidservant too terrified of losing her position to refuse his advances. She became with child and was dismissed. I am convinced Gracie is the consequence of that union; her family name matches, also her date and place of birth.'

Speechless, he stared at the middle-aged cook.

'Is Gracie aware of the situation?'

'Most definitely, otherwise she would not be here! Her mother is dead, it is only normal she contact her sole surviving parent.'

His heart sank. Yet Mrs Winters was undoubtedly justified in her suppositions for they explained the haughty elegance of Gracie and her remarkable knowledge.

Mrs Winters had not finished.

'Mr Cedric intends to be intimate with his half-sister.'

'But surely she would never agree to spend the night with her brother?!'

'We have no proof she plans to accept.'

'She must be warned!!'

'I will fetch her.'

Mr Hughes had kindly offered to replace her for the remainder of the evening. Seated at her bedside table, she abandoned unravelling the implications of overvalued stock markets, price-earnings ratios being beyond her ability to understand. In any case her mind would not concentrate on anything other than the stares of admiration as she answered Uncle Rudolph's questions. Had she made the long-awaited breakthrough, could she finally vacate the servants' quarters and move into 'their' social sphere?

A knock on the door surprised her; thankfully it was only Mrs Winters. The serious expression on her face and summons hardly surprised her; she was expecting a strong reaction from Mr Hughes.

The butler was waiting for her.

'Gracie, we wish to clarify certain matters. Your behaviour this evening was improper, but we realise it was imposed upon you. Also, well to come straight to the point, are you the daughter of Jenny Warston who worked here before the war and became pregnant after accommodating Sir Humphrey?'

So they had guessed.

'Yes.'

'You are aware that Mr Cedric has unsavoury intentions towards you?'

'Yes.'

'Gracie, what are your intentions?'

'I do not know. I so want to be recognised by my father. Not because he is wealthy but simply because he is my father. Since my mother died I have nobody ...'

Damn, she hated revealing her emotions.

Mr Hughes broke the silence.

'I cannot predict his reaction, but I believe you should act promptly, thwart Mr Cedric before he divulges his true intentions; it would be difficult for him to welcome you as a sister after having attempted to seduce you.'

The conversation was interrupted by the dangling of the service bell; the caller was Mr Cedric and he was in his bedroom.

He pulled the rope, faintly hearing ringing in the kitchen. He knew Hughes was off-duty and that the heavyset and dull-witted Angela returned home on Sunday evening. Thus, in all probability, Gracie would answer his summons. And he would be ready to provide a reception she would never forget.

Somebody knocked on the door.

'Enter.'

She entered.

'You rang, sir?'

Of course he had rung, but custom required that domestics ask the obvious.

'Ah, Gracie! Approach, there are certain matters I wish to discuss.'

She advanced, halting well before reaching the bed.

'Closer.'

She ignored his command, disobeyed him.

'What is your request, sir?'

Then he noticed something strange. Her uniform! She was wearing everyday clothes!

'Please forgive me, but I offered to replace Mr Hughes without considering changing back into my uniform.'

Which was rubbish, because she was already on duty. She had engineered coming to see him! Most interesting!

'Not to bother, there is nothing to forgive. In fact, not wearing your uniform is perfect for I wish to chat to you as a person, not as a maid, discuss your remarkable performances at tea-time and during dinner. Please approach, sit down next to me.'

'No, I must not.'

'Why ever not?'

'Mr Cedric, I would be delighted to make your acquaintance as an equal but first I wish to impart certain information.'

'As an equal'! Surely she was not stupid enough to expect a marriage proposal before undressing?

'Mr Cedric, I am your sister.'

'I beg your pardon?'

He listened in disbelief.

'Have you taken leave of your senses? You don't expect me to believe such rubbish? How dare you treat me as an imbecile!'

'Look at my face, the colour of my hair. Then reflect upon the physique of your father.'

This was getting out of hand. Forgetting his earlier intentions, he led her across the landing; his father would be reading alone.

'Father. Gracie claims to be your daughter! Please confirm she is inventing libellous untruths and will be dismissed forthwith unless she retracts everything and offers an apology.'

His father looked towards Gracie, then back at him.

'Gracie is my daughter. I have suspected it for some time; her demonstration at table this evening removed any remaining doubts. Hence, my dearest Cedric, she is your sister.'

'Yes, but only a bastard sibling half-sister.'

Whose bedding would be incestuous. Damnation. Bloody blasted damnation.

His father turned to Gracie.

'When your mother abandoned her employment, after having announced her condition, I advanced a sum of money to ensure you received an excellent schooling. She, in return, agreed never to reveal my identity and to abandon claims concerning your parentage. Did she inform you of the latter?'

'No.'

'You may be my biological daughter but I never raised you; we belong to vastly different worlds. Clearly you have inherited a generous dose of the Vaughan-Carstairs' temperament. Even so, my wife being unaware of your existence, I cannot welcome you into our family. However, you are my progeny and I admire your achievements. In exchange for remaining discreet, I would propose to support you financially.'

'In other words, buy my silence?'

'Not quite. My idea is to underwrite your continued education, help you obtain a diploma and embark on a professional career. I, and Cedric now he is aware of your identity, would remain in regular contact outside the confines of this house.'

'Thus never publicly admitting to being my father?'

'That is correct. But, in private, I would be happy to consider you as one of the family.'

He watched in disbelief as his father drew Gracie towards him and kissed her tenderly on the forehead.

'Gracie, although your mother was a servant and our relationship sinful, I admired her immensely and suffered greatly when she disappeared from my life. I truly wish to become acquainted with you, attempt to amend past misdeeds.'

She did not withdraw from his embrace, nor did she kiss him in return.

What was the little tart thinking?

'I do not expect an immediate response; you are welcome to consider my proposition for as long as you wish.'

His father's compliments about her strength of character were justified, she was worthy of being his sister, bastard or otherwise. He had better make the best of a disastrous situation, treat her with consideration, become her friend.

'If you agree to my father's proposals, I would be delighted to become your "brother". Through my many contacts I can certainly secure you a place in an institute of advanced learning. Bearing in mind your performances earlier today, the most logical choice would be reading economics at university!'

She smiled at him and held out a hand. He shook it politely and then laughed at the inappropriateness of the gesture. He placed his hands on her shoulders and kissed her on each cheek.

'Are you serving early morning tea tomorrow?'

'Yes.'

'I look forward to your visit! And please, thick-cut marmalade, instead of strawberry jam!'

Judging by the expression on her face she did not know whether to reply 'Yes, sir' or insult him for being treated like a servant.

'One further instruction, dear sister. Having entered my room, please call me Cedric!'

She smiled, a warm wonderful friendly smile that made him want to hug her lovingly.

It was time to separate. Alone in his bedroom, he reflected on the course of events, relieved he had concealed his real intentions towards her.

Meanwhile his sexual needs, at bursting point when he rang for service, remained unsatiated.

Somebody knocked on his door.

She lay on her bed, tossing and turning, unable to sleep, intrigued by the sounds of people talking further along the corridor. She recognised Cedric's voice, but could not identify the others. What on earth could they be discussing so late in the evening?

Lying in the dark, she contemplated her life, more particularly her lack of living. The maid's outburst of economic theory during dinner had humbled her, for it emphasised her own inability to aspire to anything other than light-hearted jesting about nothing in particular. If she was to achieve anything meaningful, it would have to be raising children. Cedric was the least worst contender to assume the role of father. It was him or growing old alone.

The wine had loosened her inhibitions and heightened her sense of loneliness. She rose from her bed, wrapped her negligée around her shoulders, leaving its buttons undone so her bosom could be admired. Well, at least seen. His room was next-door-but-one.

She knocked and entered.

'Can I come in?'

'You have.'

Was that a positive or negative response to her question? Before he could be more specific, she advanced and sat down on the side of his bed.

'I heard talking and could not sleep.'

He was about to say something, then refrained. He seemed dazed, saddened.

'Dearest Cedric, I was thinking about you, wishing we were better acquainted. Week-end parties are so tediously formal and prevent friendships forming.'

She studied his impenetrable expression, then realised his eyes were staring intently at her bodice.

'Come nearer, dearest Joyce. I need someone to relax with and you are just the person. Your comments about stuffy formality are spot on.'

She guided his head onto her bosom, holding it with one hand and

246

stroking the nape of his neck with the other. After several minutes he placed a hand on her ankle and started moving it upwards underneath her nightgown. She had contemplated the risk of pregnancy before leaving her room; it was the time of the month she was most fertile. Smiling to herself, she had left the sheaths in her suitcase.

His hand was well above her knee. She was not wearing panties, so nothing remained between his advancing caresses and her forthcoming marriage.

Nineteenth encounter: Frank and Sally
1936   Ealing, England

'Goal.'

'Offside!!'

Whhheeeeeeiiieee.

'Bloody linesman, blind as a bat!'

'Another ten minutes to equalise.'

'Come on, yer useless layabouts; we want a goal!!'

They watched as their team's centre-forward, he whose goal had been disallowed, reacted to his opponent's smug smirking. Without hesitation he flung the ball straight into the goalie's face, seriously flattening his nose.

Whhheeeeeeiiieee.

Fulham were down to ten players.

As a final insult, the visitors from Everton scored a second goal in the last minute of the match.

They filed out of the stadium in brooding silence; their team's third consecutive loss made relegation an unthinkable possibility. On second thoughts, an unmentionable probability. Next Saturday they would be obliged to win at Manchester City, not an encouraging prospect.

Avoiding the jam-packed pubs surrounding the stadium, they walked to the nearest District Line station. Seeing a train arrive whilst descending the escalator, they hurled themselves onto the platform only to discover it was destined for Richmond.

'Statton is bleeding hopeless, hasn't scored for weeks. Not that Whiteman is better; most of his passes went straight to an opponent.'

249

The platforms filled up with supporters, divided equally between those draped in blue, grinning and shouting, and those wearing black and red who stared silently at nothing, lost in the despondency of defeat. Luckily for other passengers and the railway authorities, those in blue were travelling east to catch a mainline train from Euston whereas their counterparts were returning to homes west of Fulham. Apart from jeers and the flinging of empty beer bottles, things were surprisingly peaceful for a Saturday afternoon.

An Ealing Broadway train arrived and they jostled into an overcrowded second-class carriage.

Arriving at the train's terminus, they exited the station and wandered along to the Rose and Crown for a pint and a packet of salted potato crisps.

He sipped at the froth of his Watney's, extracted the minuscule blue paper bag tucked inside the packet of crisps and sprinkled salt over the crunchy petals of deep-fried potato. As he munched he listened to his chums bemoaning their team's efforts, nobody and nothing escaping their wrath.

Eventually, having exhausted their frustrations, their thoughts turned to more agreeable subjects.

'So, Frank; did'jer buy it this morning?'

He grinned sheepishly.

'Five guineas from Samuels in the Broadway, with one real diamond and the rest fourteen-carat gold.'

'Blimey! Now you're really hitched! You must be bloody sure you wanna marry her.'

'You bet!'

'Where d'jer meet her?' Dickie, a newcomer to the group, was not yet versed in their past histories.

'She works at Woolworth's with my sister Sarah. They went to see a Fred Astaire-Ginger Rogers picture, after which she came home for tea.'

'You known her long?'

'Nearly a year.'

'How old is she?'

'Twenty-one.'

'Quite a bit younger than you?'

'Five years.'

'What's so special about her?'

An interesting question. Naturally, first and foremost, she was good looking, a real smasher. So he wanted to make love to her. Very much. Next, he was too old to continue living with his parents, as his mother kept reminding him. And, what clinched it, she desperately wanted to marry him.

'Dunno, really. She's great fun, got a stunning figure and her Mum says she cooks real good.'

'Seems good enough reason to get hitched.'

'Can't think of any others!'

'So where's you gonna live?'

'My Dad, who works at the Town Hall, found us a council house near Alperton; the tenants won't pay the rent because the roof leaks, and they will move. Dad will see to fixing the missing tiles, he's got friends everywhere, and we can take possession after the wedding. Since we rent there's no need for a mortgage, and we can buy furniture and electrical goods on the hire purchase. I've promised Sally a Hoover, washing machine and electric toaster which works with the new sliced bread.'

'Alperton is way out, how'll you travel to work?'

'I've got my Triumph motor-bike and Sally can catch a thirty-eight bus into the Broadway.'

'You'll still be coming to matches?'

'You bet! And be joining you for a pint afterwards, whilst the "wife" cooks my supper!!'

Everyone laughed at the joke.

It was time to wend their ways homewards. He was spending the evening with his family discussing the wedding, but they agreed to meet the following afternoon outside the Odeon to see Errol Flynn in *Charge of the Light Brigade*.

Blast! Sally's parents were coming to discuss wedding plans.

His buddies would see the film without him but everyone would congregate at The Crown after supper.

The sun was setting as he stopped at the fish and chip shop. Hopefully their cod and fries would be wrapped in the *Daily Chronicle*, *Daily Herald* and *Daily Mail*, the least greasy pages of which would be read after the meal was finished. He paid Mr Jones, grabbed the bulky bundle of fish, chips and newspaper, and walked home.

She unhooked the washing from the clothes-line, returned to the scullery and plugged in the electric iron, such an improvement compared to the old-fashioned monstrosity that over-heated on the stove and cooled progressively once you started working. Admittedly electric irons blew fuses and Mrs Hodges had been electrocuted when she touched exposed wires to see if there was any current. But they were worth the risk.

She turned on the radio in time to hear the last chorus of "Lullaby of Broadway" before Bertini and His Band played "Have You Ever Seen a Dream Walking?" with Sam Browne singing the vocals. She adored the crooner's voice and had pleaded to be taken to his latest show. But Frank claimed a prior snooker competition. Then she wanted to see Billy Cotton and His Band at the Hippodrome, but he moaned about being hopeless at dancing. Instead, they went greyhound racing.

She knew he was at the match with his pals. She hoped Fulham would win, not than she supported the club but he was always in a jovial mood after a victory.

One of her father's shirts defeated her efforts to smooth away the crinkles. Apparently a new crease-resistant fabric called Tootal had been invented in America, there was no need to iron after washing. At last male scientists had invented something useful for women! No, that was unfair, what about hair-curlers, detergents, electric kettles and plastic flowers that did not require watering?

Tootal shirts not being available in England, she continued her struggle with crease-persistent cotton. As she ironed she thought about Frank and their forthcoming wedding. She knew he was nobody super-exceptional, but he had a steady job as ticket-collector on the buses and always deposited part of his weekly wage in a Building Society instead of spending everything on booze. He was authoritative and self-assured, just like heroes at the cinema, although Hilda said he was arrogant and bad mannered. But her sister was wrong although, admittedly, some of his jokes were terribly rude. But, most important, she had fallen hopelessly in love with him. She dreamed of him every night and sometimes at work, pretending he was saving her from a burning building or robbers, just like in the films.

Of course real-life Frank was different from the hero of her dreams, but all males had faults, starting with her father and brothers who were awfully untidy. Frank picked his nose, though he wiped the mess on a handkerchief, not his trousers like some of the others. He never got completely drunk and was one of the few males she knew who didn't smoke. If only he supported a better football team...

His persistent attempts at groping where it was forbidden was infuriating; why couldn't he be patient and wait until the honeymoon? But her mother confirmed all men were the same, there was nothing to be worried about.

She was so looking forward to sharing a bed with him, lying at his side, allowing him to fondle her everywhere, absolutely everywhere. On second thoughts, not absolutely everywhere, some places were out of bounds even to husbands.

Had he known another girl? She was suspicious about Phyllis, who looked at her strangely whenever she mentioned Frank's name. She supposed it was normal he had 'done it', so she agreed to forgive premarital infidelity. However, once they were married...

They were going to be so happy together in their new house. He would do the gardening, she the cooking and housework. During the evening they would curl up in front of the hearth and listen to the radio or play records. Going to the pictures was a problem; he liked adventure films whereas she adored musicals and soppy romances. Hopefully, with two cinemas in Ealing, they would find a solution. Even better, they would go together to the Empire, where touring singing stars appeared. Gracie Fields and George Formby had played recently but Frank had been too busy to accompany her.

One day she would take her children to Saturday morning matinées. How they would thrill at the cowboy adventures and laugh at the Mickey Mouse and Popeye cartoons. Then, in the afternoon, Frank would take the boys to watch football whilst she went ice-skating or swimming with the girls. One problem existed; at Woolworth's you were sometimes obliged to work Saturdays, so Frank might be lumbered with the girls. But these were minor little worries; married life was going to be wonderfully marvellous.

Her stepfather regularly imparted his philosophy that wars belonged to history thanks to God's divine intervention; everlasting peace had been declared in 1918. Her mother's first husband, her father, had been killed in the trenches. Desperate, alone with a toddler, she had married the elderly, severely strict and serious-minded Presbyterian after a whirlwind courtship. Joshua and Hilda, her half-brother and half-sister, were so like their father and so unlike her. Which was one further reason for dreading tomorrow's meeting to discus the wedding, because Frank's family were anything but religious, especially him.

She folded away the sheets and pillowcase; it was time to light the fire in the hearth and fetch crumpets from the pantry.

'Golly! Hitler has invaded the Rhineland!'

'Will war be declared?'

'Unlikely, British public opinion is against it.'

'So Hitler gets away with it?'

'Looks like it.'

'Unemployment has reached two million!'

'Neville Chamberlain has replaced Stanley Baldwin as Prime Minister.'

'Knew that!!'

'A new pill has been invented that cures indigestion, it's called Alka Seltzer.'

'There are rumours about the Prince of Wales associating with a divorced American woman. Whatever next?'

As was usual, they were digesting their fish and chips and one of his mother's home-made puddings whilst reading the least soiled bits of newspaper. That evening there was a special bonus, several pages of *Beano* had been wrapped around the chips. Desperate Dan and Denis the Menace were in fine form.

The challenge, as they sipped on mugs of steaming Horlicks, was to announce exciting titbits of news that nobody else knew about.

'Here's one for you, Frank. The BBC is hoping to televise the Arsenal-Everton football match next August twenty-ninth.'

'Go on with you!'

'If they do it regular, there'll be no need to traipse all the way to the stadium!'

'Gosh!'

'But we ain't got no television! Anyway, if nobody attends the matches there's no point in playing. The whole idea sounds daft.'

'How about this? The Archbishop of Canterbury officially accepts the Anglican Church's acceptance of artificial birth control whereas Pope Pius in Rome claims any form of contraception is a grave and unnatural sin.'

'I wish God would make up his blinking mind.'

'Thank God we be Anglicans!'

An embarrassed silence followed his comment; talking about newspaper articles was one matter, relating them to their personal lives was another. He occasionally wondered if his parents used contraceptives; they had only conceived four children in twenty-eight years of marriage. However, far more worrisome was Sally; they had mentioned having children, but never how many. During tomorrow afternoon's meeting with her parents, rubber and whatever women used were unlikely to be on the agenda. But shouldn't the subject be raised between the two of them? Of course it should, and it was his fault it had never been mentioned.

Another unmentionable subject was his betrothed's maidenhood. She had always stopped him from exploring underneath her clothes, insisting there was plenty of time after the wedding. So if she wasn't a virgin someone else must have bagged her. Should he ask? And did it matter? According to the radio more and more girls 'did it' before getting married.

Best not ask, for she might pose awkward questions in return. He had no desire to reveal his antics with Betty and Phyllis, both of whom worked with Sally at Woolworth's.

Having prepared a list of subjects to debate the following afternoon, his mother fetched Monopoly from a drawer, her birthday present. He really did enjoy spending evenings at home with his family.

Half-past nine, her father would soon begin yawning and wend his way bedwards. She finished House *and* Garden *and returned to reading* The Railway Children. *The radio was silent; only classical music was authorised by her stepfather who condemned new-fangled jazz and swing as unchristian. Talk programmes were also forbidden; the speakers might discuss indelicate matters or mention rude words.*

Three months to go and she would be alone with Frank, her stepfather no longer able to prevent them doing whatever they wanted.

The meeting was going badly, tension hung in the air as his future stepfather-in-law repeatedly chided his family's lack of religious fervour.

'I see you subscribe to a Sunday newspaper. I must point out that such publications, being printed and circulated on the Sabbath, contravene the 1782 Sunday Observance Act. I also consider it inappropriate to listen to the radio on Sunday, for the seventh day of the week is reserved for rest and praying, thanking the Lord for creating us.'

'But it gives us something to do.'

'If you attended church, the problem would cease to exist.'

His father, never particularly argumentative, decided against debating the issue. In any case, constructive discussion with Mr Reedson, Sally's stepfather, was a lost cause.

The stepfather in question had not finished.

'I sincerely hope Frank will comport himself as befits a devout Christian and that his children will be raised in adherence with Presbyterian doctrine, ours being the only denomination to correctly interpret and apply the scriptures.'

Resisting the temptation to intone 'amen', he nodded in agreement, hoping Mr Reedson would have departed to join his Presbyterian Saviour long before his and Sally's children reached the age of church attendance.

'I see your lawnmower outside, I would not wish my son-in-law to manipulate such an implement on the Sabbath.'

Which was ridiculous, there being no time to garden Saturdays what with shopping and football. At least Sally was not supporting her stepfather, which did not mean she disagreed with him. Damnation, he knew so little about her.

They advanced to the next item on the agenda, the next point of contention

'Very expensive, a honeymoon. Wiser to use the money to buy furniture, curtains and the like.'

'But Daddy,' for the first time Sally dared protest her stepfather's ordaining of the arrangements, 'Mr Foster has offered a week in the new Butlin's holiday camp at Skegness!'

'Well, I suppose what Frank's father does with his money is his affair. But, all the same, it doesn't seem proper, frittering away good money in a commercialised encampment dedicated to potentially unrighteous pleasures.'

Which left everyone wondering what did sound right to him.

The ceremonial cutting of the engagement cake and slipping of the engagement ring on Sally's finger failed to relax the atmosphere. At least, by the time the Reedsons departed, they had finalised a wedding programme that allowed some sense of celebration to infiltrate the solemnity of getting married.

'We'll need more glasses, six for long drinks and another eight for cider and ginger beer.'

'Plus at least eight beer tankards, we get thirsty at matches!'

257

She had not considered his football chums being invited back home. Which was unfair, for she planned afternoon get-togethers with her girlfriends.

They were visiting their future house, which was being repaired and extended. The most exciting improvement was replacing the outside lavatory with a modern flush toilet. Annoyingly, the council had refused to pay for an electric water-heater to provide constant hot water; they would have to make do with a gas heater in the kitchen and cold water upstairs.

She sensed his embarrassment when visiting the bedrooms, especially when discussing where to install the double-bed. She thought about asking which side he preferred but decided the matter too delicate. It was equally awkward in the other two bedrooms, where their children would be sleeping. He had light-heartedly mentioned having boys and girls but how many children did he want? And how to 'organise' such matters?

Her mother once condescended to discuss having children, more specifically preventing them, by quoting her second husband's philosophy of 'abstinence makes the heart grow fonder'. Which, she supposed, was logical. However, one thing at a time; she should produce several babies before worrying about preventing them. Her aunt had never managed; apparently it did not happen automatically. Which must be awful.

'Give me a kiss.'

She did.

'Now we are engaged, can I fondle your bare breast?'

'Whatever for? In three weeks we'll be married.'

'Because me mates say doing such things is more fun before getting married.'

Which was not the most diplomatic way to achieve his ambition.

'The answer is no. Imagine doing it now, then discovering during the honeymoon your mates were correct.'

'Let me touch one breast. Then, after the wedding, we can compare when I caress both of them.'

How clever of him! Visiting the bedrooms and thinking what they

258

would soon be doing together had excited her; three weeks was an eternity to wait.

'Under my blouse, but not the brassiere.'

'Please!'

Interpreting the gloomy look on his face as acceptance, she pulled off her jumper.

After teasing about which one to choose, he placed his hand on the left one, rubbing gently in a way that sent thrills of pleasure coursing round her body. Then, slowly and eagerly, he unbuttoned her blouse, exposing her petticoat, an item of clothing not mentioned during their 'negotiations'. He stopped, considered the problem, and tried to slide his fingers underneath the petticoat but outside the brassiere.

He could.

So he did.

She trembled with excitement and frustration, oh how she wanted to offer herself to him. But God had ingrained respectability and self-preservation into every well-behaved girl. Then, without warning, his fingers disappeared inside her brassiere cup. She was quick, but not fast enough.

'You promised!'

'Sorry, but I love you so much.'

How could she be cross with him? She kissed him on the lips then buttoned her blouse, partly from modesty, partly because of the coldish damp permeating the unheated house.

Riding on his motorbike to The Broadway to deposit their wedding-list she tried to envisage how it would feel when, in three weeks time, he caressed both breasts simultaneously.

No tankards for beer-drinkers! Surely his mates were not expected to sip tea after their team's victories? Thankfully she didn't pick a quarrel, they had already argued enough to last an entire marriage.

It had been awkward visiting the empty bedrooms, especially theirs. He was clueless about choosing mattresses, so he allowed her to decide soft or hard. He pondered a practical problem raised by one of his mates; husbands and wives made love in the middle of the bed, then moved to their separate sides. But which side? He always slept facing left, so should he have the left half and face away or the right half and point towards her? He supposed the latter was more loving but he snored, something he had never mentioned.

Visiting the other bedrooms confirmed she wanted both boys and girls, although not how many. He enjoyed having brothers and sisters, large families were fun, even more for the children than the parents.

The upper rooms overlooked fields spreading into the distance towards the village of Greenford. The town hall agent confirmed some of the land was reserved for the construction of a 'dual-carriage highway' with two separate tracks. Since cars drove in the same direction on each track they couldn't crash headlong into each other, allowing them to drive terribly fast in complete safety. The existing A40, instead of going through town centres, would be transferred to the new highway, vastly reducing the time needed to travel from London to Oxford. Perhaps they could go there on his Triumph and have a picnic.

A roar of engines came from overhead, presumably someone flying into Northolt Airport. How exciting to sit in their garden Sundays and watch the planes landing and taking off! His future father-in-law would probably protest, flying on the Sabbath being against the teachings of the scriptures. On reflection, he doubted if God had outlawed airborne activities, aeroplanes not being invented when Moses wrote the commandments. Stupid old git, his stepfather-in-law.

He gazed at his beautiful fiancée, her breasts protruding from underneath her jumper in a most provocative manner. Oh how he wanted to see them, touch them, play with them. Perhaps his new ploy would work, the one recommended by Bill. It was worth trying. He had recently seen a magazine advertisement for padded brassieres, which might explain why she refused his requests! Yes, any ploy, however devious, was justified.

Much to his surprise she agreed to practically everything. Good old Bill! Oh the excitement of unbuttoning her blouse and the

260

sweetness of the dainty lace petticoat she was wearing underneath. Yes, her breasts looked genuine, but best to be absolutely certain. The material of the brassiere was not too restricting, it would be possible to slide a couple of fingers underneath and touch a nipple before she reacted.

They were genuine!

In three weeks he would have all night to explore them, in fact all his life.

Which was something he had not thought about. One day she would be as ancient as her mother, even look like her, and eventually be as senile as toothless Granny Granston. Best not to contemplate such horrors. What a pity he couldn't exchange a middle-aged Sally for a younger wife, like he replaced motorbikes when they were clapped out. On second thoughts, he would have become a crotchety old geezer by then; no young girl would be interested. Which meant he and Sally were destined to grow old and decrepit together.

Did old people make love? He didn't think his parents did, they never held hands nor kissed. But at what age did one cease romantic activities?

He gazed at Sally as she struggled into her tight-fitting jumper, imagining her as a white-haired granny. She smoothed out the creases from her clothes, combed her hair, twirled around in delight, preening herself in front of her delighted fiancé.

Oh how lucky he was!

She was in a quandary. They had spent hours and hours fussing over her wedding dress, veil, gloves, shoes and every imaginable item of haberdashery. Nobody, however, had mentioned underwear. Would sensible white cotton knickers disappoint him, would glamorous sheer panties shock him? What about silk stockings? Perhaps she could undress in the bathroom, walk to their bedroom in her pyjamas. Pyjamas!! Would he be expecting a flowing night-gown like in the movies? What toothpaste did he use, should they share or have separate tubes? Would she be able to read before turning out the light, as was her habit? No, it would be impolite. Unless he also read.

She sighed in exasperation, decided against asking her mother for advice and realised that, unlike fairy tales, real-life problems didn't end, they commenced with marriage.

The one o'clock news was droning on about Amy Johnson's solo flight to Capetown, battles in the Spanish Civil War and the death of A.E. Housman, whoever he was, or had been. Meanwhile he had his own worries, more personal but just as important. Should he wear a vest at the wedding ceremony? The weather was warm, no need for one, yet his mother insisted it be more hygienic. And should he change his underpants? His current ones were perfectly clean after only three days and his mother had loads of housework. He would keep them on; his wife would be thrilled to wash them after the honeymoon!

His father had reserved a room in a hotel near Hounslow for the wedding night; it was situated in romantic farmland dotted with lakes. They had decided against Butlin's for the honeymoon, it being too crowded for 'romantically inclined' couples. Instead they booked at a guest-house in Eastbourne, overlooking the English Channel. His parents had once stayed there and recommended it. It was about three hours drive on his motorbike, they would arrive in time for lunch the following day.

Then, four days later, Mr and Mrs Frank Foster would return home to start their married life together.

She was hot, sweaty, exhausted and extremely tipsy. She drank a full glass of Tizer before realising it was cider, which only worsened her wooziness. Everyone had overeaten, listened to a horrendously boring speech delivered by her stepfather and some ribald double entendres about their forthcoming nuptials from the best man.

They had danced foxtrots, quicksteps and waltzes, then the hokey-cokey, "Knees Up Mother Brown" and "Boomps-a Daisy". Her hip was still aching from colliding with her stepfather during the "Gay Gordons". Rumours abounded that somebody had laced his fruit squash with gin; judging by his ingloriously unsabbatical behaviour the plan had been highly successful.

Frank was dancing with Phyllis, who looked strangely forlorn for such a happy occasion. Tough luck, Frank was her husband. Her colleague should chat up Frank's football buddies. Admittedly they were too inebriated for the time being, but when they sobered up...

The glass of cider was taking effect; her head was spinning around the room. No, the room was spinning round her head.

Phyllis was clinging to him, refusing to let him wriggle free, return to Mrs Foster. Also known as his wife. The person he once called Sally. It was highly embarrassing, now was not the moment to reveal their clandestine lovemaking inside the garden shed. Yikes, her knee was rubbing against his pride and glory and her lips were caressing the nape of his neck.

His mother saved him. Cousin Herbert and his wife Nancy were about to leave and wanted to say goodbye.

Which reminded him the time to depart was approaching. Dancing with Phyllis had aroused certain urges, reminders of those short sharp sex sessions wedged between the lawnmower and garden furniture, hoping nothing noisy would collapse onto them. Each morning he returned to the scene of the crime to remove traces of their encounter, once discovering a brooch and another time the clip of a suspender belt. He had kept the latter as a souvenir, hidden amongst his underwear. Which meant it was now in the wardrobe of their new bedroom! Flipping hell! Could one be accused of adultery even if the 'deed' occurred before the wedding?

He checked his watch; in five minutes they would make for the storeroom where she changed into ordinary clothes, wedding dresses being ill-adapted to riding pillion on a 500cc Triumph.

And then Sally collapsed onto the dining-room floor.

Her mother slapping her cheeks and the splashing of cold water brought her round. Her eyes were soon focusing, but it took a considerable time before she could stand unaided. Then they bid farewell to their guests and made for the storeroom. It felt weird undressing whilst Frank watched; he should have offered to look away. No, that would have been stupid.

They got completely lost before locating the hotel, Frank uttering very naughty forbidden swear words when encountering the same crossroads for the third time. Thankfully somebody was waiting in the reception-hall, hardly disguising his displeasure at their tardiness. Mr and Mrs Foster signed the register and followed the surly receptionist up the stairs.

The cool night air during their twenty minute drive had effaced all traces of dizziness; she was as fresh and wide awake as a spring lamb. One about to be sacrificed. Something she was looking forward to immensely.

He was exhausted, reeking with insobriety, in a foul mood after getting lost, keen to collapse into bed and fall sleep. The only problem was that sitting behind him was a wife. Couldn't they wait until the following morning? There was no hurry, the honeymoon lasted several days.

He parked the motorbike in a shed, apologised for being late, signed the hotel register and followed the receptionist and Mrs Sally Foster upstairs to room number 17.

Twentieth encounter: Marthe and Franz
1944   Ussel, France

The rumbling became louder and more persistent; the motorcade would appear within minutes. Judging by grinding and crunching sounds intermingling with the throbbing of diesel motors, a couple of escort vehicles were accompanying the troop carriers. Not to worry, their guns would have insufficient time to swivel round and aim in their direction.

The leading vehicle came into view, an officer wearing the despised German military uniform sitting in the rear, haughtily staring ahead as if he owned the surrounding countryside. Which he did not, he merely occupied it on a temporary basis, strongly against the wishes of its population.

The explosives erupted with unexpected force, bravo Jean-Michel for his chemical expertise. Intense gunfire added to the cacophony of shouts, screams, exploding fuel tanks and the roaring of flames.

The smoke cleared and enemy soldiers came into view, staggering erratically and pointing their guns towards where they believed the ambushers might possibly be but were probably not. They were progressively eliminated. A group of survivors scurried to safety on the opposite side of the road, only to encounter snipers waiting for them.

His group advanced to the rear of the halted vehicles, ready to provide support if necessary. Yes, it was urgently required; several Germans had found cover and were responding with lethal efficacy in spite of being outnumbered, out-manoeuvred and surrounded. Grenades were lobbed into the thicket, their guns silenced, the battle was over.

With extreme caution his companions verified each enemy body, killing the injured with a bullet between the eyes before helping themselves to undamaged military equipment. Two of the least wounded were bound; they would be interrogated then executed. Four of their compatriots were dead, seven injured, none so seriously that Michel, their doctor, could not repair the damage.

A roaring was heard, a *Luftwaffe* patrol must have spotted the smoke and come to investigate. They sprawled themselves under nearby trees; no point in retreating while the planes circled overhead, they would only reveal their identity and intended destination. One of the Heinkels strafed the roadside, more in frustration than an attempt to wreak revenge.

As soon as the planes disappeared, he and his comrades climbed the flanks of the valley, seeking temporary safety before vanishing into the inhospitable Plateau de l'Artense. Once arrived at their base, they would lie low. Seek and destroy raids were inevitable following the scale of their victory; enemy soldiers would be combing every nook and cranny of the region except, hopefully, the concealed cave which had become their headquarters.

She sat in her drawing-room reading Victor Hugo. Although familiar with his novels, the injustice endured by his heroes provided comfort, confirmed she was not alone in her struggle against oppression.

She had attended mass that morning, certain traditions were inviolable, not even war would prevent her communicating with God, try to understand the reprehensible injustice of His ways. In 1940 she had prayed that He spare her husband Jean-Pierre; he perished defending the Maginot Line. She then prayed that He spare her elder son Jacques; in 1943 he was escorted away by the Gestapo, never to return. She next implored that He spare her brother Jean-Louis; he was executed for harbouring an English airman. Only Stephane remained, hiding amongst isolated mountain forests, living like a hunted animal. Would God protect him, or had He sided with the Germans?

Stephane was also risking her life. When another resistance fighter was trapped by the Gestapo in nearby Valergues, they publicly executed his parents, forcing him and his sisters to watch. Then the young patriot had been strung from a lamppost, his body left dangling in the village square in front of the schoolhouse.

If Stephane died nothing remained to make her life worth living – they could kill her with impunity.

She closed her book and walked to the kitchen, BBC London was about to broadcast its French language news bulletin. She twirled the dials, placing herself close to the loudspeaker to minimise the volume, for quisling neighbours were a permanent menace.

"Allied bombers have attacked Berlin in broad daylight. The destruction of industrial complexes throughout Germany is seriously hampering the Axis war effort. American and British troops have launched their third attack on Monte Cassino; fighting is heavy and so far inconclusive. Elsewhere in Italy Allied troops are racing northwards towards Rome."

Why, she wondered, why oh why didn't the Allies land in France, free her country from the horrors of occupation? Only Corsica had been liberated, which was a waste of effort.

"Russian troops have broken through German lines and crossed the River Dniesterr. General Dwight Eisenhower, supreme commander of Allied forces in Europe ..."

Loud knocking interrupted the broadcast. Panicking, her hands shaking violently, she had difficulty turning the 'on-off' knob.

The radio silenced and hurriedly concealed she walked to the front door trying to appear as calm as she was not.

'Madame Dulletier?'

'Yes.'

'Following the deployment of extra troops in the area, I have been billeted in your house.'

Her previous 'tenant' had been killed in a recent ambush; consequently her spare-room was available and she could not refuse. Without saying a word, without the slightest greeting, she stood aside to permit him to enter.

She recognised him. He commanded the German army contingent

267

based in Ussel. Something important must have occurred for him to arrive late in the evening without notification.

'Up the stairs, second door on the right.'

'Thank you.'

Thank heaven he was a regular army officer, most of whom exhibited a modicum of civilised behaviour. Soldiers under his authority were strict and rigidly formal, yet no gratuitous violence or other abuses had been reported. How unlike Gestapo agents and SS troopers whose mere presence made people cringe. Even worse, however, were the French security police, miserable wretches determined to outshine their Nazi counterparts in every loathsome way possible. How could Frenchmen so totally disregard the teachings of Jesus?

The lavatory flushed. Her lavatory, which had just been soiled by a hated German.

He descended the stairs.

'Madame Dulletier, I am aware of the tardiness of the hour, but I have not eaten since breakfast due to urgent matters requiring my attention. Would it be possible to procure some bread and cheese, perhaps some fruit?'

It would, but she was damned if she was going to serve him.

'I understand your reluctance. I will serve myself if you would be so kind as to show me the kitchen.'

She relented. He had asked politely and allowing him to rummage through her cupboards was unthinkable.

'Please take a seat.'

She returned carrying a tray. He was studying one of the photos on the mantelpiece.

'Please forgive my impertinence. However, I thought I recognised the church spire; is it not Saint Dizier?'

It was, but she had no intention of confirming the fact.

'I spent many summer holidays there. My grandmother was French; it was she who insisted I learn your language.'

She had been impressed by his fluency, now she knew why.

She left him alone; having a French grandmother did not pardon being a German officer.

He munched on the bread and cheese, accepting it was not her fault the bread, baked early that morning, was slightly stale. His book lay on the table, but he was unable to concentrate on the text.

He had been expecting trouble ever since the convoy was decimated by resistance fighters. It was not his fault they travelled along the D105 without taking elementary precautions. But he was the local commanding officer, hence the obvious person to condemn. He had been expecting a posting to the Eastern Front which was no longer progressing towards Siberia but retreating through Poland. Instead, he had been retained in Ussel since none of the newly-arrived SS contingent spoke French or knew the region.

He had escaped lightly, possibly because General von Gustenheim realised the true culprit was lack of morale amongst his troops. Being ejected from his lodgings to permit SS *Obersturmführer* Gruber to install himself was a minor irritation.

Although he personally had survived, at least for the moment, others would not. Revenge was in the air; before long innocent French civilians would be paying dearly, probably with their lives. Gruber was a typical example of the Nazi indoctrination machine which programmed minds to obey without compunction and without resort to moral soul-searching. His mission was vengeance, the preferred tools of his trade blackmail, terror, torture and execution. Meting out vindictive exaction on innocents did not disconcert him; in fact he probably received personal gratification from hurting and humiliating non-Germans. To what levels of single-minded sadism were human beings capable of descending?

He must be cautious, do everything to demonstrate his commitment to their cause; 'their' cause because it definitely was not his. Since arriving in Ussel he had been full of admiration for the steadfast determination of its inhabitants. He so much wanted to converse with them, prove he merited their comprehension even if not their affection. He knew, they knew, that the Third Reich was collapsing as Russia, Britain and America progressively recaptured Germany's ill-gained overseas territories. Regular German soldiers, like those under his command, supposed the inevitability of defeat; their reaction was to maximise their chances of survival by avoiding contact with the enemy. In stark contrast, the limitless capacity of SS special units to desecrate fellow humans in defence of their beloved Führer had turned them into savage animals.

He rose from the table, ready to wish his hostess goodnight, only to discover she had disappeared from view, no doubt sulking in her kitchen.

Morning classes were ended. Before leaving the classroom they paid their respects to the empty desks, those once occupied by Rachel, Simon and Ephraim. She knew the daily ritual was dangerous, maintaining it had been discussed with teachers, municipal authorities and parents. All, however, condemned that Monday morning when Vichy security police dragged away three children from her class, none as fiercely as pupils left behind simply because they were Christian. No, their friends would never be forgotten, whatever the risk.

She queued at the bakery, whispering to other customers, discussing the arrival of the menacing-looking enemy vehicles. They knew they belonged to the SS, they surmised their arrival was linked to the recent massacre and that trouble was brewing. She prepared herself for the inevitable acrimony between those supporting their country's subjugation, some of whom denounced patriots in exchange for favours such as extra food coupons, and those prepared to sacrifice everything to regain their liberty.

Madame Reguine glared at her. That some people submitted to foreign invasion was understandable but condemning those fighting to regain their former dignity was despicable. If anyone deserved disrespect it was the tartish, loud-mouthed ex-barmaid and her scrounging husband Alphonse, a pathetic layabout whose dealings with the Germans were far from transparent.

She turned away and chatted to someone else.

Word arrived that Marcel Rouffignac had been arrested in Tulle. A suspected resistance fighter, he had been visiting his sick mother and

270

walked into a trap. Screams from inside SS headquarters told of torture, the ensuing silence confirmed another martyr had died for his country.

Tulle was fifty kilometres away. Which meant Ussel's retribution was still to come.

They were collecting food from partisan farmers, the most dangerous of activities because it forced them to descend into populated valleys, visit outlying farms where the enemy might be waiting.

Whilst the main group kept watch in relative safety, Patrice and Anna descended to collect the food. They had just reappeared from within, carrying a laden bag, when the SS troopers pounced.

The farmer and his wife exited the far side of the building, running for cover. Shots were heard, they collapsed onto the ground. Their dog rushed to investigate, his furious barking turning to yelps as his body was lacerated with bullets.

Patrice was spat at, butted with rifles and kicked as he squirmed on the ground. Hauled to his feet, the torture became increasingly brutal. He was obviously refusing to reveal information to the extent that his captors eventually lost patience. A noose was tightened around his neck and the rope attached to an overhanging branch. The sadists, they adjusted its length so it half-throttled him without completely cutting the air supply so long as he stood on tiptoe. For several minutes he fought to remain alive then, either from resignation or exhaustion, his feet sank to the ground, the rope tightened and his body twitched for an eternity of seconds before hanging motionless.

Anna had been forced to watch. Now it was her turn. To the surprise of those watching the rope was tightened around her wrists, not her neck, before being flung over the same branch and pulled tight, forcing her arms above her head. Standing helplessly facing the enemy, she was stripped naked. The officer advanced holding a knife which he held to her face as he shouted questions at her. She refused to answer even when her tormentor slowly and methodically sliced off her ears and breasts. Holding one of the latter, he caressed its

271

nipple, feigning surprise she did not receive pleasure. Then he produced a stick of dynamite and forced it between her thighs. Striking a match, he held it under her chin as she screamed with pain. The second match would not ignite, the third served to light the fuse.

Since any attempt to withdraw would announce their presence, they remained immobile, mesmerised, aware of their utter helplessness against the superior firepower of the SS. But there was another reason for staying; they felt morally bound to accompany their friend in her last moments. But nobody watched as the fuse shortened into nothingness.

When the troops had departed they buried Patrice and as many parts of Anna they could assemble, before retrieving the bag of food and disappearing into the protection of the forest.

He realised the SS would in all probability inflict similar atrocities on civilians in retaliation for his group's incursions. But the obligation to continue was clear in his mind for France was not simply occupied by a foreign army; its people were being defiled and destroyed until nothing would remain of their once glorious nation.

He was early. Normally she had finished eating before he returned; that evening she was still cooking. Damn him.

He smiled at her, as always, although she refused to return the compliment. He apologised for being early, indicated his agreement to wait before eating and disappeared into his bedroom.

During the two weeks since his installation he had been impeccably polite and deferential. This was a relief because he spent most evenings at home, rarely socialising with fellow officers. Neighbours speculated he had been demoted in disgrace following the convoy massacre, meaning the SS were not his colleagues and that he was isolated and lonely.

She heard footsteps descending the stairs.

'Do you dine in the living room or the kitchen?'

'Why should that concern you?'

'Because, if you occupy the kitchen, I would appreciate reading in here, it is more comfortable.'

'I eat in the kitchen, so you may read downstairs.'

'I appreciate your gesture.'

'But not there.'

'For what reason?'

'That is my husband's chair.'

'Your husband lives here?'

'No, he is dead; but the chair is still his.'

'I am sorry.'

'For what?'

'I was expressing regret for your husband.'

'Why should that bother you?'

'From your way of speaking, your husband was killed in the war.'

'Yes, when you blasted Germans invaded my country in 1940.'

'I repeat my regrets; I understand how you must feel.'

'Heartless bullies cannot realise the pain and misery I have suffered.'

He hesitated before replying.

'My wife and daughter were killed during an air-raid on Duisburg.'

What could she say?

Eight o'clock chiming distracted her.

'BBC London will be commencing its broadcast.'

She glowered at him; never would she fall into such a despicable trap.

'Could we listen together? I very much wish to learn what is happening.'

'But your hierarchy keeps you informed?'

For the second time he hesitated before speaking.

'I have ever-decreasing confidence in the veracity of their information. On several occasions I have authenticated the accuracy of conflicting reports broadcast from London.'

'You listen!?'

'I consider it important to keep track of events.'

'If you order me to fetch a radio and you personally tune it to the station of your choice, I will listen with you.'

'Where is your radio?'

Her heart missed a beat. His question confirmed he was not fooled by the antiquated wireless placed in full view on the sideboard, which was left permanently tuned to Radio Paris, the Nazi propaganda machine, but never turned on. The powerful one that received London was hidden behind the oven.

'Wait here.'

"After yesterday's D-Day landings in Normandy, Allied troops have consolidated their positions and are advancing towards Caen. Anglo-American forces, having finally broken through German lines at Monte Cassino, are nearing Rome. Unmanned flying rockets launched by from Peenemünde in northern Germany continue to land in south-east England. Loss of lives and damage to buildings has been minor. The French Committee of National Liberation has renamed itself the Provisional Government of the French Republic and has held its first meeting in Algiers."

She switched off when the coded messages commenced. The Allies had landed in Normandy!! She clapped her hands and broke out into a broad grin, then remembered who was sitting opposite her.

'Please continue smiling.'

'But...'

'Watching someone smile is a pleasure I have not appreciated for a very long time, even if the smile be on the face of a victorious enemy!'

She studied his fatigued face.

'So you accept we will win the war?'

'That is something I cannot comment upon.'

She suddenly realised she had been talking to him as a human being, not a German officer, and that they had collaborated in the act of treason by listening to the broadcast from London.

'So they chose Normandy instead of Calais.'

'Against all military logic, which in itself makes the illogical logical.'

'So now what happens?'

274

'We Germans push the invaders back into the sea and occupy London by Christmas.'

She was about to protest when she saw a mischievous glint in his eyes.

Hissing sounds from the kitchen announced a culinary catastrophe. While she saved the food from carbonisation he wiped away the sauce oozing down the side of the cooker.

'Thank you.'

'It is only normal that I save my dinner.'

'That was my dinner.'

He mounted the stairs, and changed into civilian clothes, ignoring army regulations pertaining to the billeting of soldiers in private houses. They had agreed if anyone knocked he would change back into uniform while she dithered around before opening the front door.

He fetched his copy of *Twenty Thousand Leagues Under The Sea*, the story of an amazing U-boat and its crazy captain. As had become their custom, he read until supper was ready and then poured the wine while she served the food which, he noted, was no longer one menu for her and another for himself. Depending on the hour of eating they listened to the radio before or after the meal. That evening's bulletin confirmed further Allied advances in Europe and American victories against the Japanese in the Pacific.

He had remained impassive until mention of further 'thousand-bomber' air-raids of German cities. Had she noticed his discomfort?

'How much longer can Germany resist?'

'I honestly do not know. Something tells me Hitler will fight until the last man, human lives have no meaning to him.'

'What makes Germany so belligerent? Twice this century your country has risked destroying the world, including itself, in a quest for domination of Europe.'

'I cannot explain. On both occasions a fanatical leader managed to incite, manipulate and convince our people to support policies based on national pride and contempt for everyone else. Both times, while men were goading themselves into a frenzy, the vast majority of women sat, watched and waited, before suffering with everyone else. I am as perplexed as you.'

After a month living under the same roof she posed the question he dreaded most.

'What is the rationale for exterminating the Jews?'

'They were ruining our economy in order to grease their filthy palms. Funds were being funnelled to secret Swiss bank accounts or straight to Palestine. They were like leeches, bleeding their host nation to economic death whilst growing financially obese.'

'Does that justify herding them into camps and allowing them to perish from malnutrition?'

'They deserved to be punished.'

'Including their wives and children, including two boys and a teenage girl from my class?'

He said nothing, possibly the best response to her accusation. Was she aware of the 'Final Solution'? Should he inform her, admit to serving briefly in one of the camps when convalescing after the blitzkrieg on Poland? Should he admit his disgust for his country's leaders?

'I am sorry, I appreciate you are in no way directly responsible. Please, tell me more about your family, your wife and daughter.'

Having terminated his rambling, confused and embarrassingly overemotional evocation of family life, first as a boy then as husband and father, he asked about her childhood, her husband and sons. Her response was equally contorted and emotional. One subject omitted was her son's activities, hardly surprising in view of his supposed involvement in the resistance. Gruber had instructed him to arrest the miscreant on sight if he visited his mother, shooting him if necessary.

By the time eleven o'clock chimed he felt closer to her than anyone except Aneke, the wife he had adored and now missed so terribly. Without Aneke, there was no reason to return home, little point in winning the war.

Or was that no longer true?

He wanted to place a hand on her shoulder, show appreciation of her company, emphasise he had no personal vendetta against her. Yet he refrained; she might misinterpret the gesture, he was after all a man.

And she was a woman.

Irrespective of one being French, the other German.

She walked from stall to stall searching for groceries and household utensils amongst the mostly emptied displays. The atmosphere was upbeat; increasing certainty of victory permeated their lives regardless of the omnipresent SS. Soon the occupation would be a distant memory.

Then word of happenings in Oradour-sur-Glane reached the market and spread like wildfire. The village's entire population had been massacred in reprisal for helping resistance fighters. Over six hundred inhabitants, men, women and children, had been herded into the parish church and cremated alive by SS troopers. Midnight arrests, torture, rape and public executions, all were commonplace in their currently distorted world, but torching a place of worship packed with innocent villagers went beyond the limitations of human horror.

A silence fell upon the market, resulting in suspicious soldiers pointing weapons in their direction. A woman screamed an oath, others joined in. Someone spat in the direction of the nearest soldier, who shouted a warning and took aim.

He had learned of the massacre, off-duty troopers were boasting about the gory details and commenting how the population of Ussel deserved similar treatment for spitting and yelling insults.

He knew she had been informed the moment she opened the front door. They spoke little during dinner, avoiding the subject uppermost in their minds, but finally she could contain herself no more.

'How could human beings commit such savagery? Even animals only hunt for nourishment, killing their prey as quickly as possible.'

'I blame Goebbels and his indoctrinators at the Ministry of

Information. The youngsters they brainwash do not question the validity of their teaching; they instinctively obey a leader acclaimed as a demi-god.'

'A "demi-god"!!'

'Yes. You accept Jesus as son of God without the slightest proof. You defend his authenticity, never question the validity of his parentage, the logic of his gospels.'

'But his words are full of love.'

'But is loving a good thing? Who decides? And who decides that he who decides has the right to decide? Young Germans, those who have only known Hitler, adulate him as you adulate Jesus and react violently if anyone disparages their Messiah, or Führer if you prefer.'

'But what do Hitler and Goebbels hope to achieve?'

'Who knows? Congratulations from the Devil when they descend to hell? They cannot expect an invitation to heaven bearing in mind that Jesus, Matthew, Luke and Peter, amongst others, are Jews and would be promptly shipped to the heavenly equivalent of Belsen if Nazi leaders arrived *en masse*.'

'So why doesn't God destroy Germany?'

'SS troopers are not representative of my country; they are transitory mutants who will disappear.'

He held out a hand. She took it and then collapsed, sobbing uncontrollably. He was obliged to help her to her bedroom, momentarily seeing its interior for the first time before she closed the door behind her.

She faced her pupils; they appeared to be accusing her, along with every other adult, of creating a world unfit for them. How could she explain Oradour-sur-Glane? And now, that very morning in Ussel, Julien Deschamps had been denounced by a classmate for condemning the Germans.

'Madame, what will happen to the Deschamps family?'

'I cannot say. We must simply hope and pray for their release. Remember, they have done nothing wrong.'

'But Julien said rude things about the Germans!'

278

'That is not necessarily wicked, so long as he told the truth.'

'Madame, do you think the Germans are evil?'

'Only their soldiers. I am convinced that most Germans are decent well-behaved Christians just like us. When the war is over, I want everyone...'

The school bell interrupted her discourse.

Obersturmführer Gruber announced his long-awaited decision to punish the inhabitants of Ussel for helping resistance fighters operating in their region. These, following last week's attack on the train, had now murdered three off-duty soldiers whilst they chatted to local girls.

The girls were being held for questioning. One had admitted under torture they were accomplices, baiting the soldiers by hitching up their skirts and leading them into a trap. Gruber announced that, before their bodies were rendered unrecognisable as having once been female, they would be made available to satisfy the whims of his hard-working, devoted and patriotic soldiers. After all, there was no urgency to slit their delectable throats, and the longer they stayed alive the more they could contemplate their foolish conduct. Yes, so long as they preferred living, they would be kept alive. However, when they pleaded to die, which they would eventually, he would be more than happy to accommodate their wishes. Slowly, because a person is killed only once and the SS, most generously, would make the event as memorable as possible for the participants.

Gruber's plan of revenge was simple. Every fifth person in the telephone book would be arrested and publicly hanged in the town's main square, where they would be left dangling to ensure those surviving, including their children, fully understood who was master in Ussel. Furthermore, from then onwards, for every German soldier attacked ten citizens would be executed until either the population behaved or no inhabitants were left.

SS troopers would encircle the town at six o'clock the next morning; apprehending those selected would start immediately afterwards. His own particular role as a regular German officer was to identify citizens taken into custody, keeping *Scharfführer* Junglich informed of those still not captured.

He walked the short distance from SS headquarters to Marthe's house trying to remember if she possessed a telephone. He hoped her lack of greeting when opening the front-door was not a personal insult, just war-weariness.

'Do you have a telephone?'

'Yes, but it has been disconnected. After my husband's death I was unable to afford the bills.'

'Have you a directory?'

'But you cannot phone!'

'I know.'

She fetched the heavy volume. He almost grabbed it and flipped through the pages until reaching Ussel, then Dullutier. Damnation, she was there. No, it was Gustave Dullutier.

'If you are checking my number, it's 3415!'

If only she knew.

He verified the outer cover, it was the 1942 edition. Which version was being used by the SS? Would they substitute a widow for a deceased husband? He replaced the directory on the shelf and walked upstairs to his bedroom.

Something was wrong, very wrong.

He could remain silent no longer. The evening had been tense, he realised she must suspect something.

'Marthe, please listen carefully, there is something I wish to say. But you must promise not to do anything rash, swear not to leave your house nor attempt to communicate with anyone.'

She promised.

He revealed the SS's intentions.

'I am terribly sorry. I have been thinking of ways to save you, assuming you are on their list, but with the curfew it would be impossible to escape into the countryside. And there is one further detail; for every person on the list not in captivity by three o'clock

280

tomorrow afternoon three members of his or her family will be executed instead.'

What could he do to comfort her, atone for the mindless brutality of his countrymen?

'Why would you wish to save me?'

'Because you do not deserve to die.'

'But why especially me? After all, nobody deserves to die.'

'Because I have much respect and admiration for you.'

'Is that all?'

Before he could reply, finally admit the truth, she burst into tears. He placed his arm around her shoulders, and waited.

In the depths of her dejection an arm around her shoulders brought comfort, nothing unusual when a woman loved a man.

How was she reacting to the probability of being executed the following morning alongside dozens of her friends and neighbours? Her first thought was fatalism; she saw no way of escaping the SS troopers. Then, accepting the inevitable, she felt a desire to live her remaining hours to the utmost. Instead of sleeping she had deeds to accomplish, overdue invoices to pay and compromising documents to burn.

Another idea was forming, a means of preventing her mind from dwelling upon her rendezvous with a noose, something to prove that however corrupted mankind had become his depravity could never extinguish the most powerful force of all.

No, not religious belief.

Something more absolute in its capacity to overcome everything else; the love between a man and a woman. More precisely the physical expression of that love.

The strength of which she would prove that night, alone in her house with a very special German officer.

Author's note

When I launched into writing this initial volume words such as 'fun', 'flirtation', 'jousting' and 'joviality' came to mind. Historical research revealed the innocence of my thoughts, as those who have read the preceding pages will appreciate.

Sixty years separate Nazi atrocities from today's world. Although the mind-numbing fifties had to be survived, the sexual explosion finally came in the sixties with the pill, burning bras and rock festivals. Although far from perfect, the last forty years have shaken sexual prejudices to their rotten foundations and practically reinvented the pursuit of procreation.

All this is related in the second volume, in which the words 'fun', 'flirtation' and others reminiscent of a happier society find due prominence. Regrettably other words such as 'rape', 'prostitution' and 'adultery' also appear because today's world, even if vastly improved, still remains far from perfect.

A.S., Briançon, January 2006